The Guilty

(A Jack 'Keeper' Marconi Novel)

Vincent Zandri

PRAISE FOR VINCENT ZANDRI

"Sensational . . . masterful . . . brilliant."
~*New York Post*

"My fear level rose with this Zandri novel like it hasn't done before. Wondering what the killer had in store for Jude and seeing the ending, well, this is one book that will be with me for a long time to come!"
~Reviews by Molly

"I very highly recommend this book . . . It's a great crime drama that is full of action and intense suspense, along with some great twists . . . Vincent Zandri has become a huge name and just keeps pouring out one best seller after another."
~*Life in Review*

"A thriller that has depth and substance, wickedness and compassion."
~ *The Times-Union* (Albany)

"The action never wanes."
~*Fort Lauderdale Sun-Sentinal*

"Gritty, fast-paced, lyrical and haunting."
~Harlan Coben, bestselling author of *Six Years*

"Tough, stylish, heartbreaking."
~Don Winslow, bestselling author of *Savages*

MOONLIGHT FALLS

ALSO BY VINCENT ZANDRI

The Dick Moonlight Mystery Series
Moonlight Falls
Moonlight Mafia
Moonlight Rises
Blue Moonlight
Full Moonlight
Murder by Moonlight
Moonlight Sonata

The Jack Marconi Mystery Series
The Innocent
Godchild

The Chase Baker Action/Adventure Series
Chase Baker and the Golden Condor

The Stand-Alones
Everything Burns
The Remains
Scream Catcher
Lost Grace
The Concrete Pearl
Permanence

The Shorts
Pathological
Banal
True Stories

Bear Media LLC
4 Orchard Grove, Albany, NY 12211
http://www.vincentzandri.com

Published in the United States of America

"He looked rather pleasantly, like a blonde Satan."
~ Dashiell Hammett, The Maltese Falcon

"I'm Eve in the Garden of Eden, and he's the serpent, and I
cannot resist."
~ E.L. James, Fifty Shades of Grey

MOONLIGHT FALLS

BOOK I

In the Beginning . . .

. . . SHE FALLS FOR HIM as fast and hard as a plane crash. He has that devastatingly immediate effect on her, and she swallows up everything about him like a woman dying of an incurable thirst.

But then, he is so different from her ex-husband.

This man . . . this ambitious young man . . . he offers something so different from the tight, pit-in-the-chest, lonely relationship she's endured for six long years. This man isn't at all like the man she married. This man is kind with his words, caring with his actions, tender with his touch. When he makes love to her, he does so unselfishly and with a power so focused on her and her alone that it takes her breath away.

There are other wonderful things about him.

He is kind to her little boy. He's the kind of man to buy the little guy a train set for no reason at all other than it's a beautiful sunny Sunday. He plays with the boy. Cowboys and Indians. Reads with the boy. Carts him off to the movies. Shares Happy Meals with him. In some cases, he is more dad than the boy's real dad.

This man is exceptionally handsome, possessing the deepest green eyes she's ever before seen on a man. A tall, slim-but-not-skinny, muscular build, and thick, wavy, red-blond hair that just screams for her to run her hands through it. She considers herself an attractive young woman with her shoulder-length brunette hair and deep-set brown eyes. But not deserving of a man with such out-of-this-world looks. She feels blessed.

Unlike her ex, who is a writer, time to this man is not a commodity or something to be greedily hoarded. His generosity and selflessness seem to know no bounds, as if God placed him on this earth for her and her alone.

It's the same when it comes to money.

He's taken her places her husband couldn't begin to afford. Weekends at the Gramercy Park Hotel in New York City. A full week in Paris. Deep sea fishing and nude sunbathing in Aruba. Dinner at the most expensive restaurants and shopping at the best stores. Garnet Hill, West Elm, Bloomingdale's, Prada . . . He even bought her a new car. A fire engine red Volvo station wagon, which he claimed would be a safer ride for her and her little boy than the five-year-old Toyota Corolla she's used to driving around town.

For the thirty-eight-year-old grammar school teacher, he is a green-eyed dream come true. A knight in shining armor who has rescued her from a life of never quite making ends meet, from a husband who chooses career over family, from days filled with boredom and nights chilled by despair. For the first time ever, she has snagged the man of her dreams, and she is not about to let go. She will do anything for him.

Anything.

But then things change.

Not in a dramatic, earth-shattering way. But subtly. He begins to ask her to do things for him. Things that surprise her when they come out of his mouth. Especially when he asks her to do them with a smile on his face.

That smile.

She's never before heard of people doing the things he's talking about. Correction . . . she's heard of them before, but only when she has happened to see them on late-night cable TV or read about them in some shady, bestselling erotica novel. But then, the things he's talking about are worse than those things. They involve other things besides human flesh on human flesh. They involve tools of wood, glass, leather and steel. They involve chants and pain and spirits summoned from anywhere but heaven. He doesn't demand her to do these things with him. He merely asks her to explore the idea of doing them. To explore the possibilities. To explore the depths of her sensuality. In a word, he feels the need and the want to share her.

She feels at once shocked and afraid. But then she feels confusion

2

too. She reasons with herself that perhaps he is just being playful. Deviant, but playful. That there is no harm in what he is suggesting. She's an adult, and so is he. So long as it happens among consenting adults, what harm can come of it? Still, she resists.

But he keeps asking her to share herself. Day after day. Night after night. He never lets up. Her beautiful man, he is determined.

Other changes begin to occur.

Physical changes.

His already thin physique becomes thinner, veinier, his muscles more pronounced. The retinas in his striking green eyes always seem to be dilated now. As if he were secretly experimenting with some new drug or drugs. He rarely trims his fingernails, preferring now to grow them out like claws. And his teeth . . . he's doing things with his teeth. Having his incisors sharpened so that when he opens his mouth, he resembles a vampire.

The changes cause more and more anxiety in her. But she chooses to ignore it. He is still so kind to her. To her boy. So loving and protecting. She doesn't want to ruin what they've built together. She doesn't want to break the spell. She decides to keep her mouth shut and carry on like her life is all wine and roses.

Then one day he reveals a secret.

He takes her by the hand, leads her down the stairs into the basement. There he reveals a hidden room.

The. Room.

He reveals the room to her and all the room contains.

It makes her dizzy at first. So dizzy she thinks she might pass out. There are the four windowless, red-painted walls, a concrete floor with the drain positioned in the middle, strange devices hanging on metal hooks, video cameras, lights, and the strangest thing of all: a large, heavy, wood spinning wheel balanced atop a ball bearing-topped pilaster. A wooden wheel with four heavy leather straps attached to it that can accompany a fully grown human being. Standing in the door opening, she feels as if she is looking into a medieval dungeon.

"I had this constructed for us," he whispers. "Because I love you."

Her knees grow weak, her legs wobbly.

She fears she will faint.

But then he takes her into his strong arms and smiles that smile.

3

That's when he tells her he wants to show her something else. Something very special. Releasing her, he raises up the sleeve on his right arm to reveal a long, white, gauze bandage held in place with strips of white surgical tape. Reaching out with his left hand, he slowly, tenderly, peels away the bandage. What he exposes is as shockingly wonderful as that room is shockingly frightening.

It's a new tattoo.

But not just any tattoo.

This tattoo contains no artistic rendering. No red hearts with arrows piercing them. No Indian heads. No tribal insignias, wings, crosses, dragons, stars, or angels. This tattoo contains only a name.

SARAH, inked in deep black, with rich scarlet droplets of blood dripping from each letter.

For her, the tattoo isn't just decorative body paint. It is instead a declaration of the purest love. The tattoo means he is proclaiming his devotion and his love for all eternity.

"You don't have to do this if you don't want," he says, his blue eyes shifting from her to the sex room, and back to her. "I'll understand completely. If you like, I can close up the secret room for good."

She slowly turns away from him, focuses on the heavy wood wheel, and as much as it pains her to even contemplate being strapped to it with other people watching . . . watching and doing things to her and themselves . . . she can't help but begin to feel a hint of excitement running through her veins and between her legs. It's as if in the revelation of this basement space, along with her lover's new tattoo, a tiny door inside her has been pried open. The room, and all it contains, might still bring out the fear in her, but her love and desire for him is so much stronger.

"If it will please you," she whispers, "I will do it for you."

With that, he once more takes her into his arms, holds her hard against his chest, his hands forming tight, angry fists, his sharpened incisors biting down into his lip, piercing the flesh, drawing blood.

"Till death do us part," he whispers into her ear.

1

HAROLD SANDERS DIDN'T LOOK like a world-renowned architect who was said to be richer than God. He looked more like the grand master or head priest for one of those new, pray-for-profit, storefront Christian churches you see springing up all over the suburbs these days.

But then what the hell did I know?

I was neither world renowned nor rich and I believed in God only when it was convenient. Like when someone had the business end of a pistol barrel pressed up against the back of my head, for instance.

I guess, in some ways, not being rich or famous made me feel sort of sad, but in other ways, it provided me with an odd sense of comfort. As if in all my anonymity and humble earnings were planted a kind of peace and, dare I say it, Zen. Who wants to be rich and not have to work for a living anyway? I wouldn't know what the hell to do with myself.

I was still trying to convince myself that it would suck to be rich, and failing miserably at it, when Harold Sanders crossed his long, thin legs and cleared his throat. Not like it required clearing. More like he was insisting upon my undivided attention without actually asking for it. Considering he was the only other person occupying the room besides myself, and knowing how deep his pockets must be, I gave it to him.

"Naturally, I've done some checking up on you, Mr. Marconi," he said with a tight-lipped smile, his tone patronizing. Like an elementary school principal to a newly-arrived fifth-grade transfer.

For a brief instant, I felt like reaching across my desk and backhanding that smile right off his cleanly shaved face. But then I once more reminded myself of those deep pockets.

We were sitting in my first-floor warehouse-converted-to-office-space-and-apartment with the door shut and the view of a sunbaked Sherman Street looking positively magnificent through the old floor-to-ceiling, wire-reinforced warehouse windows. It hadn't rained all summer long, and what had originally been termed a "temporary dry spell" by the Albany meteorologists had evolved into a full-blown drought, complete with a lawn-watering moratorium and hefty fines, or even jail time, for those who broke them. It was so hot and dry in the city that the drug dealers who almost always hung outside my front door rarely bothered coming out during the overheated daytime hours. A situation which must have pleased the very rich and very accomplished Mr. Sanders upon his arrival at my downtown address in his brand new black BMW convertible.

"Please, call me Keeper," I said while painting on my best shiny, happy smile. "All my friends and enemies do."

"You survived the Attica uprising, as I understand it," he said, recrossing his legs. As I said, he dressed himself in the manner of a new-wave priest or maybe even a successful pop culture artist like Richard Prince. But he did not dress poorly. If I had to guess, I would say his black leather lace-up boots, matching black gabardine slacks, and cotton blend T-shirt didn't originate from the local Gap outlet. More like a high-end clothier in Florence, Italy. The same place he would have purchased his round, tortoiseshell eyeglasses, and maybe even the same place his thick, shoulder-length salt-and-pepper hair was coiffed. I tended to notice these things since giving up the prison warden life to become a laminated license-carrying private dick.

I leaned back in my swivel chair, locked my hands together at the knuckles, and brought them around the back of my head for a headrest.

"I was just a kid fresh out of high school. A brand-new corrections officer. Attica was the largest American-versus-American slaughter since the Civil War. Not counting the abominable Indian wars, of course, which were much worse. From a genocidal point of view."

He smiled. Probably because I'd somehow managed to use the words abominable and genocidal in the same sentence.

"Why so young?" he asked.

"I didn't feel the college path was right for me, and I definitely didn't want to go to Vietnam, so my dad pulled some strings."

Sanders smiled as though we were both a part of the same old boy crony circuit, of which I most definitely was not. What I didn't tell him is that I went on to score an undergrad degree in English. Took me six years of night classes, but I got through it.

"Sometimes it pays to have parents who can afford us a proper start in life, even if that start is on the nice side of a set of iron prison bars."

"My dad was a construction worker," I said. "He used to get drunk and lose at poker to the guards from Coxsackie Correctional."

Sanders's smile melted into a tight sour puss, as though he'd just farted out loud by mistake. Made one wonder if he were as liberal as he appeared. Or maybe he just liked to portray himself as a liberal.

"Just as well," he said. "Both my lawyer and the Albany police force spoke highly of you. Said you were a fine prison supervisor and now you are a very competent and very mature private detective."

"Aw, shucks. Now you're embarrassing me."

"They also said you were a bit of a jokester."

"You mean like a wise ass."

"Yes, indeed. Must be a requirement in your profession."

"You have no idea," I said, bringing my hand around and adjusting the ball knot on my tie so that it hung Lou Grant low under my white, open-necked button-down. "So how can I be of service today?"

He reached down toward his black-booted feet and took hold of a leather briefcase that didn't have a handle or a shoulder strap. He flipped open the fine leather lid and slid out a collection of newspaper clippings bound together with an alligator clip. He handed them to me from across the desk. I leaned forward, reached my hand over the desk, and took them from him.

"You've no doubt heard about my daughter, Sarah, and her recent troubles," he said. "Troubles with her fiancé, the restaurateur, Robert David Jr."

I knew that if I told him I had not heard about his daughter's troubles that he would find me ill-informed and, therefore, no longer a candidate for whatever job he wanted me to take on. So, considering his expensive tastes and the fact that he might have no trouble laying a hefty retainer on me, I played along.

"I'm sorry," I said, taking a bit of a gamble. "I know how hard things must be for you as of late."

"Thank you," he said, genuinely pleased with my reaction. Score one for Keeper Marconi, former English major.

While we were quiet for a reflective moment, I did my best to speed read the first couple of paragraphs on the top clipping, which bore the headline, "Manny's Owner Under Investigation in Fiancée Head Injury Case." It was about Sarah Levy, who was now divorced from the local writer Michael Levy. Seems she'd taken up with the aforementioned young restaurant owner and gotten herself into some trouble, which culminated in her landing in the Memorial Medical Center in a coma after suffering severe head injuries.

Truth be known, I had indeed heard about this case, after all. It made the local vine not necessarily because of Sarah's injuries, which were very bad, but because of the suspicious nature under which they might have been sustained on the property of one of Albany's richest and most eligible bachelors.

"You think Robert David Jr. hurt your daughter on purpose?" I posed to Sanders.

He nodded.

"The young man claims that she slipped on the ice outside his West Albany home at two in the morning. Which would be a fine explanation had he immediately called 911. She was unconscious and bleeding from a ruptured cranial cap, for God's sake."

Ruptured cranial cap . . .

"But he didn't bother to call," I said, staring down at the photo of the happy couple, which was published along with the article. Robert David Jr. was young and clean looking with wavy, if not curly, reddish-blond hair and striking, if not spooky, green eyes. Sarah was also bright eyed, her brunette hair long and lush and parted neatly over her left eye, which was brown. The two reeked of optimism and youth, even if the paper cited David's age as forty-one and Sarah's as thirty-eight. Not exactly the youth of the world, but then, love is a many-splendored thing. Until the splendor spoils. Or in this case, splits a head open.

"Why exactly didn't he call 911?" I said.

"I wouldn't be sitting here if I knew that."

"Who have you been speaking to at the APD?"

"A detective by the name of Nick Miller. While the police have obvious evidence of a violent event, they have no leads or evidence of a violent crime having been committed. See how that works, Mr. Marconi? On top of all that, the Davids aren't talking. That's exactly why Nick Miller suggested I contact you."

"So I can do his work for him," I said, not without a grin.

"Perhaps that is a secondary motive on Detective Miller's part. As I understand it, the police force is overextended these days, and the wealthy Davids are rather generous in their annual police benevolence contributions."

"I'm shocked that you'd suggest the Davids purchase their own particular brand of Albany law and order."

He recrossed his legs again. Did it with class and more than a little bit of joie de vivre.

I once more sat back in my swivel chair. Did it with blue-collar toughness and cynicism. Keeper, the hard-ass gumshoe.

"Your daughter is recovering from her injuries?" I pressed.

"She is currently in Valley View Rehabilitation Center in Schenectady. She has no short-term memory nor any recollection of the event, which occurred nearly six months ago now."

"Is she still engaged to Mr. David?"

"They have since ended their engagement," he said, his Adam's apple bobbing up and down in his neck.

"Who ended it?"

"The young man did. It was the polite thing to do. Under the circumstances."

"In other words, you're suing the shit out of him."

More bobbing of the Adam's apple along with some rapid eye blinking. I'd definitely stepped on the architect's exposed nerve endings.

"Yes, I've entered into a civil suit with him."

"How much you going after?" I said, leaning back up against my desk, grabbing hold of a BIC ballpoint, jotting down the word *lawsuit* in neat Keeper Marconi scribble. Felt good putting that English degree to work.

"Forty million," he said, with all the casualness of a man

revealing the score on a Yankees/Red Sox doubleheader.

"I see," I said. "Your lawyer's name?"

"I don't think—"

I slapped the pen down, raised my head, my brown eyes locking with his bespectacled gray-blue eyes.

"Look, Mr. Sanders," I said, "If we're going to work together, we have to get something straight right off the bat. I'm going to have to trust you and you're going to have to trust me. I'm going to be asking a lot of personal questions of you, your wife, and your grandmother if you've still got one. I might even interrogate the family dog. For sure I'm going to interview your daughter, for what it's worth. But the point is, when I ask you a question, I expect a straight answer, and I expect it immediately. Got it?"

He swallowed something. It looked like fear or respect or both. I went with both.

"My lawyer's name is Terry Kindler," he said. "And I don't have a dog at present."

I sat up straight, picked the pen back up, and jotted down the name Kindler, even though I'd personally known the litigator for years. Marconi, the conscientious.

"I'm going to need to talk with Kindler right away. Miller too. In the meantime, do you have any theories as to what happened on that cold night in February? The love birds been fighting? They not been getting along the way the soon to be betrothed should?"

"I believe Robert David Jr. hit my daughter over the head many times with a blunt object and did so in a heavily inebriated state. He then tried to cover it up by saying she fell on the ice."

"Why was she trying to leave at two in the morning on a cold winter's night? She have children from her first marriage?"

"A sweet little boy named Sam. But he was staying with his father at the time."

"The novelist," I said.

"Yes, the novelist. I suspect she was leaving because she and Robert were fighting. Robert has himself one heck of a temper."

"That so?"

"Yes, it is so. A devilish temper. I believe he hit her and nearly killed her. But instead of calling 911, what does he do? He calls his father, Robert Sr., who drives to the house, stuffs my daughter into the backseat of his car, and then proceeds to the emergency room not at the more capable Albany Medical Center, but to a smaller, very incapable hospital on the outskirts of town."

"Memorial Medical Center," I said. "North Albany."

"Indeed."

"Stinks," I said.

"Overwhelmingly," he said. "Positively pungent." The way he pronounced *pungent* was with a hard *g*. An English major notices these things.

"Two hundred per day, plus expenses. Under normal circumstances, I request a retainer of $2,500. I consider these normal circumstances."

His eyes went wide, but for only a brief second.

"Seems a little . . . excessive."

"Not if you're a world-famous architect who makes millions and who's looking for forty million more."

We both chewed on that for a while, staring each other down from across my desk. Until he slowly grew a smile, obviously interpreting my crack as a compliment masked in sarcasm. He cocked his head forward as if he were going to have to be good with my prices or else hit the bricks.

"Get what you pay for, I suppose," he said, reaching into his leather satchel and pulling out his checkbook and a genuine Montblanc pen.

"Money sings like an angel, Mr. Sanders," I said, "and I love to listen to those angels."

He wrote out the check, leaned forward, and set it on my desk beside the newspaper clippings. Then he stood back up.

I got up and came around the desk. I asked him for a card. He found one in his wallet and handed it to me.

"My cell is on there. Call me day or night. I'm not traveling right now so you can find me either at my Albany office or at my home in Bethlehem, just outside the city."

I didn't need for him to explain where the little town of Bethlehem was located. I knew it as a rich suburban haven filled with upwardly mobile and liberally educated white people like Sanders. I took a quick glance at the card.

Sanders Architects, Engineers, and Interior Designers. Offices in Albany, New York City, and Hong Kong. I thought about my own humble business: Marconi Private Detective Services, with its office

11

inside a formerly abandoned Sherman Street warehouse in downtown Albany, where the locals sold cocaine and ecstasy right outside my front, solid metal, door. But I wasn't complaining. At least it was all mine. My little kingdom on this big, blue, bitter earth.

I stuffed the card into the interior pocket of my blue blazer, my hand brushing up against the butt of my shoulder-holstered Colt .45 Model 1911.

"I'll be in touch," I said.

He held out his hand. I took it in mine and squeezed. Soft, thin, sweaty . . . maybe even metrosexual sweaty.

"Oh my," he said. "You must work out."

"I train with weights and run."

"How often?"

"Every day."

"Explains your exceptional shape for a man having solidly reached his middle years."

"I try, and I still feel like I'm twenty-one."

"Keep trying," he smiled, releasing my hand. "We don't get any younger."

"Not unless India is right about reincarnation."

I was still staring down at the perspiration Harold Sanders left behind on the palm of my hand as he casually exited my office.

Big Trouble in Little Paradise? Manny's Owner, Son Sued for $40M over Brain Injury
By Ted Bolous, *Albany Times Union* Senior Food Blogger

Have you heard about Albany's most popular high-end eatery owner, Robert David Jr., being sued up the wazoo for a whopping $40M? The lawsuit comes in the wake of the serious brain injury suffered by his squeeze du jour, the beautiful and very wealthy Sarah Levy, which left her in a coma for nearly six months. You might have read the many articles about the rather fragile situation published by the crime desk at this very paper. The lawsuit states that Robert did not attempt to assist Sarah when she allegedly "slipped on the ice" outside his West Albany home and, on top of that, actually exacerbated her injuries by not calling 911.

Wow, ya think?

Not only has Robert David Sr. and Robert David Jr.'s version of the incident been inconsistent with regards to Levy's injuries, but it's looking more and more as though the Davids are the creators of a rather insidious cover-up. According to Sarah's doctors, Sarah's injuries are more consistent with a fall from a great height or a serious head-on automobile accident, not just your garden-variety slip on the ice.

But according to David Jr., after Sarah slipped and fell, he tried to pick her up, but then accidentally dropped her not once, but several times, thus compounding her head injuries. The admittedly inebriated (Go figure!) David then panicked and called David Sr. instead of doing the sensible thing and calling 911. The two Davids proceeded to shove the unconscious Sarah into David Sr.'s car, driving her not to the Albany Medical Center (Huh!?!) but to the more out-of-the-way and far smaller Memorial Medical Center.

Okay, hold onto your bibs, but in short, it's possible Robert David Jr., Albany's richest and most eligible bachelor, has entered into a cover-up of Biblical proportions.

Stay tuned, foodie readers. This hot and spicy beef is just heating up.

2

FIRST ITEM OF DETECTING business: Wash my hands.

I stood in front of the old wall-mounted mirror in the small bathroom located down the hall from my office. The bathroom contained an old, white porcelain sink and a toilet that must have been considered state-of-human-waste-art when it was first installed in the early 1920s, back when this five-story building was home to a garment manufacturer. But now the garment manufacturer was gone baby gone, and the old porcelain god looked as though it belonged in a museum.

I couldn't help but think the same thing about myself.

Releasing a heavy sigh, I looked at my face in the mirror. As the old Chevrolet television commercial used to say, "It's not the years; it's the mileage." Not that I wasn't still my handsome old self, but my head of thick, black hair had receded with age, leaving me with a retreating salt-and-pepper growth that revealed more and more of my scarred scalp every year. I knew I could invest in one of those expensive hair-for-men treatments, but there seemed to be something extremely dishonest about that kind of thing. Vain. Selfish. Self-absorbed. Or maybe other men cared more about their appearance than I did. Metrosexuals like Harold Sanders. At least I still worked out every day, or so the architect was kind enough to notice, even if his observation did send a slight chill up and down my spine.

My face hadn't fared much better than my head of hair over the years. A couple of hair-thin scars ran down the right side of my cheek, and it's because of them that I now prefer to wear a perpetual five-o'clock shadow, lest I scare off every little kid who comes within five feet of me. Or maybe it's my excuse not to shave every day.

The scars were made by an inmate's claw-like fingernails back in the mid-1990s while I was supervising Green Haven Prison, and they look like very thin lightning bolts. Never underestimate the quickness of an incarcerated killer who weighs only 120 pounds when wet. Let your guard down for even a single second and he can kill you with a quick swipe of his hand. I was lucky he didn't remove one of my brown eyes. Then I'd be forced to wear a black eye patch, which might make me look tougher. Or even more sophisticated. Appearances aren't everything or we'd all be mannequins.

I turned on the cold water, cupped my hands under the flow, and splashed my face with it. Looking back up into the mirror, I had to ask myself out loud, "What is true love?"

My voice sounded strange and hollow inside the old bathroom with the water dripping off my face and into the sink. I experienced true love in my life only once before. With my wife, Fran. But she'd been taken away from me by a bald-headed thug whom I eventually tracked down and sent to hell by tossing him into the business end of a raging white-watered waterfall only slightly less powerful than Niagara Falls. But what was it exactly that Fran and I had all those years ago that Robert David Jr. did not have with Sarah Levy?

"Unconditional love," I whispered to myself.

That was true love in my book: When you could trust your mate implicitly and when you could forgive her for anything and everything that happened to go south in the past. Even forgiving the worst—adultery. The ultimate marriage miscue.

But then I was getting ahead of myself already. Sarah and Robert weren't married yet, and who knows if they were fighting or not on that cold night in February? Maybe her injuries happened as Robert David Jr. said they happened. Maybe she went outside to drive home at two in the morning in subzero temperatures and simply slipped on the ice, fell backward, and hit the frozen earth very, very hard. It happens to all of us eventually. That is, if you live long enough in a wintertime icebox like Albany.

I dried my face with a couple of paper towels, crumpled them up in my palms, and tossed them into the bin. Then, giving myself one more look in the mirror, I inhaled and exhaled.

"You don't really believe Sarah innocently slipped and fell, do you?" I said.

15

"Nope," I answered. "I ain't buying that shit for a minute."

"Don't say ain't. You've earned a degree in English. And you were raised better than that."

"Apparently so were Sarah and Robert. Both of them were raised with silver spoons in their pretty, little mouths."

"Go do some detecting, Keeper. And stop judging."

"Roger that."

I nodded and shot my image a quick smile. It perked me up a little to see that I still had all my teeth. So what if they were a little bit stained from the tobacco I used to enjoy on a daily basis? It's the little imperfections that make us so unique.

I exited the bathroom with a renewed sense of who I was as a human being at that very moment in time. Even if I did just finish carrying on an entire conversation with myself in the mirror.

3

DETECTIVE NICK MILLER WAS everything I could only hope to be.

Tall, slim, with a full head of gracefully graying blond hair that was cut putting-green short. His face was narrow and concave at the cheekbones, and from what I could see, he couldn't grow a full beard if someone pasted one on for him. He was also neat, dressed in pressed, navy blue slacks and a bone-colored button-down, his detective's badge hooked to one side of his black leather belt and his department-issued .9mm Smith & Wesson holstered to the other. He bore the lean build of a man who liked to run on a daily basis and maybe lift a few light weights now and again too. He also wore no wedding band on his ring finger, which told me he was probably divorced, as so many APD cops are by the time they've reached his age. Keeper, the cynical.

"You're no longer wedded?" I said while sipping a tall-necked Budweiser at Lanies Bar and Grille in Albany's far north end.

"Why don't you ask me if I'm still married?" he said, sipping carefully on a scotch and soda.

We occupied the far corner of the bar, well out of the way of a sparse late-Monday-afternoon crowd made up of mostly construction workers juicing up their livers and attitudes before heading home to ignore the wife and kids.

"I'm a pessimist when it comes to marriage," I said. "Not sure why, but I just can't help it."

Truth is, I had a happy marriage once that got snuffed out far too early by a man who had set his sights on murdering me, but who instead killed Fran.

"I am in fact divorced," he said. "Twice."

"Ouch."

He shot me a look over his shoulder.

"Thought you knew that about me."

"Never thought to ask," I admitted. "We haven't worked together all that much."

"Now we are."

"Yup. Thanks for the referral."

"Figured you could use the business."

"Why didn't you say, 'figured you might be busy as hell but maybe you could fit this one in'?"

He sipped his drink.

"I'm a pessimist when it comes to work for private detectives. Good work anyway."

I raised up my beer as if to make a toast. He raised up his glass and clinked the bottle. Sometimes a simple gesture like that is as close as you can come to being a blood brother to an Albany cop. Especially a detective. I felt honored.

"So what do you think about this lawsuit Harold Sanders has brought upon our wealthy, young Robert David Jr.?"

"Can't say I blame him. And our young Mr. David isn't exactly so young. He's forty-one, and I think he somehow beat the shit out of her, but he did so in a way that left nothing traceable."

"How can that be?"

"I've done a little research on the APD's dime. It's possible to punch with an open fist, hitting with the hard part of the palm." He demonstrated by holding up his hand, palm open, jamming it against his other open palm so that it made a loud slap across the bar. It grabbed the attention of the construction workers. "But the problem with that," he went on, repositioning his hands around his cocktail, "is that you gotta be Mike Tyson in order to deliver an open-handed blow powerful enough to put someone into a coma. Even then, it can still leave marks traceable to the perp. Theoretically speaking."

"And Sarah was in pretty bad shape when she was delivered to Memorial Medical?" It's a question for which I already knew the answer. But not the details.

He nodded. "She was a hairsbreadth from meeting her maker. Only youth and her relative physical health pulled her out."

18

"And if she'd died?"

"I'd try and slap David with reckless endangerment at the very least. Not that it would stick. But it would be something."

"Why don't you do that now?"

"They don't have a crime called 'almost reckless endangerment' yet. But if they did, I'd be using it."

We chewed on that for a minute while we drank.

"So to clarify: if he didn't hit her with his fists or a blunt object, you think it's possible his story about her slipping and falling on the ice checks out?"

"I don't. Like I said, she was in very bad shape."

"Maybe he hit her with a blunt object. A baseball bat maybe. And then she slipped and fell on the ice."

"Thus far the docs say no baseball bat. Something like that would have left a distinct mark. In today's digital age, you'd probably be able to trace the wood grain to the exact moment and place of manufacture."

"Louisville," I said, cocking my head. "Well, something had to have hit her. Or she had to have hit something."

"David claims he dropped her several times trying to get her into the back of his dad's car. But I'm not convinced that would put her into a coma. He would have had to drop her from a height of ten feet to do that kind of damage. Not the distance from his shins to the ground. It just doesn't sit right with me."

I drank some more beer and wiped the foam from my mouth with the back of my hand.

"Robert David Jr. and Robert David Sr.," I said, shifting the direction of the question and answer. "Pretty tight pair."

"Senior owns half of Albany plus a popular high-end eatery which Junior co-owns and runs." He made quotation marks with his fingers when he said the word *runs*.

"Manny's," I said. "The kid apparently lives in one of the old man's houses too."

"Yup," he said, finishing his drink and tapping the empty glass on the table to get the young female bartender's attention. "The forty-one-year-old kid does indeed live under one of the old man's roofs."

"Must be nice to be rich," I said. "Not have to pay for yourself."

"Yup," he said, as the bartender refreshed his drink with a smile befitting of her youth, long brunette locks, blue eyes, and perfectly positioned nose ring. She also smiled when she brought me a new bottle of Bud without my asking for it. I wondered if she liked older men. Scratch that . . . mature men.

"Think David and Sarah were fighting, and that's what led to her storming out on a cold winter's night?"

"You're projecting when you say *storming out*, but yeah, I'd have to guess that they'd gotten into something."

"They look like the perfect little couple. Think they do drugs?"

"He's richer than Christ Almighty and has a rep for boozing and coking, and she's divorced once already with a little boy to care for. Her architect father must have a shitload of dough, but apparently he doesn't spread the wealth with his kids, choosing instead for them to make it on their own."

"Coking. Now there's a red flag. Add this up: rich plus spoiled plus booze plus coke plus ego, and what do you get?"

"Add in a pretty horrible temper tantrum, and you've got a pretty boy who likes to beat the crap out of his women now and again if he's not getting what he wants."

"Robert David Jr. been married before?"

"Not that I know of."

"Know of anyone he used to date?"

He shook his head. "Nah, but I'm sure if you nosed around Manny's a little, you might find out. Word is that the kid bartends at night . . . when he feels like working."

"I'll make a mental note of that, Detective."

"You do that," he said, taking his first sip from the new drink.

I drank more of my new beer, leaving it half full when I set it back down. Keeper, the optimist.

"So the 40-million-dollar questions are as follows: Why did Junior call Senior at two in the morning instead of calling 911? How close does Junior live to Senior? What were Junior and Sarah arguing over—if they were arguing? And what did Junior hit her with if his story about her being dropped on the icy pavement doesn't check out in the end?"

"That's it? That's all the questions you got, Keeper? Famous PI like you?"

I drained the beer. When the cute bartender went to retrieve another from the cooler, I told her I'd had enough.

20

"Well, truth be told, Detective," I said, sliding off the stool, "I do have one more question."

"Lay it on me," he said, drinking down the rest of his scotch, gesturing to the cute bartender for one more. "That's why I'm here."

"From the newspaper clippings I read, your staff at the APD interviewed more than sixty people, but you didn't interview Robert David Jr. You really let him get away with the Fifth Amendment crap?"

Cute Bartender brought him his drink and tossed him a wink. He set his hand on her hand and gave it a squeeze. Her smiley face filled with pink blush. Score one for the single, mature cop.

"Not sure I can answer that one with a straight face."

I nodded and bit down on my bottom lip.

"Money talks," I said. "Have the Davids been making nice donations to the Albany Police Benevolence Society?"

"No comment," he said. "But yes, a little pretty green distributed in the right places can certainly get results."

"Results that border on obstruction of justice."

"*Border* being the keyword here."

"I gotta talk to Sanders's lawyer, Terry Kindler. But the man I really want to talk with is Robert David Jr."

"Go for the throat," the detective grinned, bringing his third drink to his lips.

"Hey, I used to be a prison warden." Then, in my best gestapo imitation, I said, "I haf vays of making people talk."

Miller drank and then set his glass back down onto the bar, perfectly, onto its own condensate ring.

"Just don't get arrested in the meantime," he said. "David might stink like hell, but he has his rights."

"So did Sarah Levy before somebody, or something, nearly beat her to death and left her with scrambled brains for the rest of her days."

"If you do get David to talk, you'll call me right away?"

"You'll be the first to know," I said. Then, cocking my head in the direction of his drink and my empty beer bottle. "You got this round?"

"Courtesy of the APD," he said. "We protect, and we serve, and we do so unselfishly."

I turned and headed for the door, wondering how many drinks it was going to take before Detective Miller asked Cute Bartender to go home with him. And if she would say yes.

4

AS SOON AS I got back behind the wheel of my twenty-year-old, fire-engine red Toyota 4Runner, I used my smartphone to place a call to Harold Sanders's lawyer. When Kindler's secretary came on the line, I asked for "Terry Kindler . . . Esquire." Heavy emphasis on *esquire*.

"Can I tell the Esquire what this is about?" she asked.

I told her. She told me to hang on for a moment. I hung on. Just my smartphone and me.

"Been a long time, Keeper," the sixty-something-year-old attorney said when he came on the line. "Looks like my client has already been to see you."

"Still super sharp as always, Esquire," I said. "You should donate your brain to science."

"When you can charge $300 an hour, you tend to keep your gray matter in shape. What can I do for you?"

For a brief second, I pictured the clean-shaven, bespectacled, bow-tie-wearing lawyer seated behind his mammoth mahogany desk, a panoramic view of downtown Albany visible in the picture window behind his black leather swivel chair.

"You really think you're gonna get forty mil out of the Davids?"

"You tell me. You're the one hired to scoop up the dirt."

"Figured you'd say that. I'm good at digging up the dirt. It's what I do in place of using brains and the title of esquire. You, on the other hand, dish out the dirt I scoop."

"You are indeed the best. You're in touch with your verbs too. That's why I suggested you to Sanders."

"I have an English degree from night school," I said. "Nick Miller at the APD gave your creepy client the thumbs up regarding my services too."

"My client is not creepy. He's artsy but practical. He's in line to design the new nanotech facility planned for Albany's west end. It's a massive, high-profile undertaking."

"Does Sanders really have offices all over the world, Esquire? Or is he just padding the business cards?"

"Stop calling me Esquire. I don't even know what it means . . . Well, scratch that, I know what it means, but I don't like it . . . And no, I won't discuss my client's business affairs with you, other than the little mention about the nanotech thing."

"He shakes hands like wet fish have sex. Means he can't be trusted."

"To each his own, Keeper. His daughter was nearly killed when Robert David Jr. did whatever he did to her. If the Davids didn't have more money than Oprah, Robert Jr. would be incarcerated by now."

"Always comes back to the ching, doesn't it?" I said. "Anything you can shed light on that might aid me in my investigation, oh powerful wizard of the law? You think the Davids' lawyer will talk to me?"

He cleared his throat the same way Harold Sanders did in my office a little while ago. Not because it required clearing, but because he wanted my undivided attention.

"You can try. But the Davids don't have a lawyer per se, rather a team of lawyers who work in-house. You'll never get through to them."

"Guess I'll start digging in the dirt while you collect your fee."

"Don't be a jerk, Marconi. As I said, I'm just the professional who facilitates the civil lawsuit by regurgitating the information on the proper forms and filing it with the proper county authorities. You provide the veracity to said lawsuit by digging in the fucking dirt. The rest is up to a judge and due process."

"You don't have to keep using the f-word."

"Anything else, Sister Mary Marconi? I gotta take a shit."

"You gotta go, you gotta go. I'll let you get back to your three hundred bills an hour and your esquire brains."

"Use 'em or lose 'em."

The lawyer hung up without a goodbye.

For a time, I just sat behind the wheel thinking about things. I wondered what went into building a nanotech facility. Very small machines for very small products. Very small people working on them. Like the munchkins from *The Wizard of Oz*. Or so I imagined. In any case, I obviously wasn't about to get much in the way of scoop on my new client from Terry Kindler, Esquire. And I wasn't sure I needed any in order to do my job. But at least I had made an attempt to speak with Kindler. In my mind, I crossed off a to-do item on my imaginary list. Keeper, the organizer.

It was hot out, and I wanted a cold beer in the worst way. I knew I could dance around the subject for a while, poke and prod my nose into people and things only vaguely associated with Robert David Jr. Or I could cut to the chase and talk to the real thing.

Using my smartphone, I googled Robert David Jr.'s address. Within the time it took to recite the letters *G-P-S*, I had not only the address, but also a cute, little digital map to go with it. I set the smartphone into its black, plastic, windshield-mounted port and set a course due southwest for the Albany suburbs.

5

IT TOOK ME MAYBE ten minutes to find North Allen Street, which was located in an area of Albany's concrete jungle where midtown ends and the more residential west side begins. I turned onto it, crossing over the busy Western Avenue, where I hooked a quick right, then made a quick left onto an immediately sleepy Marion Avenue. The avenue was actually more like a boulevard in that it was made up of one road that led in a southerly direction and a parallel road that proceeded north. The two roads were separated by a cute-but-narrow meridian meticulously landscaped with green grass, flowers, and trees. It appeared to be lovingly maintained no matter the cost to a neighborhood watch committee or perhaps the neighborhood beauty treatment committee.

Judging by the size and variety of the mansions that surrounded me, cost didn't seem to be a problem in this community. The neighborhood was hilly, and if I didn't know for certain that I was driving in the city of Albany, I would have sworn I'd somehow been transported to Hollywood and Beverly Hills in SoCal. Even the evening's brilliant setting sun and the relentless summer heat added to the illusion. The only things missing were the palm trees.

Just as Google promised, I found Robert David Jr.'s house about ten houses in on the right. Situated up on a small plateau, it was a three-story, tan-plaster-and-red-brick house with a postmodern design and a high-angled roof covered in red, concave tiles that one might find topping a country casa in Spain or Italy. The lawn and gardens were fastidiously maintained, and I imagined that the tall, black metal fence that surrounded the backyard also protected Junior from intruders who wanted to hop into his pool totally uninvited.

A tall, narrow window-wall made of opaque glass block was

positioned parallel to the heavy wooden front door, while a steep set of sloping steps led down to a driveway that accessed a two-car garage. I stopped the 4Runner just beyond the driveway and eyed the staircase, which was made entirely of brick laid horizontally. I thought: *If it turns out that Sarah did, in fact, accidentally slip on those steps and fall down the entire flight only to land in the driveway on her back, then I'm quickly going to be out of job, and Sanders's lawsuit is going nowhere.* I could proceed only under the assumption that what happened to Sarah outside Junior's house was no accident. Keeper, the deductive.

I wasn't exactly ready for an opening Q & A with the accused should he be home, but just eyeing the place from behind the wheel, I got the feeling that the house was, at present, empty. My gut told me to get out and do some snooping. After all, that was my job.

Snooping. Digging.

Killing the engine, I grabbed my smartphone and got out.

I made my way to the driveway first, snapping pictures with the phone's camera app. The driveway was flat and smooth and had recently been seal-coated so that it still had that smell of brand-new black tar. So much for any physical evidence that might have assisted cops in discovering precisely where and how many times Sarah might have fallen on the driveway. But then, midsummer had barely arrived and the damage had been done last winter. The time for uncovering physical evidence had long passed.

Or had it?

I proceeded up the steps of the David mansion, taking some smartphone photos along the way, staring down at the brick pavers for what they might reveal: a piece of clothing, a tuft of dark hair, an earring. Anything. But my quick survey didn't reveal a thing other than a long, winding set of steps made of brick that felt very hard under the soles of my brown Tony Lamas.

When I found myself at the top of the brick steps, I couldn't help but look through the small, glass light embedded into the door at eye level. The small, square-shaped glass was clear and gave me an unobstructed view of the home's tiled vestibule. The glass was wide enough to allow my eyes a view of the dark dining room to my right, a narrow swatch of sunlit kitchen directly ahead of me, and some of the wide-open, scarlet red living room to my left. The glass also gave me a view of the man who presently occupied the living room: Robert David Jr. himself.

I had no worries about him calling the cops on me or screaming at me to get off his dad's property while pointing a big fat gun at my face. Not in his condition. The rich young man was passed out on the couch, surrounded by empty beer bottles and overfilled ashtrays. Set out on a stainless steel coffee table was a large mirror. The mirror housed a couple of credit cards and some tightly rolled up bills, denominations not known. The party had ended too soon. There were still some fat lines of white nose candy left over. But then, I guess when Junior came to, those lines would be a much more welcome sight than your average cup of Maxwell House. Black, no sugar.

A second matching couch set up perpendicular to David's also contained a body. This one a long, leggy blonde. A blonde young woman, I should say. She was dressed only in a white lace thong and matching bra, and from where I stood, I could just about make out the colorful tattoo she possessed on the left side of her neck. The tattoo bore the shape of a serpent: A coiled red, yellow, and blue snake, its mouth wide open and bearing a long set of half-moon-shaped fangs. Every time she inhaled and exhaled, the snake looked as though it were about to strike her earlobe, which I guess was the whole point.

Being the ever-nefarious detective, I raised the camera up and snapped some shots of the two lovebirds sleeping off their party. I made sure not to use a flash so that I didn't accidentally wake them. At the very least, the photos would provide the proof I needed to present to both Sanders and the police that Albany's wealthiest and most eligible restaurateur was indeed the partier that rumor made him out to be.

That little, young piece of heaven lying on the couch beside him wouldn't look too good for him either. But then, the death bell for his engagement to Sarah had already tolled, and what the hell? It's a semi-free country. Who could blame the forty-one-year-old playboy for wanting to have a good time?

I was about to turn and head back to the 4Runner when I got an idea. I didn't come all the way out here just to take some pictures. Why not ask the kid a couple of questions? Catch him with his guard *and* his pants down. It's exactly what I set out to do when I once more checked the Google map on my phone and saw that it not only provided me with Richard's home number, but with his cell number as well. In fact, all I had to do was thumb the digitally displayed phone number on the touch screen, and Google would dial it for me.

I touched the number with the pad of my thumb and a little red box appeared with the word *dialing* inside it.

Don't you just love the digital age?

Is Manny's Owner, Robert David Jr., Hiding Out? Let's Get Your Take on the Matter . . .
By Ted Bolous, *Albany Times Union* Senior Food Blogger

Since my original post, the comments have been pouring in like maple syrup over a freshly grilled stack of buttermilk pancakes. Blueberry pancakes. What's a food blogger like me doing reporting on what might be the most scandalous assault and battery case to strike Albany in decades? Just doing my job, which is to inform, even if what I'm informing about isn't so tasty. And to make matters more interesting, it seems no one in the know (and I am in the know) has seen or heard from David Jr. since this Sanders lawsuit was officially filed in Albany County Court one week ago. Yikes! Must be the handsome Junior is spending a lot of quality time in front of the boob tube or cooking up something sexy with his new girlfriend. Remember you read it here first, and as always, buon appetito . . .

6

MY BROWN EYES PEERED through the small window embedded into the heavy wood door.

I waited for the inevitable.

When the cell phone blasted some rendition of the Rolling Stones' "Sympathy for the Devil," it startled even me. Robert David Jr. just about jumped off the couch, his body coming alive like a zombie prodded by a live electric cable. Mouthing a string of obscenities that were barely audible to me, he reached out for the phone. My cue to cut the connection and begin thumbing the doorbell.

I saw Junior raise up his head, his youngish face going from deadly pale to seething red. It was as though I'd summoned Satan himself. He stood up, a bit wobbly, in his underpants. He shuffled to the other couch, reached down, and poked the woman. Other than her right arm, which she raised up high enough to wave him away, she never moved a muscle. As attractive as she seemed dressed in nothing but her underwear, I knew that, at present, she'd taken on the guise of the living dead.

I hit the doorbell again. And again, just for good measure. Keeper, the persistent.

Robert David Jr. peered down at the coffee table and the lines of coke that were set upon it, as if for a brief second he was considering snorting a line or two for a quick breakfast pick-me-up. But he shuffled away from it, knowing that doing drugs might not be the best idea should the intruder ringing his doorbell be a cop or perhaps his sugar daddy namesake. Or so I imagined.

As he made his way painfully to the door dressed in nothing but a pair of white boxers with little red pitchforks printed on them, I was careful to take a step back and to conceal my smartphone inside the interior pocket of my blue blazer. He unlatched the deadbolt, and the door opened slowly, the hinges squeaking.

"Hope I'm not disturbing you, sir," I said, painting the widest Marconi smile on my face that I could possibly muster.

He glared at me with that flushed, narrow face, his naked torso hard and toned as if he spent his entire privileged day alternating between the gym and the tanning booth. I couldn't help but notice the mountainous bicep that belonged to his left arm. The word Sarah was tattooed on it in thick, blood-red capital letters, with little drops of blood dripping from each of the letters. Subtle. The tat seemed to go heartbreakingly well with the road map of blue veins that were popping out from his tight, thin skin. His body fat index could not have been more than 10 percent. Daily attendance to Gold's Gym and coke will tend to do that to you. So will a wound-up personality and an explosive temper, the trigger of which is hair thin.

I was determined to test that temper.

"Who the fuck are you?" he barked, biting down on his bottom lip. Hard enough to maybe pierce it with his two very sharp top incisors. Sharper than sharp, as though they'd been professionally altered.

I held out my hand, knowing he wasn't about to shake it kindly.

"Good morning," I said. "Or is it good evening, Count Dracula?"

"Listen, pal, dispense with the bad jokes. I work nights, okay? So I have no choice but to sleep all day. Tell me what you want or just fuck off."

I took a step forward and poked my head inside.

"Excuse me?" he said. "There's a lady in there, and she's not exactly decent."

"Not decent at what?" I said. "She work nights too?"

Junior inhaled, but he didn't follow up with an exhale. Swallowing all that hot air made his face grow even redder. For a split second, I thought his cranial cap might erupt like it would if we were living inside a *Looney Tune*. But if that were to happen, I would have been out of a job, and I needed the money. So I decided to temper the situation with a little Marconi charm.

"Pardon me," I said, still wearing my smile. "Where are my

manners?" I reached around to my back pocket for my wallet. "My name is Jack Marconi. I'm a private detective." I showed him my license. He gave it a cursory glance with squinted eyes. When his eyes widened again, I returned the wallet to my pocket.

"You're kidding, right? A private detective? You for real?"

"Flesh and blood."

He issued me a grin and another chance to glance at those pinpoint incisors.

"And that's a real ID?"

"Bought and paid for."

"And I don't have to talk to you."

He went to close the door, but I stuck my cowboy-booted foot against it. He tried to push it close. But it wouldn't budge.

"I train with weights," I said.

"So do I, old man," he said. "Light weights for super quickness."

"Take my advice, Count," I said. "Forget that light weight, a-lot-of-reps, cut-body nonsense. It will deprive you of real strength."

He tried to move the door again. But it wouldn't budge.

"Okay, stop calling me Count, and what do you want?"

"I'll start over again," I said. "My name is Jack 'Keeper' Marconi. And I'm middle-aged. Not old."

"And?"

"I've been hired to look into the true cause of why your former fiancée, Sarah Levy, nearly fell to her death right here on this very property this past winter. That is . . . if she fell at all."

If his narrow face were to grow any redder, it would have hurt my eyes to look directly at him.

"I don't have to speak to the cops." He fake laughed. "And I sure as hell don't have to speak to you. No evidence of a crime exists because no crime took place. Get it, Marconi? Now move your foot and get the hell off my property."

Daddy's property, I wanted to say. But just then, there was some commotion coming from the living room.

"Roberto," the woman on the couch spoke. "Roberto, come stai?"

I smiled again. "Gee, Count, I see you are a multi-ethnic type of guy when it comes to romance."

"She's as American as apple pie and gay marriage, and it's none of your business who I date. Now please leave. Or I'll call the cops."

"That's just it," I said, pulling a business card from my jeans pocket and handing it to him across the threshold. "You won't call the cops at all. Because in an indirect way, I'm working for the same cops who also are looking for the truth behind the crime that took place here. Capisce, Count Roberto?"

He exhaled, his head bobbing.

"Are you through?" he asked, his voice now raspy and filled with acid.

"For now," I said. "I'll be coming around now and again to talk. Preferably at a time that's more convenient for your . . . ummm . . . alternative lifestyle. You know, when the sun has gone down and when it isn't snowing in the summertime."

Acting on instinct, he stole a quick look over his shoulder at the coke that was still laid out on the coffee table. I removed my foot before he grew a pair of horns out from the top of his skull. The door slammed. Through the glass, I saw him about-face and pound his right fist into his open left palm. I heard the words *"Mother! Fucker!"* shouted out in frustration, as if he were undergoing a bout of road rage. He didn't march back into the living room but into the kitchen. A few seconds later, he re-emerged with a cold beer in his hand. He saw me looking at him through the door light. He raised his right hand, his bicep flexing the name Sarah like a built-in exclamation point, and he flipped me off.

I raised my right hand and tossed him a friendly wave. But what I really should have done was hold up the business end of a rosary to the glass. Turning, I made my way back down the steps to my ride, wondering how many times Sarah Levy's pretty head might have bounced off these very same brick pavers.

7

SHE WAS THE ONLY woman since my late wife, Fran, who would leave me wanting more, even after we'd made love more than one time in the same hour. She was also the only woman I could trust and genuinely call a best friend and, therefore, a most trusted confidant. I loved the way she smelled, spoke, dressed, and casually brushed back her silky, black hair. In a word, she was my angel. The truth is that Val Antonelli and I had been working together for years now. We first worked together at Green Haven Prison, where I'd been the superintendent and she, my secretary. Rather, my assistant, I should say.

And later on, when I became a private dick, she came to work for me on a part-time basis, managing the books and billing, paying my taxes, organizing the paperwork, on occasion answering the phones, and sometimes just being there for me as a sounding board and a voice of reason, especially at times when anger got the best of me.

Once upon a time, she nearly became my wife, but things got in the way, and it didn't work out. That's not to say the brown-eyed, smallish-but-beautifully-built, long-haired brunette wouldn't become my wife down the road sometime. But for now, we enjoyed what some people might refer to as a casual relationship in that she maintained her place across the Hudson River in Troy, and I maintained mine in downtown Albany. Whether she was working for me or not, we always got together a few nights a week for dinner and, on occasion, some love. This was one of those occasions when we were engaging in both.

We were lying in bed, both of us naked and allowing the cool air from the portable air conditioner to blow onto our moist skin. The bedroom in her century-old, second-floor, downtown Troy brownstone apartment wasn't large, but it had nine-foot ceilings, and the light blue walls were covered with an eclectic assortment of original artwork. The antique stand-up lamps had been turned off in favor of the gently flickering firelight that radiated from the thick, white candles that were placed on both of her two antique dressers. The neon light that originated at a quiet little bar called Footsie McGoos, which was located directly across the street, leaked in through the big double-hung window. It was a soothing blue light that worked well with the candlelight and that bathed our bodies in blue for a few brief moments at a time.

I'd just told her about my day. About Harold Sanders, his $40-million civil lawsuit, and my new job trying to find out if Robert David Jr. did indeed nearly beat Sarah Levy to death or, at the very least, toss her down the front exterior steps and then cover up his actions by calling in his father to cart her to the emergency room instead of calling 911. I also told her about my little impromptu meeting with the young restaurateur and how easy it had been to work up his red-hot temper.

We were sharing a bottle of red wine while our dinner of pulled pork simmered in the Crock-Pot in the kitchen and the sweet sound of Cliff Brown poured out of the stereo speakers, his classic jazz trumpet belting out a song called "Tiny Capers," which was recorded back in the fifties along with the great drummer and Keeper Marconi hero, Max Roach. Roach and Brown were gone now, having entered the great heavenly pantheon of jazz musicians in the sky. But the songs remained the same.

"First of all," Val said, her head nestled on my chest, "he's forty-one. He's not that young."

"I've seen him up close. He's one of those blond-haired, thin men who will always be young, even in his sixties. If he makes it that long."

"Drugs," she said. "And that devilish thing with his teeth."

"Yah," I said, smelling her rose-petal scent and feeling her hair brushing up against my arm and feeling myself getting aroused yet again. "What's with those teeth? You think he's a vampire? He sleeps all day, you know."

She laughed as the blue neon light flickered across her smooth skin and Cliff and Max played the jumpy "Tiny Capers" from the grave.

"Lots of young people are having their incisors sharpened now," she said. "Vampire-inspired tattoos are huge too. Dripping blood. Anatomically correct renderings of hearts . . . Jeez, Keeper, don't you read?"

"Read what?"

"You know. Books."

"When I'm not detecting, I'm playing drums or working out. But to answer your question, yes, I have been re-reading the great Hemingway. I'm an ex-English major, you know. ."

"Well, most kids these days aren't reading Hemingway. They're reading books like the *Twilight* series. Books about modern-day vampires who have become the new modern-day romantic ideal. They're also reading heavy-duty erotic, like *Fifty Shades of Grey*."

"Vampires have been around for centuries. Remember Boris Karloff? And erotica is just another name for porn. I should know. I am in the possession of an English bachelor of arts."

"Yes, I know. That's the second time you've reminded me in a single minute. But the new spin on vampires, erotica, and even zombies has caught on big-time with the youth of the world, which you most definitely would not know about since you are still so stuck in the 1950s, Mr. Gumshoe."

"I was born in the fifties . . . the mid-fifties."

"You're old, Keeper."

"I just proved it by making love to you twice, angel. And I'm about ready to go a third time." Staring down at my naked lap. "Soon as cute little Johnson wakes up from his cat nap."

She squeezed me and kissed me on the cheek.

"Okay," she said. "I take that back."

"Thank you. Now back to Mr. David. Despite his apparent youthful look, isn't he a bit too old to be carrying himself like a pretend vampire?"

I felt her shrug her shoulders.

"Yes and no. People are younger today. You know, forty is the new thirty and all that. Especially with social media dominating people's everyday existence. Anyone, no matter what his or her age, can create any persona he or she wants and broadcast it to millions. It's quite incredible when you think about it. I've been keeping up on what's happening between David Jr. and his ex-fiancée with the blogs the *Albany Times Union* food blogger, Ted Bolous, has been posting. Judging by their photos, Robert and Sarah seem to have had their pulse on the pop culture trigger. The most fashionable clothes, the newest music, the trendiest IKEA furniture, reality TV, the Internet, Gmail, Skype, Twitter, Facebook, Myspace, Tumblr, blogs, memes, tweets . . . You get the picture."

"Sounds like a fantasy world to me."

"The paradox being that this fantasy world has become the major reality for the young and the not so young of the world today. Thus, the fascination with fantasy-like vampire literature and, frankly, all things erotica inspired and even borderline satanic. People don't have to live in the real flesh-and-blood world anymore now that they can live inside their computers and smartphones. You don't even have to speak on the phone anymore now that you can text. And did you further know that one-quarter of America's married couples now meet through an online dating service?"

"Match dot com," I exhaled. "How sad. They probably get divorced online too."

"I can bet that if you were to search David's house when he's not home . . . and I'm not suggesting you pull a B and E here, my love . . . you'd see a bunch of books like *Dominion, Breaking Dawn, New Moon*, and maybe some fantasy and horror mixed in. Certainly David's probably read *Fifty Shades of Grey*."

"I haven't read *Fifty Shades of Grey*, and I'm an English major."

"Nor should you, smarty pants. It's a chick book."

On the stereo, "Tiny Capers" sadly ended, but happily, a song called "Walkin'" started in.

"Hey," I said, nudging Val, "this isn't the song that's supposed to come on next. I've listened to this album a million times or more over the decades, and the next song in the lineup isn't this one."

"Keeper," she said, her big brown eyes opening even wider. "You do realize that I'm not spinning an old-fashioned album on my old-fashioned turntable. We've been listening to Pandora off my iPhone, which is plugged into my very new-fangled receiving dock. Get with the twenty-first century already."

Now, instead of becoming more aroused, I felt cute little Johnson shrink to even tinier proportions.

"So what's all this got to do with Sarah Levy falling on her head in the driveway? Or, quite possibly, Robert David Jr. beating her over the head or perhaps pushing her down a set of brick steps on a cold and icy night?"

"Your boy, Robert Jr., has not only been sheltered his whole life, but he's not independent and, therefore, not dealing with reality. He's his own best avatar if you will. His own best invented persona. That's why he has such a short fuse. You don't buy into his painstakingly created fantasy, you're discounting him as a worthwhile and important human being. He's not responsible for himself, so he hasn't matured the way responsible people are forced to. His sense of reality is all cockeyed, and his development is arrested."

I listened to the music for a minute, watched the blue neon light flicking on and off our skin, and watched the dancing shadows the flame from the burning candles made against the high-ceilinged walls.

"He was pretty angry at my intrusion into his life of wine, women, coke, sin, and song."

"You knew he'd get angry. That's why you introduced yourself so early on in the investigation. You'd make a crappy spy."

"You know me all too well."

"I do. You like to piss people off. See how they'll react. I remember how you'd get information from inmates. By playing them against one another. Rewarding them after getting them to rat on other inmates who were selling contraband or hurting other prisoners."

"The best way to get a man with a short fuse to expose the truth about a given situation or himself or, at the very least, to let his guard down, is to simply piss him off. Thus far, I've succeeded in doing exactly that with Junior."

"The police don't have that luxury of pissing Robert Jr. off, do they?"

"No. If they piss off a rich forty-one-year-old brat like Junior, then daddy and the lawyer will step in and start screaming abuse. It could potentially lead to a mistrial, should that ever come to pass."

"Junior's got to be arrested first."

"It's not my job to come up with something tangible that proves what happened to Sarah was criminal. It's my job to prove the kid was liable, and that's all. That happens, Harold Sanders, AIA, gets his forty mil. If Junior ends up getting arrested, that's just cream cheese frosting on the cake."

"Hmmm," she said. "Sounds deliciously simple and easy, doesn't it?"

"Yup," I said. "Let's see if I actually find any evidence that proves the kid is not only a vampire lover but an evil killer."

"Just because David is living a fantasy life doesn't mean he harmed a hair on Sarah's pretty little head or that he's even semi-responsible for what happened to her on his property. She could have gotten drunk with him and slipped on the steps on the way out. Happens all the time. Could be that in the end, Junior's only crime is owning a steep staircase constructed of brick."

I nodded and smelled the good aroma of the pulled pork and listened to the good, heartfelt-sounding trumpet. Pandora wasn't all that bad. But I missed hearing the little pops and scratches that came from real records.

"If she really did take an innocent header on the steps," I said, "then why not call 911?"

"You got me there."

"Thus the lawsuit, the liability negligence, and the nagging pit in my gut that tells me this thing really stinks."

Val lifted her head and rolled over to face me. Her angelic brown-eyed face beamed and touched my heart like no other. Not since Fran, anyway.

"How do you intend to proceed now, lover?"

Lifting my left hand, I stole a glance at my wristwatch.

"It's too late for investigating, angel," I said. "I thought maybe we'd have some more wine and some dinner. In bed, of course."

"We could catch a vampire movie on Netflix."

"You mean like watch a movie on your computer?" It was a question.

"Isn't the digital world beautiful?"

"I was thinking we'd eat, then make love again."

I cast one last glance at cute, little Johnson, who was most definitely waking up, regardless of our conversation.

"You're younger than you know, Keeper," she smiled.

"It's what Dracula and I have in common," I said, opening my mouth, going for her neck. "Youthful, good looks and an insatiable appetite for beautiful women."

8

THE NEXT MORNING I got up extra early. While it was still dark out. I got dressed, came around to Val's side of the bed, and kissed her on the cheek while she lay sound asleep. When I kissed her, she mumbled, "I love you, baby."

"I love you too, angel," I whispered back.

I let myself out and took the steps down to the street where my 4Runner was parked. I drove through the emerging orange dawn over the Hudson River via the tall, arcing, steel-span Congress Street Bridge. From there, I caught the riverside highway that would take me to the Albany city limits and the mean streets that would appear ghost-town empty until the rush hour when all the state workers poured into the Empire State Plaza like lemmings to the slaughter.

I parked the 4Runner outside the Sherman Street warehouse and gave the three or four drug dealers who were still congregated at the corner of the old brick-and-concrete building a friendly wave. Then I grabbed the morning paper, unlocked the two heavy-duty dead bolts on the steel door and let myself inside.

Sometimes when I came through the front door, I wished I had a dog to greet me. Maybe I would have trained him to fetch my slippers for me. Maybe he would jump up onto his two back paws, lick my hand, and bark about how he loved me and missed me so much. He'd be a loyal, doting, bushy-haired Labrador retriever maybe. Or a dog-wolf, like in Jack London's *White Fang*. I'd call him Fang for short.

Fran and I had had a dog we called Alex. She was a small terrier-and-Italian-greyhound mix, and she was so kind and loving that she grew to be the child we never had. When Alex suddenly died after getting hit by a school bus, Fran was too heartbroken to ever allow herself to get that close to another dog again. I couldn't blame her at the time. Now Fran's gone too. Been gone a long time. But the pain of our permanent separation . . . the *aloneness* I feel in my veins . . . somehow never disappears.

Locking the door behind me, I entered the apartment living room and retrieved my cell phone from the inside pocket of my jacket before taking it off and tossing it onto the tom-tom of my vintage 1960s-era, blue sparkle Rogers drum set. Then I undid my shoulder holster and brought both the phone and the gun over to my desk, which was in the dining room. I sat down at the desk and opened up the lid on my laptop. Grabbing a USB cord from inside my desk drawer, I plugged my phone into the computer and clicked on the commands that would download the pictures I took at Robert David Jr.'s house.

While the pictures downloaded, I made coffee and toasted a hard roll. When the coffee was done, I poured a cup and added some 2 percent milk to it. Then I buttered the hard roll and took it into the dining room and sat back down at the desk.

The photos were set up on the screen like an electronic contact sheet. The software program that came with my computer allowed me to click on each photo and zoom in or zoom out. I could even pinpoint a specific area of the photo that I wanted to explore and zoom into it. Val was right: The digital age was a lovely thing. Or, it had its lovely moments anyway.

I ate the warm, toasted hard roll and drank the hot coffee with milk and browsed the photos.

I gazed at Junior's house from the vantage point of my 4Runner out on the street. The lush lawn was greened by constant watering, even though we were in the midst of a hellish fifty-year drought. So much for abiding by the emergency water restriction laws. The stark black, newly seal-coated driveway glimmered in the sunshine. The crescent-shaped, brick-paver staircase started at the driveway and rose up a full story until it connected with the concrete landing outside the front door.

My eyes shifted to the steps. To the close-up shots of the treads. I clicked on each picture, zoomed in on each one. Nothing special caught my eye. I then moved on to the few photos I took through the small glass embedded into David's front door. The two lovebirds sleeping it off inside the scarlet-red living room. The empty beer bottles and cans. The coke on the mirror. The credit cards used for cutting the dope into neat, little lines. The girl on the couch. Her thong underwear exposing a lovely pair of smooth ass cheeks. The serpent image tattooed on her neck. An après-party scene lifted right out of "*Hotel California,*" but it was nothing that was going to lead me to the conclusion that Robert David Jr. pushed Sarah Levy down the steps or hit her over the head repeatedly with a blunt object.

I got up from the computer, went into the kitchen, and poured more coffee.

I looked at the small pictures of Fran I still kept tacked to the refrigerator with little magnets: Fran and me arm in arm on the beach in Cape Cod; Fran trying to blow out forty candles on a birthday cake, her big brown eyes wide, her shoulder-length black hair draping her face like a veil, her skin tan and lovely; Fran standing behind thirty little children who comprised the very last class she ever taught at Stormville Elementary School. All those memories were so fresh and vivid in my brain that I could still hear her raspy voice and smell her lavender scent. I saw her smile. Felt her touch, as if an angel were embracing me.

"So what do you think about the case of Robert David Jr., Fran?" I said aloud. "Do you think it's possible to love your future wife but at the same time find no problem with nearly beating her to death?"

I waited for her answer. The answer came to me inside my brain. I heard the words as if she were speaking them.

"You know as well as I do, Jack, that no one who loves someone as much as we loved each other would ever cause physical or psychological harm. That's not love. True love means that you accept each other unconditionally. Accept each other for who you are and who you want to be. Anything else isn't love at all, but obsession."

I drank some coffee and thought about it for a moment. As usual, Fran was right. You didn't go around beating each other up in a loving relationship. I took a step back into the dining room, picked up the newspaper clippings set out on the desk, and looked once more at the photograph of the happy, "in love" couple. Junior was smiling, but there was no hint as of yet of his sculpted vampire incisors. Sarah was smiling too, and there was no hint of the brain damage she would soon incur as a result of a night gone bad with her fiancé.

I knew then that from this point on if I focused my investigation on Junior's obsession with Sarah, I just might be able to find a motive in his having attacked her. If all went well, once I discovered the motive, perhaps the method would simply fall into place.

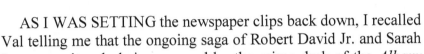

9

AS I WAS SETTING the newspaper clips back down, I recalled Val telling me that the ongoing saga of Robert David Jr. and Sarah Levy wasn't only being covered by the crime desk of the *Albany Times Union*, but also by the food blogger.

That's right . . .

Food. Blogger.

For a brief moment, I had to remind myself just what the hell a blogger was and what distinguished him from a writer or reporter. In the end, I wasn't entirely sure, although I had a suspicion that a blogger was paid less than a real reporter. Back in the kitchen, I picked up the paper and scanned the local section for the food blog. The food blog wasn't there. That's when it dawned on me that, at present, there existed two different versions of the *TU*: the traditional paper version, which was very thin these days, and the electronic version. Bingo. So that's at least one of the distinctions that separated a blog from a column and a blogger from a reporter.

I would find a blog only online.

I made my way back into the dining room and typed in the words *Albany Times Union* in the narrow box provided by my Google search engine. My search immediately brought up the link to the online version of the paper, which in this case was no longer a paper at all but a digitized representation of all the news that was fit to print in New York's Capital Region.

I scrolled along the toolbar and found that the food blog was listed under the *Entertainment* heading. It seemed odd, if not downright bizarre, to me that reports of Sarah Levy's head injuries would be listed as entertainment. But then, I still read a real paper newspaper, and from what I was being told by people like Val, these days more people got their news off their smartphones than from either real papers or the television. Every day I felt more profoundly out of the popular culture loop than ever.

I clicked on the food blog, which was penned by a man named Ted Bolous, or so Val had informed me. Bolous's byline was located directly beneath a grainy, black-and-white headshot of an overweight, scruffy-faced, white male who obviously enjoyed the free meals that must have been the major perk of his online profession. That is, judging by his numerous chins.

I scanned the first four or five blogs Ted had already written about the Sarah Levy and Robert David Jr. affair and quickly found that they didn't contain any information that I didn't already know. But Bolous's most recent piece caught my attention since it not only contained a downloadable PDF of the David-Levy lawsuit, but it was accompanied by more than one hundred comments. Try getting that pot of gold from out of real paper newspaper. Exhaling a breath, I proceeded to read:

Get Your Robert David Jr. Lawsuit Right Here
By Ted Bolous, *Albany Times Union* Senior Food Blogger
Don't say I never give you anything for free, dear foodie. I have in my tobacco-stained fingers a copy of the very lawsuit that Harold Sanders has thrust upon the David boys. All two hundred pages of it. (Don't ask me how I obtained my copy, but suffice it to say I have friends in . . . ummmm . . . high places!) Since I love you all so much, I have scanned it and attached it here as a PDF. Read away, dear food lover, and keep on churning out those comments. Reality television was never so good. We're really cooking with Wesson now . . .

Ted really had a way with words. Just by reading those sentences, I knew precisely why he had attained the coveted position of Senior Food Blogger. My God, what was next? "Double Senior Food Blogger?

I double-clicked on the link that would download the official lawsuit. While it was downloading, I scanned the first few comments while drinking down what was left of my now lukewarm coffee.

"Sounds fishy to me," wrote one person.

Another one wrote, "Maybe customers should stop going to Manny's until the Davids cooperate and answer some questions. Maybe that would get their attention."

Someone else simply typed in two words that said it all: "Cover up."

Wasn't so long ago when I'd have to stand in line at the Albany county clerk's office and pay twenty bucks for the privilege of glancing at a copy of a particular lawsuit that might be relevant to some case I might be investigating. The whole process could blow a full workday. Sometimes more if I didn't get through the document in a few hours. But all that hassle and expense had become ancient history in the new digital age. Now all I had to do was turn on my computer and do a proper search for the document I wanted. In this case, Ted Bolous was handing it to me and his readers on a silver food blogger platter while trying to make it look as though he and he alone were being entrusted with a top-secret document. Big fat liar that he was. Obviously Bolous had a flair for the dramatic.

In any case, I proceeded to stuff my face with the lawsuit . . . so to speak.

Turns out that the thick document was all presentation and not a whole lot of taste. Nothing much existed in terms of substance other than the amount Sanders was going after and a rather dry and legalized explanation of what might have occurred on the night of February 18th, along with the wrongfulness of David in calling his father to take Sarah to the hospital instead of doing the right thing by calling 911. Knowing I wasn't about to find any concrete answers to the many questions I had by sitting behind my desk, I decided that the time had come to get back in the field in order to do some real detecting.

I clicked off the PDF and looked at my watch. Going on nine in the morning. I wondered what time food blogger Ted Bolous arrived at work. Whether he worked days or nights. Assuming he wrote during the days and dined freely at night, I decided that I would pay him an unannounced visit. Heck, I might even bring him donuts. A couple of strawberry crème-filled donuts might get me on his good side.

Standing, I strapped on my shoulder holster, pulled out the two-and-one-half-pound Colt .45, thumbed the clip release, and allowed the nine-round clip to drop into the palm of my hand just long enough for me to check the rounds. Slapping the clip back home, I thumbed the safety back on and returned the piece to its holster.

Out in the living room, I grabbed my jacket from off the tom-tom and stole my keys from out of the pocket. Then with my open left hand, I came down on the crash cymbal as I would if I were drumming out the opening bars to the 1970s hit, "*Jungle Boogie.*"

"Jungle boogie, get down," I sang on my way out the steel door and onto an overheated Sherman Street.

10

AS I RELOCKED THE deadbolts on my front door, one of my neighbors approached me.

"Beautiful morning, Warden," called out a muscular black man who was dressed in a tight, black T-shirt, Levi's jeans, and black lace-up combat boots. "Need a little pick-me-up, boss? Something for the nose?"

"Just had my coffee, Blood," I said. "Anything else would give me a heart attack."

"Was a time I could sell the Brooklyn Bridge back to the New York City if I wanted to," he said.

"But these days you are the patron saint of prison reformation, Blood," I said, heading for the driver's side door of the 4Runner, but not without pulling a twenty spot from out of my jeans pocket. I handed it to my former Green Haven inmate as I opened the door and got in. "Thanks for keeping an eye out on the ride," I added. "My weekly payment."

Blood took the bill and stuffed it into his pocket.

"Pleasure doing business, Keeper," he said as a young, white male dressed in a business suit came around the corner of my building. When his eyes caught mine, he cautiously backed up and out of sight.

"Looks like a buyer, Blood," I said.

"The dealers got to make a living in the age of mass unemployment, right? I try and make sure they don't sell no heroin or injectable shit though," he said. "That stuff's for the uptown Clinton Avenue junkies. That's what I tell them. You wanna sell on my street, you sell recreational shit to recreational-minded suburban white-breads. End of story."

The middle-aged, former-convict-turned-college-graduate, and self-appointed Sherman Street Watch Committee chairman tossed me a wave and made his way around the corner to keep an eagle's eye on the drug deal that was about to go down—for which he would no doubt collect a sizeable percentage, albeit silently and anonymously. I closed my car door, turned the engine over, and opened the windows to let out some of the heat that was already building up so early in the morning.

As I pulled away from the curb and headed down the one-way roadway toward Lark Street, I took a glance at Blood in the rearview mirror. He was standing maybe twenty feet away from a young dealer, a black man dressed in a polyester track suit, his head covered in a do-rag. The customer was handing the dealer a business-letter-sized envelope that was no doubt filled with cash. Blood looked on as though he were refereeing a boxing match, his big arms crossed over his considerable chest. The dealer and customer both smiled profoundly at each other before parting ways. It was a curious dance of black-market economics and a clash of two opposing cultures, not altogether different from that which I once knew all too well inside the concrete jungle.

Jungle boogie . . .

Fifteen minutes later, I was sitting inside the 4Runner with the window down and Cliff Brown going on the cassette tape deck. Cliff could really bring tears to my eyes when he belted out "*Somewhere over the Rainbow*" on his trumpet. I was probably the only man in Albany who still owned a cassette tape deck stereo in his ride. But hey, at least I knew the outdated music machine was never going to be stolen at night while I slept, even if I stupidly left the doors unlocked down on Sherman Street.

Resting beside me on the passenger's side seat like a little square bundle of joy was a box of a dozen Dunkin' Donuts all laid out, nice and neat and colorful in a bright pink box. As luck would have it, the *Albany Times Union* awarded its star bloggers with their own parking spaces. I figured the best way to run into the very man I intended to see was to park in his designated space.

I waited for the time it took Cliff Brown to play three songs and ate a blueberry cake donut, which I washed down with a large coffee and milk. No sugar. When the older-model, compact, tan Honda hatchback pulled up behind me, the driver hitting his horn, I knew I had my man. Without hesitation, I quickly reached over, opened the glove box, hit the Play/Record button on the microcassette player I stored inside it, and then covered it with a pair of black leather gloves. I wasn't sure if Bolous would have anything earth-shattering to tell me. But if he did, I'd at least have a record of it.

I slapped the glove box closed and held my ground while chewing on a second blueberry cake donut. It was still warm and practically melting in my mouth. Heaven in the shape of an *o*.

Turned out Bolous wasn't as fat as his official *Albany Times Union* headshot made him out to be. He was, instead, terrifically out of shape. I watched the tall, skinny-yet-bloated and paunchy, double-chinned man approach me from the vantage point of the side view mirror. As the writing embossed on the mirror glass warned, he was closer than he appeared, so when his knuckles wrapped on the window, it startled me a bit. I thumbed the button that allowed the window to roll down electronically.

"Yes," I said, swallowing some donuty goodness. "Can I help you?"

"You're parked in my spot, dude."

I pretended to appear wide-eyed and startled.

"Is that a fact?" I said, staring through the windshield at the plastic and wood sign that said *Reserved for Ted Bolous*.

"Oh my god," I said. "You're not *theee* Ted Bolous? The famous food critic and blogger? Wow, I'm a big fan, and now I'm actually parked in your spot. Wait till my friends hear about this."

He smiled. That was a good sign. He fancied himself a local celebrity.

"Yes," he said, dragging out the *s* in *yes* as if he were a snake, or maybe just more in touch with his feminine side than the average male. "As a matter of fact, I am Ted Bolous."

He was wearing a blue blazer over a brown T-shirt that said *Lorna Del Ray* superimposed over a rustic beach scene in sunny SoCal. His jeans weren't regular Levi's 505s, like my own, but skinny jeans. They fit so tightly that his considerable paunch spilled over his thin leather belt like uncooked pizza dough. On his feet, he wore little leather booties that weren't exactly boots or loafers, but something in-between. He wore thick, black, square-rimmed eyeglasses, and his hair was black and very thick and parted in the middle. He sported an unusually wide mouth that was surrounded by a very trim beard. If I had to guess, my new friend Ted Bolous was not only a foodie, but a pop-culture monster. And—dare I say it—a metrosexual who might get along swimmingly with my client, Harold Sanders.

"Would you like me to back out, Mr. Bolous?" I said.

"That would be the idea," he said, hiking up the black computer bag, which was strapped to his narrow shoulder.

"Listen," I said, "perhaps I should introduce myself." Then I told him who I was, who I presently worked for, and why I was parked in his space.

"Jesus," he said, "do I look like I'd want to speak with you? Maybe you should back out now before I call in security."

I reached for the donuts and held them up to the open window.

"There's a large coffee in it for you too," I said.

He looked one way and then the other. I could practically hear his stomach growling from inside the 4Runner.

"Just back out," he said, "and let me pull in. Then I'll give you five minutes. But no more."

"Swell," I said. "You seem like a strawberry crème guy to me."

He smiled at that, his chubby cheeks blushing red.

"For your sake," he said, "I hope the coffee's still hot."

11

WE SAT IN MY 4Runner with the electricity on but the engine off. That way, Cliff Brown could provide a low-volume soundtrack to my conversation with the locally famous Mr. Bolous.

Ted was munching on one of the strawberry crèmes with one hand while holding his still-hot coffee, to which he'd added four sugars, in the other hand.

"I really have to watch the sweets," he commented, eyes staring deep into his coffee. "I'm forty-three now. Diabetes could be looming around the corner like a sugary black hole."

I sipped my coffee and contemplated his not-quite-accurate black hole metaphor.

"Exercise is key," I said.

"I'm too busy eating to exercise."

"I would be too if I ate for free."

"Comes with the job," he smiled.

"The blogger's life," I said.

"I'd rather be fictionalizing," he said.

Fictionalizing . . . He pronounced it as though he'd invented it. Maybe he did.

"Lately you've been writing not only about food and restaurants but about Robert David Jr. and Robert David Sr."

He nodded and sipped his coffee.

"The Davids own one of the most popular, if not the most popular, gourmet restaurants in Albany. When something happens that involves them—and potentially the future of that establishment—I feel it my duty to write about it."

"And to open up the forum to the law-abiding public," I said.

"Yes, I invited my readers to post comments as moderated by me."

I gave him a slight love tap with my elbow and a wink.

"Move like that just might increase readership. Am I right?"

He pursed his lips and cocked his head.

"Perhaps," he whispered.

"You sure are smart, Mr. Ted," I said. "I bet you'll be writing for *Gourmet* in no time. Or maybe you'll have your very own series on the Food Network like Rachael Ray. Don't you just want to eat her right up? Yummo."

He was trying hard not to show how right I was in my assessment regarding his hopes and *fictionalizing* dreams, but his face beamed red under all that scraggly facial hair. It didn't take a genius to know that Mr. Bolous craved serious fame. He finished his donut and with hardly any movement or physical exertion, somehow managed to snatch up the second strawberry crème.

"So what kind of answers do you want from me?" he asked.

"You know Robert Jr. pretty well," I said.

"He's not my best friend."

"But you're close enough to have been trusted with a copy of the lawsuit, which you then sprung on the public."

"Professional courtesy." He shrugged. "Quid pro quo."

"You eat for free," I said, "and you take care of him in other ways by keeping him and his restaurant in the news."

He ate one more donut and drank more coffee.

"Tell me something," I said. "Do you think Robert Jr. is capable of trying to kill someone like Sarah—even accidentally?"

He swallowed.

"How should I know?" he said. "I'm the last person on earth you want speculating about something like that. The suit, that Mr. Sanders has brought against the Davids, is some pretty serious shit. Attempted murder, negligence, and conspiracy to cover up the truth. I just write it the way I see it, and right now, I'm just as confused as the APD as to what happened to Sarah back in February."

"I'm just asking you your opinion, off the record, if you think the kid could do such a thing."

He swallowed and looked at me.

"You wearing a wire, Marconi?"

I made the sign of the cross, knowing that the tape recorder in the glove compartment was doing its job. Not that Bolous had told me much of anything thus far.

"On my late old man's grave," I said. "This is all on the up-and-up. Straight, no chaser."

He shrugged his shoulders.

"Robbie parties a lot. He works the bar and manages to get pretty hammered most nights. It's possible they had a fight, and it got out of hand. But I don't think he would do anything to intentionally hurt Sarah. I was under the impression they were very much in love."

"Have you ever witnessed him being violent to anyone else?"

His face went a bit pale then. He looked at his watch and downed the rest of his donut.

"Look, Marconi," he said, "my editor is going to be on my case if I don't get inside."

He opened the door while Cliff Brown quietly wailed his trumpet from the grave.

"So you have been witness to one of his violent episodes?"

"Seriously," he said, "I gotta go."

He got out and closed the door. Hard.

I watched him make the short trek into the *Albany Times Union* building and enter through an unmarked employee entrance that required a key on his key ring. I guess that way he could avoid the legions of blogger fans, who no doubt awaited him at the building's front door.

I knew that I'd shaken him up a little with the violence question. I could only wonder where and when he'd witnessed the Robert David Jr. temper. I reached into the glove box, lifted up the pair of black leather gloves, and pressed the Stop button on the tape recorder. I rewound the tape to the beginning. I couldn't be sure, but it was possible that Sanders and Miller both might like to hear Bolous's opinion of Junior's violent predisposition. They might also be interested in how quick the blogger was to end the conversation once the subject came up.

I thought about Harold Sanders and his forty million reasons for me to prove Robert David Jr. did, in fact, hurt Sarah Levy and then proceeded to cover it up along with his father. I thought about Sarah Levy sitting inside a rehabilitation center, her brain still scrambled from the incident. I thought about Robert Jr., his cocaine, his sexy new girlfriend, his vampire teeth, his bleeding Sarah tattoo, his green eyes, his devilish smile. His violence. I thought about Robert David Sr. and the crucial role he played in all this.

I looked down at the donuts. Still eight left.

I didn't have a third large coffee to go with them, but maybe by now, Albany's biggest land developer already had had his caffeine fix for the day. I pulled out my smartphone, Googled Robert David Sr., found the address for David Enterprises down on Broadway and turned over the engine. Driving out of the *Albany Times Union* parking lot, I pulled a left onto the suburban Albany Shaker Road and headed east toward the Hudson River.

It was time to shake up the sugar daddy.

12

DAVID ENTERPRISES WAS HOUSED in an unassuming building located in an unassuming part of town. The three-mile stretch of Broadway located in North Albany had, over the years, become a more-or-less deserted relic of what it once was in the 1940s and 1950s, when it was filled with young men and women who worked in the many department stores, steel mills, fabric outlets, and eateries that lined both sides of the busy street. But now that the department stores had closed in favor of the shopping malls and the steel mills had packed up and gone south of the border to Mexico or east to China, dozens of historic brick and plaster-coated high-rises and other buildings sat vacant and rotting.

David Enterprises was obviously an outfit that saw the value in renovating some of these old buildings, since it was housed inside one of them. Pulling into a small parking lot located adjacent to the turn-of-the-twentieth-century, four-story, brick building, my immediate thought was that Robert David Sr. couldn't be all bad if he were making a solid investment in Albany's future by giving new life to its once-rich past. But then, for all I knew, his operation was just a front for something more insidious. Keeper, the suspicious.

I grabbed the box of donuts, or what was left of them, and exited the 4Runner. I crossed the hot, sunbaked parking lot and took special notice of a spit-and-polish, black, four-door Mercedes sedan parked in the spot closest to the front entrance, Its front grill was only inches away from a pilaster-mounted iron placard bearing the embossed name and title *Robert David Sr., President and CEO*. Gave me chills just to be standing on the same plot of land as someone who might be president of anything. Made me wish I had more donuts with me.

I entered the vestibule of an old building that had recently undergone a renovation that transformed the place into something high-tech and sophisticated. Other than the thick glass walls that framed the waiting room and a safety glass security door that led into the main office, the interior was entirely open, the exposed brick walls painted black, and the floor underfoot consisting of the building's original rough plank floor, which had obviously been refinished and re-planed. Temporary partitions and enclosures separated workers from one another while track lighting wrapped its way around the upper walls and across the open ceiling overhead.

To my right, I found a reception counter that at present appeared entirely unoccupied. To my left was a leather couch and couple of matching chairs. In front of that was a glass-and-metal coffee table covered with all the right magazines: *Architectural Digest, Food & Wine Connoisseur, Metropolis Design* . . .

The wide wall behind the couch was covered with framed photos of the many properties the Davids owned. There was a series of full-color glossies that featured some of the same abandoned buildings I'd just seen located on Broadway and also some of the newer steel-and-glass towers that lined both sides of State Street in downtown Albany. A nice interior shot of Manny's front bar was placed beside a few shots of its brick-and-glass exterior.

The wall also bore some shots of a business-suited Robert Sr. wearing a hard hat and donning a shovel while standing in the center of a group of other suited professionals who were also wearing hard hats and donning shovels. Each of them had one foot pressing down on a spade, which had been painted gold, and the other foot planted firmly on hallowed ground that was about to be broken for a new building that was no doubt financed by the Davids. There had to be a dozen different versions of the same groundbreaking ceremony. Standing on one side of David Sr. in at least two or three of those photos was Albany's mayor, Gary Jennings, looking tall, barrel-chested, and tanned. Standing on the other side of David Sr. was a ravishing, tall, blonde-haired woman dressed in a black mini dress with a matching jacket. I knew her as the county prosecutor, Jennifer Waters. Good to know David Sr. had Albany politics on his side.

One last photo showed the proud father and son standing before the bar at Manny's, their arms wrapped around each other, their smiles beaming, each of them sporting a full head of reddish-blond hair and a similar long, thin, clean-shaven face that beamed with identical bright green eyes. They may have been father and son, but they looked more like brothers. There was something about their smiles that was both pleasantly attractive and yet pleasantly devilish.

"Can I help you?" came the voice of a woman from behind me.

I turned quickly, but then slowly and coolly approached the reception window.

"My name is Keeper Marconi," I said. "I'm a private detective. I was wondering if I might get a few minutes with Mr. David."

She was a tall brunette with long hair, bright brown eyes, and thick, sensuous lips. She was wearing a fire-engine red wraparound dress that revealed its share of cleavage and just a hint of an expensive, black lace underwire push-up bra.

"Do you have an appointment?" she said. "Mr. David is extremely busy at the moment."

"He'll talk to me even if I don't have an appointment," I said. "I'm convinced of it."

She smiled out the corner of her red-lipsticked mouth.

"And how is that?"

I raised up the pink box.

"I have donuts."

Her grin turned into a smile, which turned into a giggle. Keeper, the lady's man.

"Tell you what," she said. "A calling card will do for now."

I slipped the box of donuts through an opening located at the bottom of the glass. Then I fished out a calling card from my pants pocket and set it on the counter beside the donuts. The receptionist took the card, looked down at it, and then looked up at me again.

"Can I tell him what this is regarding, Mr. Marconi?"

"His son and Sarah Levy."

Her smile faded.

"Just a minute," she said. Turning, she walked toward the interior of the office building, offering me a parting shot of her perfect, valentine-shaped posterior.

My heart was still racing when she returned a few seconds later.

"Mr. David cannot see you right now," she said. "But if you care to make an appointment, he will be happy to speak with you at a later date."

I came closer to the window, so close I could see my breath clouding the glass. As a former prison supervisor, I knew there had to be a button or an electronic release of some kind that would unlock the interior safety glass door. I also knew it had to be located somewhere inside the reception cubicle. If I had to guess, it would be mounted to the wall just a few inches to the left side of the reception window.

"Are you sure he can't see me now?" I said.

When she brushed back her long, brown hair with her right hand, it gave my already thumping heart a start.

"I'm sorry for the inconvenience," she said while resting her perfect figure on a stool that was set before the counter and, at the same time, producing an iPad, which no doubt contained an electronic version of David's schedule.

"Well then, do you mind if I steal a donut?"

She raised up her head and gave me a glare.

"Suit yourself," she said. "You paid for 'em."

I reached in, opened the box, and squished a couple of the jelly donuts so that the red jelly oozed out of the dough like lava. Then I gave the box a little shove and dumped it all in her red lap.

"Oh my!" I barked. "How clumsy of me."

She issued a shriek and jumped off the stool. Her pretty face assumed an expression of horror as the crushed jelly donuts and a chocolate frosted donut attached themselves to her skirt. That's when I began to feel along the wall to the left for the switch. Sure enough, I found it on my first cast. I pressed the doorbell-like device, and the interior safety glass door popped open. Retracting my hand, I pulled it back out of the opening before she could take it in her pretty little mouth and bite it off in anger.

"Sorry about the dress," I said.

"Asshole," she said. "Total. Fucking. Asshole."

"Next time I promise to bring a full box of donuts," I said, slipping inside through the open door.

13

I WASN'T THROUGH THE door a half dozen steps before a uniformed security guard grabbed hold of my right arm with one hand and pointed the lights-out end of a .38-caliber Smith & Wesson in my face.

"Easy, killer," I said. "I just want a little face time with your boss."

The guard was bigger than me. Wider. Stronger. Fatter in the gut. Shaved head, black goatee, and biceps that looked as though they were about to burst through his blue uniform shirt. If I had to guess, he was an APD officer forced into early retirement or even a New York State corrections officer washout.

"Please unhand our guest," came the voice of another man.

I gazed in the direction of the voice. Down a long, narrow corridor created by workstation walls, all of which had the overcurious and somewhat alarmed heads of David Enterprise workers sticking out from behind them. Standing there tall and well dressed in a navy blue double-breasted suit accented with a silk red tie was the CEO himself—Robert David Sr.

"Sir," barked the burly security guard, "this man just snuck into the office when he was politely asked to leave."

"Hey," I said, "I brought donuts."

David ran his right hand through his full head of thick, nearly white hair and stepped forward.

"Well, if he brought donuts, he can't be all that dangerous," he said in a voice that was neither high nor low, but even toned. The voice of an educated, erudite man.

The guard let me go. Not without a small shove for good measure. "Thanks, Lurch," I said, straightening out the sleeve of my jacket.

"Do you carry a pistol, Mr. Marconi?" asked David.

"Yup," I said.

"Would you be so considerate as to surrender it to my security officer?" he requested.

Without protest, I reached into my jacket, pulled out the .45, and handed it to the monster, grip first.

He smiled as he took it, as though it were his for keeps.

"Easy with that, Lurch," I said. "You don't want to hurt yourself."

"Keep it up," he said through gritted teeth. "I'll find out where you live."

I turned to David Sr.

"Your rent-a-cop could stand to learn some people skills."

"That's quite enough, Rodney," David said. "Why don't you help yourself to one of those donuts Mr. Marconi claims to have brought us." Then, with a gentle-but-sweeping gesture of his open right hand, David Sr. said, "And the rest of you, please get back to work. The floor show is officially over." He didn't command his people to get back to work, so much as he asked them to.

"Please, follow me, Mr. Marconi," David said, turning and making his way toward the opposite end of the building.

Rodney took off for the reception counter and the now crushed donuts.

I followed David, knowing that all eyes were peeled on my behind.

14

"NOW THEN," SAID THE David Enterprises CEO as he settled in gracefully behind his desk, "What's this all about, Mr. Marconi?"

As if you don't already know . . .

I was seated in an expensive leather chair in front of the desk inside an office that was larger than my Sherman Street flat. Like the rest of the office building, the walls consisted of exposed brick that had been painted black in some areas and red in others. The ceiling was open, the mechanical workings and lighting fixtures exposed but also painted an industrial black. Trendy. The floor was wood with a few expensive, imported rugs placed here and there. To my right was a kind of sitting area with a couch and matching easy chairs that faced a gigantic wall-mounted plasma TV. To my left were floor-to-ceiling industrial-style windows that faced Broadway and beyond that, the Hudson River.

The door opened behind me, and I instinctively turned to get a glance at who it could be.

"Pardon me, Mr. David," said the same beautiful brunette in red who met me earlier at the reception counter. "Will you be wanting coffee?"

She looked as stunning as ever, even after the donut attack. Not a trace of strawberry jelly on her red dress.

I turned back to David. He issued me one of those sweeping hand gestures as he had to his crew only moments ago. It was sign language for, "Would you like a coffee?"

"Please," I said, throwing a smile over my shoulder at the brunette. "Milk, no sugar. Oh, and I like it hot." I tossed her a wink with my right eye when I said *hot*.

She rolled her eyes as though it were going to cause her pain to facilitate my need for caffeine.

"Mr. David?" she said.

"I'm fine, thanks, Victoria."

She closed the door, leaving us alone.

"Victoria," I said, rolling the name off my tongue and lips as if it tasted of milk and honey.

"Excuse me, Mr. Marconi?" David said, sitting back with ease and grace in his black, tall-backed, leather swivel chair, setting his elbows on the armrests and cathedralling his fingers together.

"Your secretary," I said. "Her name is Victoria. How apropos for such an attractive woman."

He smiled and rested a prominent chin onto his clamped fingers.

"Yes," he said, "Victoria has her talents. But I wouldn't go around referring to her as a secretary. She might bite your nose off. Refer to her instead as my special assistant."

"Sounds like an important job," I said.

"It is, indeed," he said, raising his chin up from his fingers. "My day is extremely busy, and she has a way of organizing it so that it runs as smoothly and beautifully as her silk, black panties."

I couldn't help but grin when he said panties. Which is exactly what he was looking for. He was trying to find common ground with me by proving he had an eye for the girls.

"How nice," I said, noticing that his desk was empty of anything that suggested work. Other than a black telephone, not even a laptop computer occupied the long glass desk.

"So what is it you are so anxious to ask of me?" the CEO said, getting right to the point.

Before I could answer him, the door opened, and my coffee arrived. Victoria breezed in and set it on David's desk. The coffee was served in a real china cup and saucer emblazoned with a hot red *D* and *E* that made up the David Enterprises logo. She set a silver spoon onto the saucer, and as I watched her leave the room, I couldn't help but picture those black panties clinging to the smooth skin underneath her red dress.

When the door closed behind her and the oxygen returned to the room, I said, "I've been hired to investigate the Sarah Levy case."

I looked for a reaction.

David gave me nothing. Not even the blink of an eye or the rise and fall of his Adam's apple. He did, however, sit up straight in his chair, setting his still cathedralled hands onto the desk.

"And what is it exactly that you feel the need to investigate and who are you working for?"

Again . . . as if he didn't already know.

He smiled when he spoke, as if hiding his anger. His teeth were perfect. I wondered what he would look like with sharpened vampire incisors. Probably just like his angry namesake son.

"My client," I said, "who shall remain confidential, is concerned that you and your son, Robert Jr. covered up a possible assault with the intent to kill."

He maintained that smile. No blinking. No swallowing. Even his red tie remained completely vertical and ninety degrees to the floor. Chalk one up for Mr. Calm and Composed.

"And what is it you want from me, Mr. Marconi? An admission of guilt?"

"Maybe you can tell me why your forty-one-year-old son lives in one of your houses. You also employ him. He seems to bear no responsibility of his own."

"The domestic and business arrangements I share with my son are none of your business, not to mention that of your mysterious client who most certainly goes by the name Harold Sanders, the formerly in-demand architect."

His use of "formerly in-demand" took me a bit by surprise. I asked him why he would say such a thing about an obviously talented individual. That is, judging by the metrosexual's manner of dress along with the hefty retainer check he laid on me.

"Sanders is a capable architect. But his talent is limited. Commercial construction is way down, and so is his once-thriving business. No wonder he wants money from me that he doesn't deserve." He looked away and shook his head. "You ask me, he's exploiting his daughter's misfortune in order to line his empty pockets."

"He has an office in Hong Kong," I said. "He must be doing something right."

David Sr. went wide-eyed and laughed.

"*Had* an office in Hong Kong for about five minutes," he said through a giggle. "He's strictly Albany material now, and barely surviving that."

I didn't know whether to believe him or not or if the state of Sanders's finances really mattered all that much. So long as his checks didn't turn to rubber every time he signed them.

"Good to know you two won't be in-laws anytime soon," I said.

He lost his smile when I said it.

I decided it was a good time to cease with the low blows and change the course of my questioning.

"Why didn't you tell your son to call 911 when he called you in the middle of the night asking you to come to his aid over a severely injured and unhappy Sarah Levy?"

Now he swallowed. And blinked. Score one for Keeper.

"The David family isn't used to dealing with such emergencies. We are a peaceful, responsible family that has contributed more than most to this fine capital city. After Sarah slipped on the ice and hurt herself, my son panicked and called me first. He loved Sarah very much. He would never willingly hurt her or anyone else."

"Yet you didn't insist he call 911."

"We both thought it would be quicker if the two of us were to drive her."

"How far away do you live from your son?"

"About six and a half minutes by car."

"How long, in your humble estimation, sir, would an ambulance have taken to make it to the scene?"

"Certainly more than six and a half minutes."

I smiled.

"Good answer," I said, knowing it had been rehearsed. "But at least an ambulance is manned by EMTs, who have access to knowledge and equipment that can save lives should they require saving."

He stood up. "I haven't spoken to the police this much regarding this non-matter, and I certainly don't need to discuss it with you. I trust our conversation is over?"

I gazed at my coffee cup.

"I haven't had my coffee yet, Mr. D.," I said.

"My apologies," he said. "Perhaps you can get some coffee on your way home."

"Not going home," I said, getting up.

"Oh, and why is that?" he said, coming around his desk and

heading for the office door.

"I'm going to make a flyby to your crib. Talk to the missus. I bet her coffee is better than yours anyway."

His face went so red it matched his tie. He swallowed and began blinking rapidly. Yet another score for Keeper.

He opened the door, but then he slammed it closed.

"Let me warn you, Mr. Marconi," he said, turning to me. "If I find out you are harassing me or any members of my family, I will come down on you like a pack of rabid wolves."

"Oh my," I said. "That doesn't sound very peaceful to me."

"Joke all you want. But I'm dead serious."

"So am I, Mr. D.," I said.

He opened the door. I stepped out. I heard the door close behind me. Hard.

Up at the reception counter, I asked the rent-a-fat-cop for my piece. He wiped powder and jelly from his mouth and handed it to me. There was jelly stuck to the grip. Red jelly.

"Oops," he said, his cheeks full of dough. "My bad."

I grabbed a napkin from off the counter and wiped the jelly away. It was still sticky when I shoved it into my shoulder holster. But I chose to deny him the satisfaction of knowing that.

When I turned for the interior door that would let me out of the building through the vestibule, I caught site of Victoria. The lady in red. I nodded at her and smiled. To my dismay, she did not smile back.

"You have my card," I said. "Call anytime. For any reason."

Knowing I didn't have a chance in hell of ever seeing her dressed in only those silk, black panties, I let myself out and never once looked back.

Comment by HiImBi

The one thing I can't stop thinking about is the lawsuit price tag: 40 million freaking dollars. I mean, what would be happening if Robert Jr. worked at Target or Wal-Mart? What if his daddy-o were a state worker or worse, unemployed? Bet there wouldn't even be a lawsuit if those were the circumstances. Somebody stands to make a lot of money out of one poor woman's bad luck.

Comment by Jillypoet

Duh, HiImBi, have you checked into the cost of rehabilitation these days? Poor Sarah Levy deserves the best care she can get. Doesn't matter if her own father is a wealthy architect. The cost of the lawsuit will certainly defray costs that can break even a rich person. I think you're just jealous of people who have more money than you. Rich people are human too.

Comment by HiImBi

COMMENT DELETED BY MODERATOR

Ted Bolous, *Albany Times Union* Senior Food Blogger, Responds

Let's all get along, people, just like the fine ingredients of a devilishly hot chili con carne. ☺

15

THE DAVIDS DIDN'T LIVE in a house. They lived and thrived on a country estate. The giant main house was a Moby Dick white, three-story colonial with big square pillars that supported a large portico. The driveway that led up to it was about a half mile long. Or so it seemed. The driveway wasn't gravel-covered or even blacktopped like the driveways of the common proletariat. It had been laid out by masons with stone pavers, making it look a lot like a yellow brick road without the yellow. The long drive was bordered on both sides by tall pine trees, and the grounds were meticulously maintained and lush and green, despite a searing hot, dry summer only the devil could love.

I pulled up to the end of the driveway where a three-car garage faced me. Two vehicles were parked outside. The one closest to me was a pristine but older model Mercedes sports convertible with the top down. The vehicle beside it was a white Range Rover. It had a small, red-white-and-blue flag-shaped emblem stuck to the back windshield that contained the letters L and G. I knew the letters stood for the Lake George Yacht Club, which was located about fifty miles north of Albany where the Adirondack Mountain region began.

I killed the engine and got out and took the long stone path that led me up the short flight of steps onto the portico landing. I thumbed the doorbell. It didn't ring so much as gong. It took a moment or two for the door to open. When it did, I wasn't greeted by the woman of the house, but instead by a small man. A middle-aged man dressed in worn dungarees, work boots, and a denim work shirt. His leathery skin was suntanned, if not sunbaked. He asked if he could help me in an accent I took to be Mexican. I told him who I was and that I wished to speak with Mrs. David if she were available. Pulling out my PI license from my back pocket, I showed it to him, for what it was worth. He examined the license for a second or two, and then he asked me to step inside.

To say the setup was opulent would be putting it mildly. Black-and-white marble flooring, perhaps imported from Italy, provided the base for a large wraparound staircase that looked as though it had been designed for the Gone with the Wind movie set. Suspended directly overhead was a chandelier so large and crystal filled that I could only assume it had been imported, perhaps from Moscow or Venice. The walls of the foyer were painted white, and they supported several long, gold-framed mirrors. I took a step forward and, looking over my left shoulder into the living room, caught sight of a fireplace so big that a man could stand inside it. A tall man. Mounted to the cherry-paneled wall above the fireplace hung an oil paint portrait of the woman I took for Mrs. Robert David Sr.

The image of a tall, white-gowned, blonde woman with a considerable bust proved mesmerizing, to say the least. Her hair was shoulder length and parted over her left eyebrow. But that wasn't what captured most of my attention. Her striking blue eyes were responsible for that. They drew me in so hard I thought I might levitate off the floor and find myself floating toward the portrait as if in a dream.

"Do you like my painting?" said a voice from above. A deep, sultry voice that didn't break me from my spell, but instead added to it. Swallowing a breath, I raised my head and caught sight of Mrs. David in the flesh.

"Must have taken ages," I said, looking up. "And cost a bundle."

"Indeed," she said from the top of the stairs.

From where I stood down below, she appeared to be a tall woman. Unlike in the portrait, she wasn't dressed in a gown, but instead wore a bright red tennis skirt, red-and-black sneakers, and a tighter-than-tight, acrylic black, sleeveless athletic top that showed off her second best attribute next to her blue eyes. She began the slow descent down the staircase, not as though she was greeting a most unwelcome private detective into her home-sweet-home, but instead as though she were meeting a prom date.

She didn't bounce down the stairs, but descended them like a runway model, one step at a time, one foot in front of the other, showing off almost the entire length of those long, personally trained legs. I did some quick calculations in my head. I knew that if she had a forty-one-year-old son, she had to be, at minimum, in her late fifties. Had I not known she was the mother of a young, middle-aged man, I would have pegged her as somewhere around thirty-five, max. Watching her descend the length of that wraparound staircase, I felt the air escape my lungs and my heart beat a paradiddle against my rib cage. Someone once sang a song, "I'm Always Falling in Love." Such was the inherent risk of my profession.

Finally, she got to the bottom of the staircase and approached me. I was entranced by her eyes. And pretty much everything else she owned, and she knew it. She held out her hand. I took it in mine. Unlike Harold Sanders' handshake, hers was firm, warm, and inviting.

"I'm Penny David," she said. "My husband phoned to tell me you were coming. Lucky for you, my tennis lesson was just about over." She smiled naughtily. "Of course, I haven't had time for a shower. And now I'm a little . . . wet."

"Excuse me?" I said.

She giggled, running both hands down her red skirt, smoothing out the wrinkles.

"Oh, I can see how that sounds," she said. "I'm a little wet with perspiration. I hope you don't mind."

I swallowed, my mouth and throat desert sand dry.

"No problem," I said. "We're all human animals, after all."

The little Mexican man entered back into the vestibule.

"Iced tea is served on the patio, madam," he said.

She turned to him. "Thank you, Juan." Then back to me. "Shall we?" she offered. "I'm positively parched."

"By all means, Mrs. David," I said. "Please lead the way."

She turned and started walking, adding a little swing to her tight, red backside.

Naturally, I was all too pleased to follow.

16

SHE BEGAN THE SLOW march through the foyer into the kitchen, where she stole a pair of white-rimmed Jackie O sunglasses off the counter. She slid the sunglasses on and made her way out a back glass-and-wood door that accessed a stone patio shaded by a large and intricate trellis of white wood slats, which were covered in vines. She pointed to one of two round metal tables that were further shaded by country club green umbrellas. The chosen table had a tray with a pitcher of iced tea already placed upon it, along with a couple of tall drinking glasses filled with ice plus one whole lemon and one lime. Set beside those was a large kitchen knife. Without a word, Penny grabbed hold of the knife and began to slice up lime and lemon wedges with all the speed of a Ginsu chef preparing a beef teriyaki for eight.

Turning to me, she smiled.

"I'm very good with a knife," she said. "I was once a sous-chef for several restaurants in France and later at The Globe on Park Avenue in Manhattan. That's where I met David Sr., during a tour my boss gave him of our kitchen."

I sat down while she took a seat directly across from me. Leaning forward, she rose up out of her seat just enough to lift the pitcher off the tray, her boobs nearly spilling out of her tight black top. She poured us each a glass of iced tea, then set the pitcher back down onto the silver tray.

I took the glass in my right hand. It was cold and the wet condensation was already beginning to drip down the sides of the glass. I took a sip and felt the pleasantly cold liquid against the back of my dry throat.

"Delicious," I said, wiping my mouth with the back of my hand.

She drank and set her glass down. Gently.

"Juan is an amazing tea and lemonade maker. An artist really. And the meals he creates are simply fabulous. He outdoes even me." She puckered her lips and blew a kiss to no one in particular. I thought my heart would stop.

"So tell me something, Mr. Marconi," she said. "Do you carry a gun on your person?"

"Yes, ma'am," I said. "Comes with the job. I'm fully licensed, if that's what you're getting at."

"Oh, I believe you. Entirely."

"How swell. I'd like to speak with you about your son. About Sarah Levy too."

"Is it long and hard?" she asked, taking another sip of the drink.

My heart didn't stop, but it skipped a beat or two.

"I'm sorry?"

"Your gun," she said. "Is it long and hard? Or one of those thick-but-short ones? What do they call them again?"

"Snub-nosed revolvers."

"That's it," she said. "Snub-nosed revolvers."

"If you must know," I said. "Mine's long, hard, and thick."

She laughed again and tossed me a wink with her right eye.

"Well, you asked," I said.

"That I did," she said. "So what would you like to know about my stepson and his former fiancée?"

"Stepson," I said as if it were a question.

She perked up and set her glass back down.

"The first Mrs. David is most definitely dead." She was quick to explain. Then she said, "You didn't think for one teensy-weensy moment that I was old enough to have a son David Jr.'s age, did you, Mr. Marconi?"

I'm not sure why, but I felt a wave of relief suddenly splash over my body.

"Not for a moment. To be honest, I found myself a little confused when I first laid eyes on you."

"Are you trying to tell me I'm beautiful?"

The throat went dry again. Something was telling me that the present Mrs. David Sr. wasn't getting precisely what she needed from the hubby. Maybe his gun was short, thin, and soft.

"How did the first Mrs. David die?" I inquired.

She shrugged her shoulders.

"From what my husband tells me, Joan fell off a ladder while working on these very same vines above our heads. Picking grapes in the fall. She made her own wine, the original Mrs. David, which I find rather interesting, if not honorable. Can you imagine that? Making your own wine from scratch?" She lifted her right hand so that she showed off her long, stiletto-like fingernails. "These days, manicures cost far too much for me to risk breakage by doing manual labor."

"No more sous-chefing?"

"Take a look around you," she said with a sweeping gesture of her right hand. "Would you?"

I had to laugh.

"No," I said. "I guess I wouldn't."

I drank some more tea and made a mental note of how the original Mrs. David entered the afterlife only a few feet away from where the present Mrs. David and I were enjoying some exceptionally good iced tea on a hot summer's day.

"Mrs. David," I said.

"Penny," she interrupted.

"Penny." I smiled. "What's your take on what happened between Robert Jr. and Sarah on February 18th?"

She sat back in her chair and looked over her right shoulder as if staring at a bird that was nesting in one of the many oak trees that bordered the huge property.

"I'm not sure what to think," she said. But then she perked up again and pulled her Jackie Os off. "You want the truth, Mr. Marconi?"

"Keeper."

"Keeper," she said. "How very interesting."

"Nickname," I said. "From prison."

I didn't tell her from which side of the bars I was bestowed said nickname, and judging by her corner-of-the-mouth grin, she found the ambiguity rather interesting. Perhaps even titillating. Keeper, the tease.

"Well, Keeper, I think they got all coked and boozed up. They fought, and she ended up falling down those front steps. That's what I think. Not that it matters much."

"It does matter," I said, silently wishing I'd brought along my

74

tape recorder. Not that she would have agreed to my recording our conversation, and I didn't want to take a chance on concealing it.

"Why would they fight if they appeared to be so happy?"

"David and my husband aren't exactly alike," she said. "In fact, you could say the apple most certainly did fall far from the tree."

"Meaning?"

"Meaning my husband is straighter than a board and just as stiff. Only not stiff in the way I would have preferred."

I wanted to tell her that I'd gathered that, but I decided against it. Instead I said, "David Jr. is a partier: a bon vivant and a playboy."

"All of that for sure," she said. "He also has some . . . well, let's call them hang-ups."

"Go on," I said.

She slid her Jackie Os back on as if what she was about to tell me were easier to say while donning a mask.

"I'll be frank with you, Keeper," she said. "David is into some devilishly weird sex."

"And you would know that how?"

"I'm his stepmother, after all. Not his real, biological mother." She exhaled. Dramatically. "If you . . . get my . . . ummmm . . . drift."

Yes, I got her drift. All too loud and all too clear.

"I see," I said. "I can only assume that those moments when both of your respective ships have passed in the night have been entirely consensual?"

"Sensual without the *con*," she said. "In a very devilish way."

"Devilish?"

"David likes it rough. He likes threesomes, foursomes, parties, girls, boys, whatever he can fuck and be fucked by. It's like a hobby for him. The perfect hobby for a bartender whose daddy owns his own bar."

"Sarah Levy doesn't seem the type."

"Indeed, she's not. And I believe, therein, you have the source of their conflict. Perhaps even his motivation for doing what he just might have gotten away with." Opening her mouth just slightly, seductively setting the pad of her manicured index finger upon her pouty bottom lip, she said, "Or perhaps . . . just perhaps, Keeper . . . I'm talking out my cute, tight little ass."

She might have been talking out that tight little ass for sure, but her words made sense to me, at least judging from the scene I encountered this morning.

"Penny, is your husband aware of these little trysts you've shared with his son?"

"Oh God, no," she said finishing up her drink. "He'd have me drawn and quartered and hung up to dry on the plate glass wall of some downtown building he owns."

"You don't know me. So why confide in me? If you were to testify in a court of law precisely what you just revealed, I believe the Davids would, at the very least, be found liable for Sarah's head injuries. It would mean the end of your Shangri-La, so to speak. To be honest, while I was driving all the way over here from your husband's office, I expected a door slammed in my face."

She smiled again. That's when I heard her sneakers come off and felt something push up against the interior of my thigh. It kept moving until it gently pressed against my sex. That something was a bare foot to which was attached some very curious toes.

"I'm a pretty good judge of people, Keeper," she said. "And I've taken an immediate liking to you."

"My lucky day," I said, downing the rest of my tea, feeling her never still, bare foot against my hardness.

"Listen," she said, "Juan is going into town and I'm alone all this beautifully torrid Tuesday afternoon. There's a pool around the corner. It's very, very secluded. Would you care for a skinny dip?"

She reached down with both hands and pulled off her top, exposing her precious tanned C-cup titties. For a beat or two, I couldn't even move. I'd been rendered paralyzed by her beauty. But then just as quickly, I knew that if I lost total control, I would get myself into more trouble than I could handle.

I stood up.

"I appreciate the offer," I said. "But for now . . . over the course of this investigation . . . I have to play it straight." Then I came around the table, took her in my arms, and laid a big wet one on her delicious lips. When we both came back up for air, she was still holding onto me, but I pushed her out of my arms.

"I'll let myself out," I said, heading for the kitchen door.

"Keeper!" she called out.

I turned to see her beautiful half-naked, half-dressed in red, presence gazing back at me.

"You're right," she said. "Your gun truly is long and hard."

"The David boys are lucky men," I said, and then I left before I changed my mind about that swim.

17

ONCE INSIDE THE 4RUNNER, heart still pounding, I consulted with my smartphone app for a quick search on the name Mrs. Joan David. My search resulted in a short list of articles, most of them having been published by the *Albany Times Union* long before it was publishing blogs by the likes of the fictionalizing foodie, Ted Bolous. The headlines were all pretty much the same: "Albany Entrepreneur's Wife Dead in Backyard Mishap," "David Manslaughter Investigation a No Fault," "Robert David Sr. off the Hook," and "Joan David Falls from Ladder. Dead at 54." There were a few others, but I'd already gotten the drift.

I decided to get to the bottom of the situation by placing a call to Nick Miller's cell phone so I could be sure to get him, even if I stood the chance of annoying him with yet another interruption. He answered after the second ring.

"Joan David," I said.

"What about her?"

"She's dead."

"No kidding. How big is that rock you've been sleeping under?"

"It might have helped if had you told me her husband was investigated as a possible perp in her death."

"She fell off a rickety old stepladder in the backyard while picking grapes. Some people thought it possible that she was pushed by someone. Namely, her husband. It was pretty well known that they fought like cats and dogs. But not only was that possibility never proven, Keeper, but Bob David Sr. had never proven himself a man with a temper capable of doing something like that. Plus he had a rock-fucking-solid alibi."

"What about the evil-tempered kid?"

"Sure, he would be capable. Theoretically. But he was away taking cooking classes and working on his tan on the old man's dime in the south of France. Rock-fucking-solid alibi number two."

For a quick second, I pictured Juan, the caretaker and superb iced tea maker, but then I thought better of it. The little, gentle, man just didn't seem to fit the profile.

"Listen, Keeper," Miller went on, "I see where you're going with this, and I can't blame you. But don't waste your time and mine driving a road that leads to nowheresville. Capisce?"

I felt a little deflated at the notion of nowheresville, and I wasn't sure why.

"Roger that, chief," I said. "It might be a little painful for you to have to reopen an investigation that just might, in the end, prove the APD made a major foul up mistake ten plus years ago that inevitably led to the fucked-upness of Sarah Levy's head."

Heavy silence filled the phone like bad gas.

"That all for now, Keeper, you asshole?"

"Yes, sir," I said. "Thank you for protecting and serving me."

"Fuck you," he said before hanging up.

18

I STARTED THE 4RUNNER, pulled out onto the suburban road in the direction of the downtown. It didn't take long for me to notice the black Lexus hatchback that was tailing me from behind. This isn't like television or the movies when a car suddenly starts following you from maybe one hundred or more feet away and you're immediately convinced that the driver isn't just any schmuck who happens to be heading in the same direction you are. This guy made it obvious he was tailing me by practically ramming into the 4Runner's tailgate. Maybe he wanted me to know he was following me or maybe he was simply crappy at his job. It's also possible he was just an out-of-control tailgater and not someone intent on following me at all. Didn't matter. The effect it had on me was the same.

Road rage.

I was driving on a downhill that was bordered on both sides by woods and the occasional home set inside them. At the very bottom of the hill was a traffic light which, at present, was red. I had two choices: Hit the brakes, fishtail, and take a chance on the son of a bitch smashing into me. Or I could floor it, see how badly he wanted to crawl up my ass.

Stealing a quick, if not fleeting look at the black-haired, black mustached, and aviator sunglasses wearing man behind the wheel, I decided to go with the second choice.

Putting pedal to the metal, I gunned it.

19

THE 4RUNNER HAD ALREADY seen its twentieth birthday. Technically speaking, she was an old girl. But old isn't the word for how she ran. In celebration of her twentieth—and the fact that for a change, I had a little extra money in the bank—I had her completely overhauled. The engine was a brand new eight-cylinder, turbo-charged model outfitted with a hemi. It would give me zero-to-sixty in the time it took you to say, "Get ready. Get set. Go!" The tires were outfitted for rough terrain but could negotiate a city street like a Formula 1 circuit racing car. They were expensive at $1,500 a piece, but my girl and my life were worth it. The interior was updated with airbags and instead of shoulder-strap seatbelts, I had the option of a shoulder harness should I need one. Right now, I needed one, but I did not enjoy the luxury of pulling off onto the soft shoulder and rigging it up. I would have to take my chances as is.

I had already hit sixty by the time I neared the traffic light. It hadn't turned green yet and vehicles were motoring through it in both east and west directions. I glanced into the rearview and saw that the dark-haired man had removed his sunglasses as if they impeded his eyesight. His eyes were wide and full of fear. I knew the face of fear. I saw it every day in the faces of both guards and inmates when those prison gates slammed closed behind us, locking us inside the concrete and metal razor-wire cage.

Eyes back on the road.

The light was still red. Cars hugging the road that ran perpendicular to the one I was driving were still motoring through it. I tapped the brake to slow me down so that I could make the turn without flipping. I was driving an SUV. SUVs are easy to flip at just a fraction of the speed I was going.

The Lexus was still on my tail. His front fender had to be separated from my back fender by only a few inches.

The light turned green. I sped through it, leaning into a left-hand turn, the back end of the 4Runner fishtailing, the thick tires spinning, burning rubber, spitting up gravel and smoke. Until they caught and I was thrust forward, the 4Runner leaning heavily to the right side, but regaining its balance soon enough.

I floored the pedal once more and hooked a quick right, fishtailing again, but coming right out of it, and speeding down a two-lane bypass that led back in the direction of the city.

When I looked in the rearview, I could no longer make out the Lexus. Had the driver wiped out at the bottom of the hill? Or did he just spin out? I never had time to look. When he appeared to me again in the driver's side-view mirror, I knew that he'd only spun out. He was gaining on me. Whoever he was, he wanted me bad.

The speedometer approached ninety.

Cars pulled off the road. I had no choice but to veer around the ones that didn't. Another traffic signal was located at the very end of the bypass where the road narrowed into a basic two-way street that ended within a half-mile at yet another road that ran perpendicularly to it. That road spanned the length of a long highway bridge that rose one hundred or more feet over a major Interstate highway. Only thing I could do was try and negotiate an immediate right or left as I drove onto the bridge. I also had to make certain I did so at a speed that wouldn't propel me over the opposite side of the bridge railing, plunging me to certain death. I could only wonder if the man driving the Lexus was aware of this.

I blew through the red light. Then made it onto the two-way street. Through the windshield, I made out the entrance to the bridge and the metal railing that separated the road from a one-hundred foot drop. I tapped the brakes again, reducing the speed to fifty. That's when the Lexus bumped against my tail. I stole a glance in the rearview. The man had a pistol gripped in his left hand while he tried to bump, grind, and steer with his right. His window came down and he stuck the gun out and fired.

My back window exploded and a small bullet hole appeared in the passenger side of the windshield. The entrance to the bridge loomed largely only a few feet away. So did a red and white stop sign. But I ignored it and swung the wheel to my right while, behind me, the squeal of slammed-on brakes and locked-up tires filled my ears.

The 4Runner bucked and fishtailed, but managed to hug the bridge road.

But the Lexus hadn't fared so well.

It was going too fast to make a left or right turn. Instead, it rammed the railing, blowing a hole right through it. But it hadn't gone all the way over. The car was balancing and teetering on its middle, the back end still resting on the bridge and the front end entirely exposed to the elements. I hit the brakes, slowed the 4Runner down to twenty MPH, and made a U-turn.

I approached the Lexus, hoping it wouldn't go over the side.

Not yet.

Not until I managed to get some answers out of the soon-to-be dead driver.

20

I PULLED UP TO the wobbling car, got out of the 4Runner, leaving the door open and the engine running. Thus far, no one had gone by or stopped to lend a helping hand in any way possible. But I knew they soon would. Coming from out of the near distance now, the sounds of sirens. Police sirens.

Pulling my .45 from its shoulder holster, I made my way around to the driver's side of the car, my heart still beating not in my throat but in my mouth. I put my hand on the Lexus door. It teetered like a school yard see-saw with a fat kid occupying one end and another fat kid on the other.

The dark-haired guy inside went wide-eyed.

"Make! It! Stop!" he screamed. He was still holding his gun, but he was too afraid to use it. Too paralyzed with fear even to flex a tendon on his pinky finger.

I rapped on the door panel with the pistol barrel.

"How's it going in there?" I smiled.

Behind me, I heard the sound of a tractor trailer. It sped by without stopping. The sirens, however, were getting louder with each passing second.

"I just shit myself," he said through the open window. "That's how it's fucking going."

I pointed to my right ear with the barrel.

"Can't hear you," I said.

"Get. Me. Out. Of. Here," he said.

"Who do you work for? And who sent you?"

"Fuck you," he said.

I opened the door. The car lurched forward, made an ugly metal against concrete grinding sound as it slid on the chassy a few inches toward certain body-spattering doom. I stepped quickly back thinking it was going over for sure. But the teetering calmed down, and the see-saw balance game resumed. Lucky bad guy.

I looked at the dark-haired goon. His round face was pale with fear. Hands trembling.

First, I reached inside, pulled the gun from his hand, tossed it over the side of the bridge. Then I repeated, "Who sent you to do a shitty job of following me? Or was that just a really shitty job of trying to kill me? Was it David Sr.?"

He didn't answer. Maybe he'd rather go over the side than answer me.

"Okay," I said, "have it your way."

I went around to the hatchback, started rocking on it.

He screamed.

"Please! Please! Don't!"

I came back around.

"Give me a name," I said.

"Robert David," he said.

"Robert David Sr.?" I pressed.

To my surprise, he shook his head.

"Junior," he said. "The kid sent me."

"That so," I said, just as the sirens got so loud I knew the cruisers were about to round the corner and drive onto the bridge. Reaching into the car, I grabbed hold of his dark jacket and yanked him out. He fell onto the concrete road while the vehicle rocked slowly backward, then slowly forward, then back again gaining momentum. Until finally the entirety of its weight shifted to the front and it slid off the edge of the bridge, making the tumble to the highway below. I could only hope that it hit the soft shoulder of the Interstate and not the highway itself. If the latter were the case, then I could only hope the unlucky motorists saw it coming.

I listened for a brief second or two and never heard so much as a pin drop.

Taking a quick glance over the side, I could see why. The Lexus had plummeted onto the soft, grassy no-man's-land that abutted the highway

Pocketing my .45, I walked back to my ride.

"You're just gonna leave me here?" he said, from where he lie on his back on the bridge road shaking like a wounded doe.

"The cops are coming," I said. "Somebody's got to explain this mess to them."

"They'll arrest me."

"That would be the point, wouldn't it?"

I got back in the 4Runner, shifted the tranny into drive, and made a U-turn heading back toward the inner city. I hadn't yet made it off the bridge before the first blue and white took the corner toward the scene of the accident, and one very shaken, very lucky, black-haired goon.

21

WHEN I PULLED UP IN front of my Sherman Street home, Blood was still standing outside, standing guard over the neighborhood like an urban sentinel. He stood stone stiff and gazed at my bullet-wounded 4Runner.

"Who shot you up, Keep?" he said as I slipped on out.

I told him.

"You should have let the dude go over the edge. Now he be out on bail and back to shoot your ass again. He might not miss this time. You see what I'm saying?"

"Crystal," I said. Then, digging into my left-hand pocket for whatever cash I had on me, handing it to him. "You think you can manage to get your people to make the necessary repairs, as soon as time permits?"

He looked down at the cash gripped in his hand, thumbed through it, giving it a cursory count.

"Couple hundred bucks," he said. "Well, that will get you in within the hour."

"I'll have another two hundred for you, plus whatever the repairs cost. And a little icing for your mechanic."

He cocked his head, pretended to think about it for minute.

"Deal," he said.

"How are things in the 'hood?" I said, slipping the key to the 4Runner off the ring, handing it to him. "Dealers happy today?"

Slowly, he shook his head, pursed his lips.

"Terrible. Getting so the Sherman Streeters can't make an honest living in a dishonest trade."

"Not a big market for pot and blow?"

"There's a market. But kids nowadays, they want bath salts, X, and heroin. We don't sell that shit on Sherman. Coke and ecstasy is bad enough."

"You free tonight for a freelance project?"

"What you got in mind?"

I told him about Robert David Jr. and his love of coke and booze and the high life.

"Heard about that dude," Blood said. "Bartender up there on Lark Street. Word around town is he fucked up his girl. Tried to beat her brains in or something."

"Whatever he did, he didn't do a good enough job," I said. "Because in the end, she lived."

"Bet she got one hell of a story to tell."

"Apparently she can't remember a thing."

"Or maybe she too scared to talk."

Blood had a point. Maybe Sarah Levy was scared. Scared to tell the truth about what happened. Scared of what Junior might do to her if she did. Standing there in the heat of the city, I knew that the sooner I got a face-to-face with the head trauma victim, the better. It was going on noon. It would probably take Blood's people two hours to fix the 4Runner at most. I'd use that time to try and make sense of things and to do a little more in-house detecting. I would also check in with Sanders.

"So what's this freelance project you got in mind for me tonight?"

"I want you to see who Junior buys his junk from. Who, where, when, and how."

"You want me to get some film of him in the act?"

"If you can manage it."

"Can't promise anything. But I can try. It will cost you though."

"I have a rich client."

"The best kind."

"No, sir," I said. "The best kind are rich, beautiful women who are single."

"You ever get one of those?"

I shook my head.

He laughed.

"Hang in there, Keeper. One day you find the right woman."

"Had one of those once," I said. "Sort of have one again."

"*Sort of* don't count in love and war."

"Just ask Sarah Levy," I said. "Her fiancé *sort of* tried to kill her. Maybe."

"Bet he'd like to sort of try and do it again. That is . . . if he can get at her."

I stared into his deep dark eyes before I turned for the front door to my building. His words sent a cold chill throughout my body. I could only pray that Blood, the Sentinel of Sherman Street, wasn't also a prophet

Sarah Levy Said to Be on the Mend
By Ted Bolous, *Albany Times Union* Senior Food Blogger

Your delicious food blogger just received word that Sarah Levy, while near dead only a few months ago from the injuries she suffered in the driveway of her then fiancé Robert David Jr.'s house, is recovering rather quickly. While I'm told by those who wish to remain anonymous that she still can't recall a thing having occurred on the night of February 18th, she has asked for Mr. David Jr. by name on several occasions.

One wonders what will happen when, and if, her memory finally does return.

Will she spill the beans on a story entirely different from the David boys'? Or will her version fit in nicely and neatly with theirs, thereby making the $40 million lawsuit all but null and void?

Starving and inquiring minds can only wonder..

22

THE FIRST THING I did when I got inside was place another call to Miller.

"You responsible for that fucking car wreck on the bridge off the bypass?" he posed.

"I'd be a liar if I said I wasn't somewhere within the vicinity when it occurred."

"Not even a full twenty-four hours on this job and you're pressing some pretty sensitive buttons."

"You got the goon in custody?"

"No reason to hold him. He claims to have lost control of his ride. He was pretty shaken up."

"He took a shot at me."

"Like with a real gun?"

"Sure."

"Then why'd you let him go? I would have held onto him with your testimony and your ride as a body of evidence."

I told him about the goon's piece I stupidly tossed over the bridge. Then, "It's not time to start tossing people in the clink when the real man we want is free to sharpen his teeth and do as much coke as his nostrils can snort. The goon, or goons, will be back. This time I plan on being ready for them."

"Using yourself as bait to try and hook the biggie fish. Nice strategy. You get anything out of the goon? Who he works for directly?"

"He claims to be working for Junior. But that could be bullshit."

"Junior? Junior can't tie his own shoes without daddy's help."

"But say Junior is willing and capable of hiring goons like him who are willing to blow my brains out? That means you, Detective Miller, have a much larger problem looming."

"And what would that be?"

"Should Sarah Levy suddenly regain her memory, she's going to want to sing like a bird."

"Not if Junior can help it. Is that what you're trying to tell me?"

"Exactly."

"I'll try and get a security detail to watch over her room at Valley View Rehab."

"Not a bad idea. If it's okay with the APD, I'm going to take a trip out to visit her later this afternoon."

"Let me know how it goes."

"Are you asking or telling?"

"Stupid question even for you," he said, cutting the connection.

23

I WENT INTO THE kitchen and made some coffee. When it was done, I added some Crown Royale and milk to make it a Coffee Royale. I took a careful sip. That taste brought me back to my grandfather, Pasquale. When he first came to this country back in the 1920s as a teenager, he drove beer trucks between Albany and Connecticut. When prohibition came along, he drove the same trucks along the same route, only under the cover of night, the cargo no longer beer but bathtub gin. He'd been chased on more than one occasion by the Feds who were referred to as G-men at the time. He'd never been caught or shot at. There were times he swore they didn't want to catch him. The Feds had their hands out, and rum runners paid well for the privilege of not being arrested.

In later years, my grandfather took to more honest work as a mason contractor. He often worked downtown on the city high rises that were springing up all over the place, having been placed in charge of several crews who would plaster the many brick and block exteriors. During his lunchtime, he'd drink Coffee Royales with a local priest who often joined him for weekly visits to the whore houses down on Green Street. Simpler days. Simpler times. Far away from the digital age.

I drank more of the coffee. It warmed my insides on a day that was already hotter than hell. I tried to back up a bit and think about this whole thing. I started from the start. With Harold Sanders. The slim, artistically dressed architect was convinced his future son-in-law did something bad enough to his daughter's head it caused her to enter into a nearly irreversible coma. The kid then tried to cover up his wicked actions by enlisting his daddy to drive her to the hospital instead of calling 911 and bringing in a potentially lifesaving EMT.

Now that Sanders had gotten nowhere with the cops, he'd entered into a civil lawsuit with the Davids. In turn, he'd hired me to dig up enough dirt on them both in order to win a settlement worth forty million. Unlike a lot of lawsuits in which the defendants don't have a pot to piss in no matter the lawsuit amount, the Davids were richer than God. Should they lose the lawsuit, they would be forced to cut a check and the check would be a good check. Which meant Sanders was relying on me to do a good job. Heck, there might even be a five-figure bonus in it for me.

But thus far, it looked as though the Davids were doing the job for me by just being themselves. Not only did I now possess some pictures of the kid seated beside a mirror full of coke and a mostly naked blonde bombshell with a snake tattoo on her neck inside his home, but I'd been chased by a goon in a black Lexus hatchback who took a shot at me. Then there was the rather threatening face-to-face with Mr. David Sr. while his wife, Penny, thought nothing of offering me her body just as she'd done with her stepson so many times before. Or so she claimed. She'd also revealed that little bit about Mrs. David Number One having died from a fall off a ladder while picking grapes under the backyard arbor. An accident that, in my mind and still tight gut, might not have been an accident at all. When I added it all up and combined it with the testimony from food blogger, Ted Bolous, about Junior's nasty temper, the Davids were not exactly the Waltons.

But still, none of this meant that Sarah simply hadn't walked out the front door on a cold winter's night, slipped on the ice, and fallen down the steps. Without some kind of solid proof of Junior having caused her to fall or some kind of evidence that proved he hit her over the head with something, Harold Sanders would be shit out of luck. So would the APD.

I drank some more coffee.

It tasted weak.

I decided to add more Royale Crown to it.

I tasted it again.

That little bit of extra whiskey did the trick. Maybe the Coffee Royale was serving its purpose. Calming me down over one hell of a rough morning. But it wasn't quieting the little noise inside my gut that was telling me I'd stepped into something that stank. What made the noise all the more disarming wasn't the fact that I'd almost been killed this morning, or that I was uncovering information that would make it look as though the Davids were at least capable of killing someone. What bothered me most about the noise was the name it kept calling out.

It was calling out the name of my client: Harold Sanders.

24

I STILL HAD AN hour to kill before I'd get my 4Runner back. I decided to spend that time productively, which meant I'd call Harold Sanders and more or less demand he meet me on Lark Street within the half-hour.

I did it.

He told me he was in the middle of a project meeting and asked me if it could wait. I told him I didn't care if he was in a meeting with I.M. Pei and, no, it couldn't wait. We agreed on a small Italian restaurant just around the corner from his Albany office and less than a mile from my warehouse.

"What the hell," I said. "You can buy me lunch."

"Shouldn't you be buying me lunch with the money I'm paying you?"

"I'm not that kind of business client, Mr. Sanders," I said. "I'm a save-your-ass-and-make-you-a-lot-of-money-you-probably-don't-really-need kind of client. See you in thirty."

The Italian restaurant I met him at was located on a State Street corner, directly across from the Albany Institute of History and Art. It was called Francesca's, and it was a wood, two-story building that had been somebody's home once. Perhaps Francesca herself. But now it housed around a dozen tables inside what used to be the place's dining and living rooms. It was as close to a traditional, family-run Italian trattoria as Albany ever would see.

We were the only customers having lunch that day, as though the owner opened up for us and us only. Francesca was a short, seventy-

96

something, heavy-set woman, with thick black hair and a considerable bust. She wore a black dress as though in perpetual mourning for a now-dead husband whose framed portrait hung on the wall by the register.

When she greeted us, I couldn't help but notice her thick Italian accent. I asked her from which part of Italy she originated.

"No Italy," she answered sternly. "Sicily." Then she looked at me for a brief moment or two, not with interest, but suspicion. That suspicion told me she wasn't lying when she claimed Sicily as her home turf. I told her that my family originated from the mountainous Marche region along the Adriatic coast and she just glared at me for a moment more and shook her head. Italians from the south love to hate Italians from the north. And vice versa. It's a never-ending war. For the purposes of lunch, however, I hoped we might find some common ground.

Sanders and I were seated and handed our cardboard menus. There were only three main dishes available. One chicken, one meat, and one fish. Polo, carne, pesce. When Sanders chose the pesce and a glass of Chianti, I went with the meat and a Moretti beer. Made me feel tougher than he was. Which I was anyway. He was dressed all in black again, just like yesterday when I'd first met him. But he wasn't wearing a jacket. Just black jeans and a black T-shirt that looked as though it'd been professionally pressed. His hair was perfect. Thick, long, gray, and artsy.

Francesca brought our drinks and set out two small plates of insalata, one for each of us. In between the plates, she set a basket of fresh, sliced Italian bread.

"So why the impromptu meeting?" he said, sipping his Chianti.

I drank some Moretti beer. The cold aromatic beer felt good against the back of my dry throat.

"I've discovered quite a bit about the Davids and I thought you should know about it," I said. "Not the least of which is that they are very dangerous and that they believe you're broke and that's the real reason behind your suing them."

He smiled and shot me this squinty-eyed look as though to say I was being overly dramatic. He sipped more wine and set his glass back down.

"Look, Mr. Marconi," he said, dabbing at the corners of his mouth with his cloth napkin, "if this is your way of trying to get

more money out of me, I'm afraid you'll have to do better than that."
Shaking his head, disgusted. "Broke . . . Now that's a good one
indeed."

"I'm not trying to get more money out of you," I said. "I'm trying
to issue you a warning. A facts-of-life warning. This lawsuit you've
initiated has begun to stir up the hornet's nest. And I don't like
hornets. Hornets have stingers, and it hurts when they sting."

He ate some salad. The dressing was a simple virgin olive oil and
red-wine vinaigrette.

"I thought you were tougher than that, Mr. Marconi," he said
after he swallowed what was in his mouth.

"My reputation precedes me," I said. "But death awaits me, and
I intend to put it off for a while if I can help it."

"Has your life been threatened in any way?"

"You hear about the accident on the bypass bridge this morning?"

"Traffic was tied up for miles," he said. "You had something to
do with that?"

"One of David's employees took a shot at me."

"Looked to me like he nearly got himself killed in the process."

"Turns out I'm a better driver than he is." I ate some salad. It was
delicious. Tangy and textural and cool. "I saved him from going over
the side of the bridge only after he told me who he worked for. I also
let him off with a warning. That whoever comes after me again
won't live to tell about it."

"There's the Keeper Marconi I hired."

I drank some beer. What I couldn't get over was the fact that
Sanders, all one-hundred-thirty artsy-fartsy pounds of him, seemed
to be enjoying this exchange.

Our pasta dishes arrived. A simple Spaghetti Pomodoro. I
wrapped up a forkful and ate it. The pasta melted in my mouth. It
was homemade.

"Please give me the bottom line here, Mr. Marconi," Sanders
said. "Are you still willing to work for me? Or have the David boys
scared you off? Maybe you think my checks are no good."

The architect knew how to press my buttons, and he was playing
me like the keypad on an iPad.

"I'm sticking with it," I said, "because I honor my commitments.
I also don't think it will take very long to prove that the Davids are
not exactly simple, law-abiding citizens. For one, Junior is a drug

addict and, from what I'm told, a sex addict with an unusually violent temper. A devilishly violent temper, or so food blogger, Ted Bolous, tells me. The old man feels the need to hire security guards and goons who are willing to kill in order to keep him protected. But I'm sure you knew that already."

He drank some wine and I sipped some beer.

"Actually," he said, "that's why I hired you."

"You telling me you had no idea what kind of family your daughter was getting mixed up with when she agreed to marry Junior?"

He cocked his head.

"It's no secret around town that Junior won't be up for a Boy Scout of the Year Award anytime soon," he said. "But if what you're telling me is correct—that he has a serious drug and sex problem as well as a history of violence—then that will only aid me in my cause."

"Indeed it will and I will write it all up in my report to you. But what I won't be able to write up is precisely how he harmed your daughter. That is he did anything to harm her at all."

He set his fork down and wiped his mouth.

"You have to believe that if I weren't certain of foul play, I would never have entered into this lawsuit nor would I be wasting your time and my money, Mr. Marconi."

I finished my second plate just as the third plate arrived. It was a small sizzling steak with a side of roasted potatoes.

"Here's your bottom line," I said. "How would you feel if I told you I know how to prove beyond the shadow of a doubt that Junior did try and kill your daughter and that I can do so without having to produce a single shred of hard evidence?"

He finished his second pasta plate and started in on his grilled pesce—head, tail, and all. Just as it would be served in Sicily.

"You have my undivided attention."

I ate some steak. It was tender and hot and juicy.

"In light of my little run-in with the goon this morning, I believe it's only a matter of time until Junior feels like maybe he should try and kill your daughter again. Do it right this time."

He dropped his fork and sat up.

"You really believe that?"

I smiled.

"It's my job to believe such realities, Mr. Sanders. It's also my job to issue you the necessary warnings."

"What do you suggest we do? My daughter is still slowly recovering. She's not capable of taking care of herself much less protecting her life and limb. And, of course, I have my business dealings to contend with."

"Of course you do," I said. "You'll be relieved to know I've already alerted Detective Miller at the Albany Police Department, and he is sending out a protective detail to Valley View."

"That certainly comes as a relief."

"I'd like to interview Sarah after lunch. With your permission, of course."

He shook his head.

"Don't you think she's been through enough?" he said. "My wish is to keep my sweet angel out of this."

"Your angel is already major-league involved, and I need to get an idea of how much she remembers about the night of February 18th."

"She remembers nothing," he said, drinking the rest of his wine, then holding up his empty glass for a refill.

"According to Bolous's blogs, Sarah seems to be recovering nicely and making progress every day. It only stands to reason that eventually she will regain her long-term memory. And when she does, it's very possible she will recall precisely what happened that night."

"And if she does?"

"She just might reveal the identity of the man who may have attempted to kill her. And that identity will more than likely match that of Robert David Jr."

"If that happens," Sanders said as Francesca grumpily set a second glass of Chianti before him, "do you feel it's possible Junior will try and have her killed in order to silence her?"

"Wouldn't you?" I said, drinking the last of my beer.

His face turned sickly pale, and he didn't seem to have an appetite any longer.

"Looks like your job description is about to change somewhat," he said.

I ate some steak.

"From this point out," he added, "I not only want you to prove

Robert David Jr. is responsible for nearly killing my daughter, but I want you to protect her from it happening all over again."

25

BY THE TIME I made it back on foot to my warehouse after lunch, my newly repaired 4Runner was parked up against the curb, awaiting my inspection. Not only had the front and back windshields been replaced, but Blood's people even gave it a thorough wash and wax.

"You like, Warden Marconi?" Blood asked as he approached on the sidewalk.

"Superior job as usual," I said watching the early afternoon sun glisten off the vehicle's red hood.

"I've made contact with some of my peeps," he said. "By end of the night, I'll know exactly what kind of shit Robert Jr. is doing and who he's getting it from."

"Just add your service fee to my tab, Blood," I said, opening the door and slipping inside the 4Runner. The leather seats were slippery with a new coating of Armor All silicone protection. "It's got the new car smell all over again."

"I pay attention to details, Keep," he smiled. "Topped off the tank for you too."

I closed the door, knowing that without a doubt, I would soon possess information that would prove Robert David Jr. to be a regular purchaser of illicit drugs. It wouldn't prove he almost killed Sarah Levy. But it would bring me one step closer to proving he was fully capable of a real bad guy.

Driving to Interstate 90, the highway that would take me west to Schenectady and Valley View Rehabilitation Center, I called Robert

David Sr.'s office. His lovely assistant, Victoria, answered.

"David Enterprises," she said in her low-toned, sultry voice. "How can I help you?"

"Are you free for a drink tonight?" I said.

"Who is this?"

"I'll give you a hint. You once wore my donuts."

I heard her exhale.

"What is it you want, Mr. Marconi?"

"I've already told you. A drink sometime."

"I'm involved with someone, and even if I weren't, I'm not exactly your type."

"And what type is that?"

"Sophisticated comes to mind."

"Some women confuse me for James Bond. We both carry guns, you know. Danger is our middle name."

"Like I said, I'm busy."

"Would your big boss happen to be in?"

"He's busy too."

There was a little commotion in the background. Then I heard the sound of a palm being pressed down against the receiver. After a few seconds, Victoria came back on the line.

"Hang on for one moment, please."

I was immediately put on hold. My port-mounted cell phone filled with the sound of Muzak. *The Girl from Ipanema.* I concentrated on the highway while I tapped out a rhythm to the music with my thumbs against the steering wheel.

Then David Sr. came on the line.

"What can I do for you, Mr. Marconi? I was under the impression our communication had come to an end."

"That's because you tried to make my life come to an end. A very tragic and violent end, you might say. By the way, congrats on the new trophy wife."

I pictured him swallowing a rock.

"I have no idea what you're talking about. And leave Penny out of this."

"How's your goon feeling? He was pretty shaken up when I let him go free. I could have sent him over the side of that bridge. But I wanted him to face something worse than death. I wanted him to crawl back into the rat hole you all live in, and I wanted him to tell

103

you he failed at disposing of me. You know, next time he tries to kill somebody by running them off the road, tell him not to use his gun. If he uses his gun to spray bullets all over the place, it won't end up looking like an accident. It'll look like murder in the first. In any case, all this bumping off business doesn't bode well for your lawsuit defense now does it, Mr. David Sr.?"

"I don't employ goons as you say, but I do employ a crack team of brilliant young lawyers to handle my affairs including this silly case. And I would never do something as stupid as having you intentionally harmed."

"I could ask your first wife, Joan, if she might back up your statement, but . . ."

"Why you cold-hearted son of a bitch."

"Cold ain't the word for it," I said, my eyes on the road, recognizing the exit I needed to take about a half mile up ahead. "Should the goon I let live this morning have been arrested and revealed who he worked for, he might have said a Mr. Robert David Jr. Which we both know is the same as him working for you since you cut all the checks. Oh, and the police are perfectly aware of all this. Just wanted to let you know that."

I hung up before he could get in another word edgewise. I stared at the phone mounted in its car dock for a while, thinking it was very possible that David would call me back. But he didn't. I was almost disappointed that he didn't as I turned onto the exit, paid my toll, and started making my way toward a very damaged Sarah Levy.

26

VALLEY VIEW REHABILITATION CENTER was housed in
a series of century-old brick-and-stone buildings that could have
doubled as an Ivy League University. There was a black iron fence
that surrounded the place. The kind of fence made up of sharp spikes
that would impale you should you attempt to climb over it. There
was a small guard shack at the entrance where visitors were required
to take a ticket before a yellow, wood slat gate like the kind you see
at a railroad crossing, was raised up allowing you entrance to the lot.

As I drove onto the lot and searched for an empty space, I could
see how meticulously cared for the Valley View grounds were. I
wondered about water restrictions in the city of Schenectady since
the lawns were green and lush, and so were the shrubs. There were
many flowerbeds and shade trees and wide gravel paths that
provided access to and around them. There were some male and
female nurses dressed in surgical green and hospital white who were
wheeling patients slowly over the gravel paths, the peaceful view no
doubt aiding them in their recovery.

I parked the 4Runner and got out. I cut across the lawn to the
administration building which also served as the rehab center's main
entrance. Once inside, I inquired at the information desk about Sarah
Levy. The middle-aged woman behind the desk was reading the
latest copy of *People* magazine. The major topic featured was the
tumultuous break up of Katie and Tom Cruise. I knew this because
I caught a quick glimpse of both Tom and Katie's shiny happy
Scientology faces printed on the glossy magazine cover as the
woman slapped it down, pulled off her reading glasses, and exhaled

an annoyed breath. Without a "Welcome to Sunny View Rehabilitation Center," she silently checked the chart set out on the counter directly beside Tom and Katie.

"Are you family?" she robotically asked.

"I'm a private detective working for Ms. Levy's father, Harold Sanders. He should have called by now warning of my arrival." I smiled when I said "warning." I had to be careful when I smiled. It could cause even the coldest of women to melt on the spot.

She looked back down at her chart as if a notation about my permission had been added to it. And by the looks of it, it had.

"I.D., please?" she said, setting her reading glasses back on the crown of her pug nose.

I pulled my P.I. license from my back pocket, slipped it out, handed it to her through the opening at the bottom of the glass separator.

She looked at it as though she knew what she was doing.

"Picture looks like you," she said, handing it back to me.

"Captures the essence of my charm and charisma pretty well, don't you think?"

Finally, her stone face showed the first hint of smile. Coldness officially melted.

"Ms. Levy is in B Wing. Room 415," she said. "I'll call upstairs and let them know you're coming."

"You're a doll," I said.

"Wish my husband would tell me that."

"Maybe you should give him a little now and then," I whispered under my breath as I turned and made for the elevators.

"I heard that," she said.

I took the B Wing elevator to the fourth floor. When I got out, I could see that the place was laid out just like a regular hospital, with a nurse's station in the center of the wing and four separate corridors that branched out from it. The station was brightly lit and the circular counter was filled with computers and other electronic gadgetry that escaped my pedestrian status. I inquired once more at the desk as to the location of 415. The heavy-set young woman at the desk told me that Donna from the front desk had called and told her to expect my arrival. She pointed in the direction of Sarah's room. Then she told me not to expect too much. Sarah was recovering nicely, but she still retained only short-term memory. Much of her long-term memory had either disappeared for good or hadn't yet returned. Once I told her I understood, she told me I had only fifteen minutes and no more.

"So make it quick," she said.

"I intend to," I said. Then, "Are you aware that Tom and Katie Cruise have broken up?"

She glared at me. "Wow, a real comic in my presence."

"Must be the terrific valley view," I smiled.

"Oh, and by the way," she said, "Donna at the information desk told me to tell you she gives her husband plenty." She followed up with an overly dramatic wink of her right eye.

"Tell her I'm glad for the hubby," I said, winking back. "Maybe she should tell it to Katie and Tom. Could rehabilitate a marriage made in Hollywood."

I turned and immediately made my way to Sarah Levy's room, not knowing exactly what to expect.

27

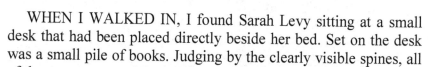

WHEN I WALKED IN, I found Sarah Levy sitting at a small desk that had been placed directly beside her bed. Set on the desk was a small pile of books. Judging by the clearly visible spines, all of them were penned by the same author: Shel Silvertstein.

From where I stood inside the open door, I could see *The Giving Tree,* which was set on the desk beside the open book she was presently reading aloud, which was *Going Up.* Her choice of clothing amounted to a simple purple nightgown that ended somewhere around her knees and her feet were bare. Her hair wasn't long and lush like in the newspaper photos, but instead, cropped and sort of choppy. As if she cut it herself with scissors.

I stood in the doorway and watched and listened for nearly a full minute before I made my presence known. Her voice was enchanting, its softness and youthfulness drawing me in like a child listening to his mother while she read a bedtime story. But then I remembered the fifteen-minute time limit and I wrapped my knuckles on the heavy wood door.

She turned, looked up at me and smiled.

"May I come in?" I said.

"Are you . . . the . . . detective?" she said. As I said, her soft voice was enchanting, but it was also slow. Her speech not slurred as I more or less expected. Just slow in its delivery.

I introduced myself and told her I was working for her father. Then I stepped into the room and came around the bed to her desk. There was a chair set beside it. I sat down in it and gestured toward her pile of books.

"Shel is one of my favorites," I said. *"The Giving Tree* still brings tears to my eyes."

She nodded, but I'm not sure she understood me entirely.

"I'm having trouble reading," she said, this time slurring her words just slightly. "Since my accident, I have not been . . . myself."

"What accident is that, Sarah?"

Her smiled dissolved then, and she went back to staring at the open book set on her desk. It was then I noticed the thin, purplish scar that ran its way up from the base of her skull, up past her right ear. It explained why her hair had been cut so short. The area must have been shaved not too long ago to accommodate the surgery to relieve the pressure on her swelled brain.

"When I fell," she said. "Fell . . . on . . . the ice."

"Do you remember *how* you fell on the ice, Sarah?"

She shook her now fragile head. Slowly.

"I'm trying to remember. But I can't seem to come up with a picture of that night. When I try to remember, my head begins to hurt and I become very tired."

"Do you remember your fiancé, Robert?"

"Yes," she said, with another slow nod. "Robert. I remember Robert. I miss Robert. Robert does not come to see me."

"Do you recall if you were fighting on the night your accident occurred, Sarah?"

"Robert and I love one another," she whispered. "We're going to be married soon." She rubbed the now vacant area on her ring finger where an engagement band should have been.

"But even when two people love each other they can still have fights. Is it possible that you and Robert were fighting on that night?"

"I. Can't. Remember."

"Do you remember why you decided to go outside to your car at two o'clock on a very cold and dark winter morning? Were you trying to get away from Robert? Were you afraid of something?"

Her body was beginning to stiffen up at my questions. She wouldn't make eye contact with me as if it would hurt her head to do so. She remained glued to that book. But I'm certain that she wasn't seeing the words or the black and white images sketched out on the pages. I'm convinced she was trying to replay the events of that night in her mind. She was trying to draw her own pictures inside her battered brain. She was trying to recall a series of events and images. But they just wouldn't come. I was certain of it.

"Try hard for me Sarah," I pushed, knowing I could only go so far until she might break down completely. "Is it possible Robert hit you? Or pushed you?"

"No. No. No," she began to mumble. "Robert loves me. Robert. Loves. Me."

"Did he push you down the steps, Sarah? Please try and remember."

She was crying now. Openly weeping. Once more, I thought about my mini tape recorder sitting idly in the 4Runner where it wasn't doing me any good.

"Robert loves me," she said again. "We are going to be married."

"Did he push you down the steps so that you hit your head?"

"Robert loves me," she said through the tears. "Robert is angry. Robert is so, so, so angry." She got up from her chair. "Please don't be angry with me, Robert! I'll play with you, Robert!" Screaming now. "I'll do what you want me to do, Robert. I'll do it for everyone. Don't hit me, Robert!"

A man came rushing in then. A tall man dressed in a white lab coat.

"What in the devil is going on here?" he said. He was more or less shouting under his breath.

I stood up, told him who I was and who I worked for.

"I'm trying to find out what Sarah remembers of the event back in February. Her life could be in danger."

"What danger?" he said, taking hold of her trembling hands, guiding her the few inches to her bed, and helping her lie down in it. "Please wait for me out in the hall, Mr. Marconi," he added.

I did what he told me to do. I went out into the hall and waited while the chubby nurse standing behind the nurse's station shot me red hot glares. When the doctor came back out, he closed Sarah's door, but not all the way, as if she were a toddler taking her afternoon nap. He didn't tell me his name, but I could read it plain enough from the plastic-coated I.D. pinned to a breast pocket that also held a couple of ballpoint pens.

"Tell me, Dr. Saviors," I said. "What exactly does Sarah recall?"

He was tall and slim, and his dark hair was receding. I pegged him for maybe forty.

"Not a lot, I'm afraid. The extent of her injuries are simply too severe to allow her any semblance of long-term memory."

"But she must remember something," I said, "or she wouldn't become so upset."

"She's upset because she gets frustrated," Saviors said. "Tell me something, Mr. Marconi, wouldn't you be bothered if you had absolutely no recollection of your past whatsoever? Who you are? Where you grew up? If you were married or not? Had children?"

"She remembers, Robert," I said. "She remembers him enough to recall her love for him, and his anger for her."

He began to shake his head, almost violently.

"Reactions," he said. "Like touching a dead man with an electric probe."

I wasn't sure whether to believe him or not. But then, why would he lie to me? Unless, of course, he was taking under-the-table money from the Davids too.

"Is it possible she will regain her long-term memory?" I said.

"Yes, it is," he said. "But it could take many more months. Her rehabilitation is progressing well, but it is a slow, painstaking progress. By all that's right in the world, she should be dead. Her brain was severely swelled when she arrived at the emergency room back in February. Emergency surgery saved her life."

"You're, of course, aware her fiancé never called 911."

"I'm aware of it, and I don't like it any more than you or her father likes it. But it's not my place to judge the Davids and their actions. Lots a people would panic under similar circumstances."

I glanced over my shoulder at the nurse. Still glaring. I stuck my tongue out at her.

"One more question, Doc, and I'll make a swift retreat before your support staff impales me on the metal fence outside. Do you think it's possible Sarah was hit over the head with something? Or maybe pushed down a set of ice-covered brick steps?"

"Are we off the record here, Mr. Marconi?"

"There never was a record to be on in the first place. I don't work for the cops. I work for me and my current employer."

"Her head injuries are severe. A simple punch to the head, even from a man who is strong and in shape, wouldn't cause the amount of damage done to this young woman. But a fall, perhaps down a long and steep flight of steps, might indeed result in the same kind

111

of trauma. That is if the back of her head slammed every tread on the way down."

"Okay," I said, "thanks, Doc. You should know that if she does eventually recall the events that resulted in her injuries and it turns out Robert David Jr. had something to do with them, then she might find herself in danger. Or maybe she's in danger anyway."

"You feel that her former fiancé might attempt to silence her? Or is this your attempt at being dramatic?"

"I've alerted the police to the possibility. That's how strongly I feel about it. No drama, Doc. I promise." I issued him the two-fingered Boy Scout salute when I used the word "promise."

"I would prefer not to see policemen hanging around my rehabilitation center, Mr. Marconi. It's bad for business."

"I understand," I said, as I stole one last glance at the now peacefully sleeping Sarah through the narrow door opening. "But then, so would a murder."

About-facing, I made my way toward the nurse's station where I shot the chubby nurse a Marconi smile.

"Have a nice day," I said.

"I will now that you're leaving," she said.

I stood waiting for the elevator to arrive, feeling her eyes burning holes in my backside.

28

FROM BEHIND THE WHEEL of the idling 4Runner, I placed a call to Miller's cell. He answered after only one ring. I told him about my meeting with Sarah.

"She really can't remember a thing?" he said. "Sure she's just not afraid to admit she remembers something or everything?"

"She didn't seem afraid to me, or like she was putting on some kind of act. She seemed lost. Lost in her own brain damaged world. But she did seem to remember one thing about Junior that raised my red flag."

"I'm here," Miller said.

"In one breath, she kept telling me how much Robert loves her. Not *loved*, as in the past tense. But loves."

"And?"

"And then she started spouting off about Robert getting angry with her. She doesn't like it when Robert gets angry. Her words corroborated exactly what that Bolous said. That Junior has anger issues. I got the testimony on tape."

"Oh yeah? What exactly might Junior be getting angry about with his lovely, wealthy Sarah?"

"She said that if she didn't *play* at what he wanted her to play at, then he'd become very angry."

"Play," Miller repeated. "As in play a game? A game created in hell?"

"What else could it mean?"

"Any ideas?"

"Judging from Junior's lifestyle, his games could range from sexual to drug-related to satanic to all of the above."

"Sarah seems like a nice girl, Keeper."

"That she does. Not the type to play any of Junior's perverted and evil reindeer games."

"You gonna give your client a full report on all this?"

"Not yet."

"Then what's your next move?"

"I'm going to have a drink at Manny's in a little while, and see what I can sniff out there. Then, if Junior is working tonight, I might do a little more snooping around Marion Avenue."

"Keep, you should know better than to admit to a B-and-E prior to committing it. Especially over the phone with a union-dues-paying officer of the law."

"I wouldn't have to be committing a B-and-E if you guys could grab yourselves a simple search warrant. Tell you what. Junior's been violating the lawn-watering restrictions. At least try and bust him for that."

"I feel another one of my fuck yous coming on, Keeper."

"Allow me to try another angle. Think you can help me out with the silent alarm once the intrusion comes up on the scanner? You might have to make a few calls on my behalf to dispatch once the security company gets wind of the trip. "

"Jesus, this conversation isn't happening. But I'll see what I can do. And yeah, it'll require a phone call or two, but nothing entirely too impossible so long as you're quick and efficient about it."

"That's the spirit, copper."

"You know if I didn't need you right now, Keep, I'd have nothing to do with you."

"Gosh, and here I thought our love was all one-sided."

"Text me before you get there and, for God's sakes, try not to leave any evidence behind, please. You get caught, this thing is shot and I don't know who the hell you are."

"Hey Mitch, it's me you're talking to here. Jack Marconi . . . *the* one and only."

"Thank Christ Almighty for that," he said.

This time I raced to hang up before he beat me to it.

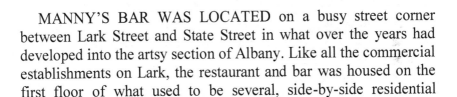

29

MANNY'S BAR WAS LOCATED on a busy street corner between Lark Street and State Street in what over the years had developed into the artsy section of Albany. Like all the commercial establishments on Lark, the restaurant and bar was housed on the first floor of what used to be several, side-by-side residential brownstone apartment buildings.

The bar was old even by Albany standards. Very old. Probably dating back to the late 1800s or more. But the Davids had managed to renovate the place into a modern drinking and eating establishment complete with fancy overhead lighting, a rich scarlet interior wall finish, and an ear-pleasing digital sound system. They also made sure to keep in the old by making the refurbished antique wood bar the place's focal point. The ornate mahogany counter extended the entire length of the room, reaching all the way to the dining room.

It was early still. Not even five o'clock when I hooked a quick right just as I entered through the front glass and wood door, and bellied up to the bar's near corner. Marconi's number one rule of private detecting. Never enter into a place you can't easily get yourself out of. Planting myself this close to the door felt entirely like the right thing to do. Keeper, the cautious.

There was a woman dressed in tight black Levis jeans and matching black T-shirt tending to the bar. She was standing all the way at the opposite end, where she was washing out wine glasses in the small sink and placing them stem first, vampire bat-style, on an overhead rack to dry. She'd heard me come in but wanted to finish what she was working on before she approached me.

It wasn't until she made it more than halfway that I noticed she was the same woman I'd seen yesterday evening lying passed out on Robert David Jr.'s couch. The tall blonde, with the killer body and the tattoo of a white-fanged snake coiled against the smooth skin on the right side of her neck. Now that she was standing only a few feet away from me I could see that the snake started down at her shoulder and extended upwards to her earlobe. Cute. I wondered if her boss and lover was hanging around anywhere. Maybe in the kitchen. I was banking on his presence.

She tossed me a smile that was decidedly forced.

"What can I get for you?" she said. Her voice was low, raspy. I pictured the way she looked in her white, lacy thong underwear. It made me blush.

I ordered a bottle of beer. She retrieved it for me and set it onto a coaster that said, "Bass Ale."

"Glass?" she said.

"Strictly cowboy for me," I said. Then, "What made you go with the snake?"

She shot me a quizzical look, as though I'd asked her what brand she uses for a conditioning rinse. It took a beat or two, but eventually what I asked clicked inside her pretty little brain.

"Oh, the snake," she said, bringing the tips of her fingers to the coiled blue, red, and brown snake tattoo. "I like snakes. I find them enchanting and mysterious."

"Looks like it's about to bite your neck. You like neck bites?"

Her faced turned a distinct shade of hot red.

"I don't even know you," she said.

I reached into my pocket, pulled out a card, and set it on the bar.

"But your boyfriend knows me," I said.

I looked at her neck, wondering if Junior had tried to pierce her neck with his teeth. Tried to draw blood like a real vampire. It was impossible to tell from where I was sitting and from where she was standing behind the wood bar. She looked the card over and then looked me up and down.

"You're the one came to the house last night."

"That would be me. I'm looking into how and why Sarah Levy can't even remember her birthday, much less what happened on February 18th, when her brains got scrambled on Junior's property."

Her pretty face went stone stiff, the blood draining out of it.

"What's your name?" I pressed on.

For a split second, I didn't think she was going to tell me.

"Daphne," she said after a time.

"Like on *Scooby Doo*? Really? Wow."

"What do you want from me?" she said.

"I just want to ask you a couple of questions, Daphne. Before you get busy."

She stole a glance over her shoulder. Other than a high school age busboy who was busy setting up the back dining room tables for the dinner hour, the place was empty as a morgue.

"Do I have to speak with you?"

"No."

"Then maybe you should leave."

"I don't want to."

She exhaled. It made the snake move.

"What do you want to know?"

"Are you Robert's new girlfriend?"

"Sort of."

"Meaning?"

"We see each other when we feel like seeing each other."

"So if this were Facebook, your relationship status would qualify as, 'It's complicated.'"

"You go with that, Mr. Detective."

"You aware that Sarah Levy thinks Robert is still in love with her? That he's still going to marry her?"

"At this point, she probably still believes in the Easter Bunny, Mr. Marconi."

"True. Very true. And how very sensitive of you to say so. How long have you been doing drugs with Robert?"

She took a step back.

"This conversation ends now. Enjoy your beer and leave."

"But I'm just getting started," I said. "Do you feel Robert is capable of hurting someone he loves out of an uncontrollable anger?"

"Leave," she said, her right hand in the air, waving at me to be gone.

She disappeared into the back room and for a few moments, I thought I might never see her again. But then I heard a commotion, and someone else emerged from the back room altogether. It was Robert David Jr. Judging by the scowl on his face, the baseball bat in his hand, and the red horns protruding from the top of his skull, I could see that he was not happy.

Thus far, things were going pretty much as planned.

30

OKAY, MAYBE JUNIOR DIDN'T have actual horns growing out of his skull, but he was threatening me with a baseball bat. He was wearing the same black jeans and matching black tee that his sig-"it's complicated"-other was wearing. The tightness of his clothing accentuated his lean musculature when he stomped his way down the length of the bar to me, patting the palm of his free hand with the fat end of the cut-off baseball bat.

I drank some beer.

"You really gonna hit me with that thing, Junior?"

I pictured that same bat slamming into the back of Sarah's head.

"I might," he said, that scowl now bearing those sharpened and whitened vampire fangs. "I thought I told you to butt out of my business, Marconi."

"Your business is entirely my business, Junior," I said, taking another drink of my beer, setting it down carefully onto the Bass Ale coaster. "I believe that sooner than later, it will be police business also. And then, take it from someone who knows, it will be maximum security prison business. That's when your pretty little fantasy life will come to an end and you will become the skinny boyfriend of a big, black, buck male."

I wasn't pressing Junior's buttons. I was slamming them home with a framing hammer. And my methodology was working too. He proved it by doing something extraordinary. He raised up his right leg, stepped up onto the bar's interior work counter and, twisting his body, jumped up onto the bar top so that he landed on the aforementioned skinny ass. Then he quickly swung his legs around, slid down onto the floor and stood before me, that shortened baseball bat still poised in his right hand.

I looked into his eyes.

The eyes were glassy, pupils contracted to maybe half their size. I knew what I was I looking at. I'd seen it in prison many times when inmates smuggled in speed or crystal meth. Something that would serve as a quick high and a cheap substitute for fine cocaine.

"Wow," I said. "A floor show and everything."

Out the corner of my eyes, I saw Daphne reappear. She had an unlit cigarette nervously poised between two fingers of her right hand.

"Time for you to be long gone, Marconi," he said, as he took a step toward me, raising up the bat as if he intended to strike me with it. "The cops have no evidence of nothing."

"That's a double negative, Junior," I said, as I got up fast, grabbed hold of the bat, yanked it out of his hand. At the same time, I took hold of his arm, wrapped it fast around his back, pushing the wrist up toward his neck. I shoved the arm hard, and nearly brought his shoulder to the point of dislocation. But not quite.

The pain was so intense he immediately dropped to his knees and yelped like a girl. I pressed the bat against the back of his skull and pushed his head down, chin against chest.

"Robert don't!" Daphne screamed, coming around the bar and making her way to us. "I'm calling the police."

Dropping the bat, I reached around and turned the deadbolt on the door. Then I reached into Robert's back pocket and pulled out his wallet. I shook it upside down so that the credit cards and money spilled out of it onto the floor. I kept on shaking the leather wallet until a small clear plastic packet of white powder emerged. Tossing the wallet, I picked up the packet. Then I let go of Junior's arm and, raising my right leg, pressed the flat sole of my boot against his backside and pushed. He went down hard onto his face.

"By all means, Daph," I said, "call the cops. I'll be happy to show them what you two like to do in your spare time."

There were a couple of suited young men standing outside the door. They tried to open the door. But it wouldn't budge.

"Yo!" the first one called out as though we were in a *Rocky* movie. "You open or what?"

All three of us ignored him.

Junior raised himself up onto his knees and tried to work the pain out of his shoulder by shrugging it and spinning his arm around in slow circles.

"No cops, Daph," he insisted. He got back up onto his feet. Wobbly.

The guy at the door tried it again, as though it would magically open this time.

"Hang on!" Junior yelled through the picture window glass. Then, looked at me. "You touch me again, and I will kill you."

"I'm sure you will," I said. "It will only add to your newfound reputation."

"Robert, shut up," Daphne said. "You're already in trouble."

I eyed the guys standing outside the door. One was short and round. His buddy behind him was tall and thin. Abbot and Costello. I shoved the packet of dope into my pants pocket, unlocked the door, and pushed it open.

"It's hot outside, boys," I said. "Good time for a cold one."

I eyed Junior as I slid my way past the two customers and out onto the searing sidewalk. I could still feel the angry heat permeating off his lean body all the way to my parked 4Runner.

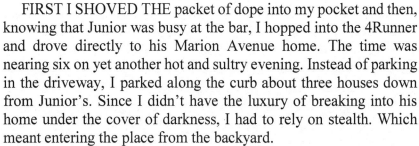

31

FIRST I SHOVED THE packet of dope into my pocket and then, knowing that Junior was busy at the bar, I hopped into the 4Runner and drove directly to his Marion Avenue home. The time was nearing six on yet another hot and sultry evening. Instead of parking in the driveway, I parked along the curb about three houses down from Junior's. Since I didn't have the luxury of breaking into his home under the cover of darkness, I had to rely on stealth. Which meant entering the place from the backyard.

I got out of the 4Runner and walked along the street for a bit, until I came to the house that was located next door to Junior's. It was a three-story brick house set on a heavily wooded lot. Hooking a right onto the property that bordered the two lots I entered into the wooded area where it hugged Junior's privacy fence. I followed the fence line all the way back into the dark woods until it ended at a ninety-degree corner. Making my way around the corner I stepped onto Junior's property and searched for a breach in the wood slat storm fence.

What I found didn't actually qualify as a breach, but I did find an area at the bottom of the fence that was half rotted away from constant exposure to the thick, damp woods. Using my boot like a battering ram, I kicked the wood in. It didn't take much effort before I was able to make an opening that would easily allow my five-foot-nine, one-hundred-eighty-five pound body access. Lying myself down on the pine-needled floor, I crawled through the opening in the fence.

Once through, I stood up and quickly made my way across the

green grass and onto a smooth concrete and inlaid stone patio that surrounded the Olympic-sized, in-ground pool. The pool was filled with crystal clear, blue water. One of those space-age, robotic vacuums that didn't require a human operator was busy cleaning the pool floor in random arcs and sweeps. Surrounding the pool were potted plants and black wrought iron furniture. A wood Tiki bar was stationed near the shallow end. It had three bar stools set out before it. Fancy.

I made my way past a long iron table that was big enough to support a large dinner party and then came to a set of sliding glass doors. I knew that if the place contained hidden video surveillance as a part of a much larger security system, that I had already been snagged. Which meant at this point, it didn't matter if I skillfully jimmied the glass doors open or simply tossed a chair through the glass.

Vying for the neater, safer alternative, I pulled out my Swiss Army knife, opened the big blade. I fit the blade into the narrow space between the door frame and the door, and methodically moved it back and forth until the lock released. Sliding the door open, I let myself into Junior's private world.

32

STANDING ONLY A COUPLE of feet inside the house, I listened for any kind of alarm.

Nothing.

No dog either.

I pulled a pair of Latex gloves from my blazer pocket and slipped those on. Even if it might be proven later on that I broke into Junior's house, it still wouldn't do me or the police any good to have my prints contaminating a possible crime scene.

I stood in the sitting room which contained a long sectional couch and some bookshelves. There was an LCD TV mounted on the wall and a big black coffee table. Some original artwork hung on the wall. I hooked a left and made my way through the same living room where Junior and Daphne had been sleeping one off the evening before. The place had been cleaned up since then, the mirror returned to its rightful place, the metal coffee table immaculate. Not a trace of any partying left over. If I had to guess, I would say the place had been cleaned by a pro. Probably an outfit for which Senior, no doubt, footed the bill.

I took a look at the kitchen.

It was large and full of stainless steel. Like the rest of the place, it was so clean it looked as if it hadn't been used for cooking, much less eating, in recent days or weeks. But then, I could only assume Junior took his meals at the restaurant. That is if he ate at all. Maybe he simply survived on other people's blood. The dining room was

124

attached to the kitchen. Again, the same story. Clean. Immaculate. Sterile even.

I walked back out to the vestibule and took the stairs up to the second floor. The master bedroom was located to the right. I went in and took a quick look around at the king-sized bed which was made up with a black satin comforter and matching black pillows. The walls were painted a dark blue. Covering much of them were bookshelves. The shelves were crammed with books. I took a quick look at the titles. Many of them were the same ones Val had mentioned to me the night before. Titles being gobbled up by the Facebooking, videogame playing, texting-while-driving, youth of the world. *Dominion, Dead Until Dark, Club Dead* . . . There were a few zombie titles added to the mix, *Cure, Eating Miss Daisy, Faster Zombie Cat! Eat! Eat!* . . . and also, as Val also suspected, a bunch of erotica titles: *Wallbanger, In Flight, Rock in the Heart,* and, of course, *Fifty Shades of Grey*. But not only were there at least a dozen copies of "Fifty Shades" on the shelf, there were dozens more of its sequels: *Fifty Shades Darker, Fifty Shades Freed,* an entire "Shades" trilogy, and more.

I snapped a few quick pictures of the bookshelves.

"I'll be damned," I whispered to myself. "Leave it to Val."

I shifted my eyes to other areas of the room. The drapes were long, thick and dark, and had they been closed, the room would have been devoid of any light whatsoever. Clearly Junior liked his darkness in order to sleep. More evidence of his fascination with the vampire life? Maybe.

I opened the drawer on the end piece set alongside the bed. A Kindle e-reader was stored inside it, some tissues, a tube of KY jelly, and not much else. Picking up the Kindle, I turned it on. The first book that popped up was *Fifty Shades of Grey*. As if Junior wasn't getting enough of the same material from the paper versions. I glanced at the books collected in his digital library. They were identical to the ones that were stored on the walls beside me. Turning off the Kindle, I set it back in the drawer and closed it.

There was no TV hanging on the wall. No sound system either. The room was intended pretty much for sleeping. I moved over to the dresser of drawers and opened the top one. It was filled with socks and underwear. Boxers, not briefs. Good choice. I felt around inside the drawer for anything that might not feel like fabric. Again, nothing.

I noticed the bathroom set off to my right. I went inside it and stared at the shower and toilet. Clean as a divine whistle. I opened the glass shower door. There was a large bottle of shampoo and a matching bottle of conditioner set on the small metal shelf. I closed the door, shifted the couple of steps to the medicine cabinet and opened the door. The cabinet could have served as a mini pharmacy. There had to be two dozen bottles. Uppers and downers galore. I pulled the smartphone from the pocket inside my jacket and snapped a picture. Then I closed the door, exiting the bathroom.

Out in the hall, I checked the other bedrooms.

One of them was made up as a guest room, and the other had been made into an office. The room was finished off with cherry wood paneling. It looked like an office only a lawyer could love. Or perhaps a doctor who liked to audibly record his daily patient notes at home. There was a laptop computer sitting out on the desk and not much else. I opened it. It immediately booted up to a sign-in screen. I knew I would never be able to come up with the right password, so I didn't even bother. Plus time was getting tight. I wasn't sure how long I had before Miller would have the alarm system re-engaged and the cops would have no choice but to pay a call to check for a possible intruder. Unplugging the computer, I closed it back up, stuffed it under my arm, then took it with me out into the hall and down the stairs.

Standing in the vestibule, I took one more look around. I noticed a door that looked as though it might lead to another room. I opened it. The door led to a staircase that went down into the basement. I knew that I had to check it out. Setting the computer on the counter in the kitchen, I came back out into the vestibule and started down the stairs, careful to hit the switch on the wall to my right that lit the space up in electric light.

At the bottom of the stairs, I looked upon a spacious room that was outfitted with free weights, a treadmill, and a stair climber. The walls were covered with floor-to-ceiling mirrors and I nearly jumped out of my skin when I turned to see myself standing there. I walked across the room to an area that contained a couple of solid wood doors. I opened the first one. The interior was a dressing room. I opened the second one. Another dressing room. I opened the third one. A half bath. I closed the door, inhaled and exhaled.

"There's got to be more to this place than meets the naked eye," I said aloud.

That's when I leaned my shoulder against the white wood wall paneling and that's when I felt it move. Turning toward the panel, I reached out with both hands and pushed it. It moved again. Not a lot, but enough to tell me that there was something unusual about the paneling. Running my fingertips along the left side of the panel, I came upon a kind of secret, invisible opener that had been designed to be flush with the wood paneling. My heart pumping in my throat, I twisted the opener counter-clockwise and felt a mechanical release. I pushed on the panel once more and the very narrow door opened onto a hidden room.

A room that sucked the breath from my lungs.

Fifty Shades of Robert David Jr.
By Ted Bolous, *Albany Times Union* Senior Food Blogger

I've known of the man and enigma that is Robert David Jr. for nearly ten years. Ever since he got into the food business and I got into the writing business. He was going to be the next Wolfgang Puck and I was going to be Truman Capote. Turns out, he's a bartender and I'm a blogger. But through the years, I'd always assumed I knew Robert Jr. as well as anyone who keeps a sort of friendship at arm's length can. But then the problem emerged with his fiancée, Sarah, which landed her in Valley View Rehabilitation and Junior's reputation on the legal chopping block. The rumor mill churns, of course, and as of late, this blog has mostly been dedicated not to food, but to someone who is living a secret life.

What do I mean by secret?

Sources are telling me that Robert Jr. isn't obsessed only with food. That he is also obsessed with something else. That something involves men and women and lots of them. All in one playroom, doing nasty things without their clothing on. Sounds as if there are fifty shades to Robert David Jr. after all.

It's funny because I always thought I knew the man, and perhaps the rumor mill is all wrong. But then, what if it's right?

Appetizing comments anyone?

Comment by Bobbie
Honestly, Ted, I've really loved reading this blog for years now, but opening the forum up to comments about Robert David Jr. and his poor, injured ex-fiancée and some rumors about their bizarre sex games is nothing short of a disgrace.

Comment by HiImBi
Eat, Pray, Love, F$#%, Kill . . .

33

THE ROOM WAS NARROW, but deep.

The walls were painted black and red and they seemed to pulse or radiate from the red and yellow lights that went on automatically as soon as I opened the door. There were a few of the same floor-to-ceiling length mirrors mounted to the three walls before me and I could see my own reflection in the far one. It made me shiver.

Set in the center of the room was a large wooden wheel-like device. It was angled in order to accommodate a live human being who would simply lean back against it before being strapped to the hard device with four, thick leather belts. Judging from the position of the belts, the victim's arms and legs would be spread out wide.

Hanging down from the walls, by means of metal hooks, were all sorts and varieties of whips and chains. There was a metal shelf set beside the open door that housed leather masks fitted over head-manikins, some small stainless steel knives, scalpels, a harness, more chains, a muzzle, and a large round cueball-like device that was probably used as a gag. I stepped into this torture/sex chamber and looked down at the floor. The floor was finished with black paint and in the center, under the wheel, was a drain. I took a closer look at the wheel and could see that it bore the many stains of human fluids including waste and blood. Looking at it from behind, I could see that it was mounted on a heavy-duty hinge device which meant that it was capable of spinning the victim at all sorts of odd angles, just to further enhance the torture experience. Or so I assumed.

When I looked up at the ceiling, my eyes filled with a rendering of a satanic symbol which consisted of a large red star with a pyramid superimposed over it. Painted in the center of the pyramid was the face of the devil. A traditional devil that was something a Renaissance artist might have devised. A red, evil, smiling face, razor-sharp fang-like incisors, horns protruding from the head, long hooked nose, long pointy chin, sharp triangular ears . . . My hands were shaking when I pulled out my smartphone and started taking pictures. I shot the torture wheel, plus close-ups of the floor, the drain and the fluid stains that surrounded it, and finally the ceiling. I took shots the whips and chains against the wall. I got enough on digital film to prove that Robert David Jr. was no altar boy when it came to his particular brand of sex and religion. If what happened in that room could be called sex. But certainly there was a kind of worship going on. There was enough visual evidence on my phone to at least give Miller and his boys the fuel they needed to secure a search warrant for the David home. Once that happened, they could bring in forensics and allow them to search the area of Sarah's accident with a fine tooth comb.

My heart solidly lodged in my throat, I closed the door on that evil room of torture and made my way back upstairs, that much closer to heaven.

34

I GRABBED THE COMPUTER from the kitchen counter and made my way to the back sliding glass door. But then it dawned on me that it wouldn't make a hell of a lot of difference at this point if I simply exited the place by means of the front door. It would also allow me to take a closer look at the front staircase. Maybe some evidence, no matter how small, still existed despite an entirely contaminated crime scene. Rather, *potential* crime scene. Evidence that might lead the police to the conclusion that something bad and something violent happened here on a frigid night in February.

Crossing back through the kitchen and the vestibule, I unlatched the deadbolt and made my way out onto the concrete landing. A landscape of shrubs and gravel flower beds hugged both sides of the wrap-around brick paver staircase. Reaching down, I pushed back the shrubs, hoping to find something that might connect me with Sarah Levy. Problem was, it was now six months after the fact and the weather, not to mention some meticulous landscaping and home maintenance, had pretty much white-washed the crime scene of anything significant.

It took me a good five minutes to make my way all the way down the steps. Call it dumb luck or serendipity, but it was while searching the vegetation on both sides of the last stair tread that I found the little red bead. Just a plain little red bead that might have been a part of a string of beads, like those that might come together to form a bracelet. Costume jewelry, Val called it. Cheap, but colorful jewelry that was usually made up of beads and other trinkets that made for a fun, carefree look. Knowing it was entirely

131

possible that Sarah's fingerprints could still be found on the bead, I pulled my cotton handkerchief from my back pocket and picked it up. I wrapped the bead in the cloth and stuffed it into my back pocket. That's when I peeled off the Latex gloves and shoved them back into my blazer pocket. Turning, I began the trek back to my 4Runner, knowing that I would be pressing my luck by hanging out at Junior's house even for one minute more.

35

I DROVE BACK IN the direction of downtown and my Sherman Street warehouse. It was going on seven o'clock, and I was hoping that Blood might be back from his little research mission to find out precisely what kind of drugs Junior was doing and where he got them from. When I made the turn from Lark onto Sherman, he was standing outside the door to my building, a wide smile plastered on his round face.

I parked along the curb, grabbed Junior's computer, and got out.

"You must have something for me, Blood," I said. "That smile doesn't come from drinking or drugging."

"Damn straight," he said. "I pretty much get high on life these days. That little ten-year stint in Green Haven will do that to a man he pay enough attention to the concept of right versus wrong. Can't say the same for your Robert David Jr. though."

I didn't bring up the fact that, at present, Blood was more or less a silent partner in several recreational drug sale operations on Sherman Street alone. But for the former inmate, it would be as close as he would ever come to being entirely legit while being his own boss. And somehow his business didn't seem any less legal than most of the trading going on down on Wall Street.

"Got some news for me?" I said, unlocking the deadbolt.

"Let you know soon as you make me some coffee."

"Deal," I said, opening the door.

A few minutes later we were standing at my kitchen counter. I was drinking a beer and Blood was sipping hot coffee with milk. He was busy reprising his early evening mission, which included a clandestine meeting with a drug dealing kingpin who resided in Albany's South end and who, for the purposes of my agenda, would go nameless. I would also have to go without the video or photos I'd been hoping for. Take it or leave it.

"Your boy Junior got himself quite the rep," Blood said, his hands wrapped around the white coffee mug as if he needed the warmth coming off it in the middle of a hotter than hell summer.

"What makes him so special from your garden variety dope hound?" I said.

"He don't like just any kind of drug," Blood said. "He is one of those special-order-type of white breads. And he got the money to pay for it too."

"So he's not doing coke?" I asked while retrieving the little white powder-filled packet that fell out of his wallet onto the floor of Manny's bar.

I handed it to Blood.

He looked down at it, nodded, and handed it back to me.

"Coke," he said. "Can tell by the way it's packaged. Maybe save this for your police buddy."

I set the coke packet onto the kitchen counter and, for now, forgot about it.

"So we know Junior's doing his share of coke anyway," I said. "But then I've known that for almost a couple of days now."

Blood nodded emphatically.

"Oh shit, yeah, he doing that junk. And some crank. And some LSD. Basic college kid stuff. But his special order is something else altogether, Keep." Taking another sip of the coffee. "You ever hear of Molly?"

Molly. I thought about it for a minute. I'd been exposed to a lot of drugs in my time. In the prison system, even a stolen canister of Ajax could be cut up and reconstituted into some kind of hallucinogenic. It could even be mainlined if you knew precisely what you were doing. On occasion, a desperate inmate might be rushed to the infirmary for OD'ing on 409 All Purpose Disinfectant. Or some generic state-issued toilet bowl cleaner. Life inside prison was lonely. It also came cheap.

But the truth is, I wasn't as up on the street trade as I probably should have been, considering my new line of work. And Molly, whatever the hell that might be other than a kind of innocent, if not pretty name, eluded the hell out of me.

"I give up," I said, drinking some beer. "What it is?"

"You know what it is already," he said. "You know what X is?"

"X or ecstasy. We had it listed as a Schedule 1 narcotic in the joint. A hallucinogenic and a stimulant. Popular with the college kids who like to party and sex it up all night. Quite a few variations of it around, including a new form of mescaline."

"Very good," Blood said. "And yet another variation called 'Molly.' A very different variation."

"How so?"

"Molly isn't a variation of ecstasy so much as an extraction. A purer form that accentuates the sex part of X."

I drank some more beer. It felt good and cold and sudsy going down my parched throat.

"The sex part," I said. "The chemical that causes heightened sexual arousal."

"Precisely," Blood agreed. "Add to that some stimulants in the form of coke or crank and you got yourself one very horny, very energetic individual."

"Someone capable of attacking another person if suddenly enraged?"

Blood drank the rest of his coffee, set the empty mug back down. I went to refill it, but he put up his hand.

"Too much caffeine makes my heart race," he said. "And I gotta be my best out there on the mean streets, you know what I mean." And then, "Does a man taking Molly and a soup of other narcotics have to be enraged to kill someone? Are you kidding, Keeper? Somebody ingesting even half of what Robert David Jr. is doing has to experience only a slight annoyance in order to enter into a full-blown rage."

I thought about Sarah and her head. I thought about how Junior called his father onto the scene instead of 911. Because, not only would he risk being nailed for having done something bad to Sarah, he would have been identified as being under the influence of alcohol and some pretty heavy-duty drugs. I also thought about the little red bead lying at the bottom of the steps in the gravel bed.

I drank the rest of my beer, went to the fridge, opened it, and popped the cap on another.

"You know what I think, Blood?" I said, taking the beer with me back to the counter. "I think what we have here is a psycho killer who just didn't get it right the first time."

"Or maybe he never intended to get anything right at all. Maybe the drugs just make him a crazy man. Maybe he's sorry for what he did to Sarah. Maybe he couldn't help himself. Or shit, maybe she really did just fall down the steps on her own, like he said."

Blood was right. From the beginning, I set my sights on Junior being guilty and never did give a whole lot of thought to the possibility that he might be innocent. But then, I wasn't hired to prove him innocent. I'd been hired to look into the possibility that he assaulted his fiancée with the intent to kill her, or at the very least, that he was liable for her injuries and the brain damage she suffered. Thus far, I hadn't uncovered anything disproving my theory that he was a silver-spoon-fed vampire-loving psycho who attacked his fiancée in a drunken and drugged up rage. But then, I hadn't uncovered anything that didn't disprove his innocence either.

There was the man who tailed me and took a shot at me, but that didn't prove anything other than his being—one, a lousy tail and, two, a real reckless jerk for taking a shot at me. A real pro assassin would not have missed, nor been stupid enough to try and air me out with a handgun that he held out the open window of a speeding car. That kind of shooting works only in Hollywood.

"You through with me, Keep?" Blood asked after a time.

I nodded and padded my pants pockets. They felt a bit light.

"You good with adding this to my tab?" I smiled.

"Guess I gotta be good with it."

"Got one more project for you if you got the time, Blood."

I cocked my head in the direction of the computer sitting on the kitchen table.

"You lift that from Junior's house?"

"Yup."

"Isn't that illegal?"

"Technically."

"You ain't scared about being arrested?"

"Cops know I broke in. They helped me break in. Sort of."

Blood shook his head. Laughed.

"Fucking white cops. And they call us darkies crazy."

"'Darkies' went out with segregated public bathrooms."

"I'm a walking encyclopedia of black history," he smiled. "And it's not even Black History Month. So what's it you want me to do with that thing?"

"Got somebody who can figure out the password so that I can access his files?"

"What you plan on finding out?"

"Not sure. Maybe some condemning emails. Maybe some pictures or videos. Who knows?"

"Could be a gold mine of information," Blood admitted.

"Yup."

"Hate it when you say 'Yup' all the time. White people says 'Yup' and 'Nope.' You gonna keep on doing that?"

"Nope."

"I got somebody who might be able to crack the password. Might take a day or so. I'll add his fee to your tab."

"That's good enough for me."

He went to the table to pick the laptop up. But he hesitated before touching it. I reached into my blazer pocket, tossed him a pair of clean Latex gloves.

"You reading my mind, Keeper," he said, smiling.

"We're more alike than you think, Blood," I said.

"Yes, we is," he said, slipping on the gloves then snatching up the computer. "We two bad apples from very different trees, we is."

"Martin Luther King Jr. would be so very proud," I said.

36

SOON AS BLOOD WAS gone I once again contacted Detective Miller and arranged to meet him at the Lark Tavern to show him the pics I'd taken at Junior's residence over a beer and possibly a burger. I also thought that now would be a good time to hand over both the coke and the tape I recorded of my conversation with Ted Bolous outside the *Albany Times Union* building. He agreed to meet up in half an hour. Since the Lark Tavern was located on Lark Street, less than a mile west of my place, I decided to hoof it.

By the time I arrived, Miller was already drinking a beer at the long wood bar. He was wearing his usual uniform of dark gray blazer, white button-down shirt with a white cotton T-shirt underneath, and a pair of dark slacks. Black lace-up shoes for footwear. Also as usual, his blond hair was cut immaculately short, his face shaved clean. Not that it required shaving in the first place.

"Took you so long," I said, bellying up to the bar.

"Cut out earlier than expected," he said. "You could have messaged me the pictures. Or emailed them."

"Call me old-fashioned," I said. "'Sides what are you complaining about? You seem to be enjoying yourself."

I pulled my smartphone from the interior blazer pocket, went to Gallery, then My Library and pulled up the series of pictures I'd taken at Junior's house.

"Get a load of these and tell me what you think," I said.

He did it.

Meanwhile, I ordered a tall-necked Budweiser from the college-aged young woman who was tending bar. She had on a black tank-top and her ample chest was covered in colorful tattoos. She wore a nose ring too. Her blonde hair was pulled back tight into a ponytail. Ahhh, youth.

Miller handed me back the phone and took a drink of his beer.

"I'll need copies of everything, naturally," he said. Then, wide-eyed, he added, "Wow, Junior's got some serious fucking issues."

"Ya think?" I agreed, reaching into my blazer pocket, producing the micro-cassette tape of my little talk with Albany's most famous food blogger. "And some well-known anger issues to go with them," I went on while I handed over the tape to him. "Just have a listen and you'll hear scoop right from Bolous's gravy-stained mouth."

He stared at the tape in his hand for a minute, then slipped it into the chest pocket on his blazer. That's when I dug into my pockets and realized I'd left Junior's coke on my kitchen counter.

"You still own a real tape recorder?" he asked. "You're so twentieth century, Keeper. I'm surprised you own a smartphone. You realize you can record with it if you want?"

"My girlfriend thinks I'm still so 1950s and I don't know how to record with my phone."

He took a sip of his drink and shook his head.

"So what kind of interesting illegal chemicals is Junior filling his veins with?"

I told him about the coke that was sitting out on my counter first, but then I told him about the good stuff. The Molly. When I was finished, I pulled out the handkerchief that contained the red bead I'd found in the gravel bed beside the lowest stair tread on the exterior staircase outside Junior's house. I unwrapped the handkerchief and exposed the bead as though it were some kind of diamond in the rough.

"Present for you," I said.

He stared at the bead.

"You thinking what I'm thinking, Keeper?"

"You've got a man with an obvious drug problem, a temper, vampire fangs, and who knows what the hell is going on inside that satanic basement sex chamber."

"More like a torture chamber."

"Prints," I said. "You need prints. Then you can grab yourself a search warrant."

He cocked his head at the red bead.

"Starting with this here bead," he said. "I can test it for prints. If only Sarah's prints are on it, we're SOL. It won't prove anything other than what we already know. That she was present at the house at some point."

"But if Junior's prints are on it too, then it at least suggests the two might have had a struggle in the driveway which might have led to her bracelet snapping off and her falling and hitting her head. Just for starters. Think you'll be able to convince a judge enough to get him to sign off?"

"It's still a stretch," he said. "But it's more possible now than ever, thanks to you. Problem is, these pics don't mean anything since you took them by illegal means. Doesn't mean I can't get a judge to look at them though."

"I took his laptop too."

He shook his head.

"Jesus, Keeper. Anything else you've done that will fuck up our chances of nailing this asshole?"

"I think it's possible we can find some very good stuff on that computer, Nick. Anyone who goes to that kind of elaborate basement setup is saving the best footage for himself. Capisce? You ever read the book *Fifty Shades of Grey*?"

"Can't say I have. But I can say this: you need to put the computer back before I can grab a warrant."

"I have somebody working on the password now. When they break the code, I can download the contents of the computer onto a zip-drive. You go ahead, grab your warrant all the same. I'll arrange it so that you can simply bring the laptop with you when you make a surprise visit to the place. It will be as though it never left his upstairs office at all. And besides, if he bitches about it, who are people going to believe? Him or Albany's finest?"

"Yeah, toss up," he said. He got up, finished his beer. "You talk to Sander's lawyer, Terry Kindler, yet?"

"Once," I said. "Not much of a conversation though."

"Now that you have some meat to mull over with him, might be a good time to grab his attention again. Maybe even show him some of these pictures. You should give him a copy of the tape too."

"You think if we put the pressure on the Davids, they might be willing to cooperate with the police? Maybe even accept a plea if it appears charges will be pending?"

"That would be the strategy," he said. "Just might get Sanders and Kindler their forty mil too."

"I'm going to talk to Sarah's ex," I said. "He should be aware of the dangers facing her should she begin to remember what happened that night. What about her security detail? I was there this morning and it wasn't all that secure."

"I'm working on it," he said. "Not the easiest thing in the world providing a very personal, and very expensive I might add, police bodyguard protection unit when technically speaking, there's no real and imminent danger. It's also the Davids we're talking about here. Our benefactors."

"But we both know better than that, don't we?"

"We do."

"The first Mrs. David," I interjected. "Joan. Sure she wasn't pushed off that stepladder?"

He exhaled as if every time I brought the subject up I was also stepping on his big toe with my boot heel.

"Can't be sure of anything," he said. Then, pulling out a ten-spot, he set it on the bar. "I got yours."

"Mighty large of you," I said. "But you're still avoiding the Joan David issue."

"Keep working this job the way you been doing, Keeper," he said, stepping away from the bar. "And in the end, I might actually buy you that burger."

"Talk about motivation," I said. "I don't think I'll be able to sleep tonight."

He snickered and left.

I stayed and drank two more beers while the tattooed bartender texted her boyfriend. For a time, I thought about getting a tattoo. Maybe a big coiled snake to match Daphne's. Then I was reminded about how my youth had fled the scene a long time ago and I decided against it.

I ordered another beer instead.

37

BY THE TIME THE sun went down I was feeling hungry enough for a good meal. Sometimes I did my best relaxing while cooking. Some people like to watch TV. I like to toss a little Miles on the record player, and slowly make a meal. Even if that meal is for only me. Maybe if I were to ask him nicely, Ted Bolous would allow me to guest blog sometime about the relaxations of cooking. Maybe when he stopped blogging about the Davids, and the lawsuit Sanders was trying to crush him with. The lawsuit I was trying to validate through my superlative detecting skills. Keeper, the modest.

With Miles delicately jazzing out to *Ninth Life*, I filled the two-and-one-half quart pot with cold tap water, added a couple teaspoons of salt, and set it on the stove, turning the gas burner flame to the high setting. Then I got the cutting board out and sliced up two fresh vine tomatoes, some onion, and a little basil. In a frying pan, I added a couple of tablespoons of extra virgin olive oil, some crushed garlic, and a half teaspoon of butter. When it began to simmer, I added the tomatoes, basil, and onions. In the cabinet above the stove, I found a can of tomato sauce, opened it, and added that to the mix. Covering it, I let it simmer while the water came to a boil. When it did, I added a pound of linguini and lowered the flame to medium high.

I was opening a bottle of Hobnob pinot noir when I saw the face staring in at me from the window above the kitchen sink. My immediate reaction was to go for my gun. But it was hanging on my bedpost in my bedroom. Slowly gripping the paring knife that was sitting out on the cutting board, I saw that the young woman who was standing on my fire escape had a coiled snake tattooed on her neck and that, judging by her eyes, which were wet, puffy, and red, she'd been crying. I asked her to come inside by pointing to the back fire door, which was located off the dining room. Setting the knife back down, I inhaled a calming breath, made my way into the living room, and opened the door for her.

"I'm so sorry to intrude like this," Daphne said in between sniffles. "But I really need to speak with you."

I looked over her shoulder to see if she'd been followed. I couldn't see anyone in the immediate vicinity, of course, that didn't mean Junior or one of David's goons didn't have their eyes peeled on us at that very moment.

"Come in," I said.

She stepped inside. I closed the door behind her and locked it.

Then I went for my gun.

"How long you been standing out there?" I said, having re-strapped my holster and the .45 it housed to my shoulder. "And did anyone follow you?"

"I'm not sure how long," she said, wiping her eyes with the backs of her hands. "I got here maybe a half hour ago. I saw that you weren't home so I waited down in the back parking lot until I saw your kitchen light come on."

She reached into her leather jacket and pulled out a pack of smokes.

"You mind?" she said.

I got up, brought her over one of mine and Fran's old ashtrays, a ceramic clam she picked up at an antique store one bright Saturday a year or so before she died. I also brought over the wine and two glasses. I poured the wine and asked her if she'd eaten.

"I work in a restaurant," she said. "I'm always eating." Then, smiling sadly. "That's why I smoke."

"If you change your mind, I hate to eat alone," I said, but she responded to my offer with silence. That's when it dawned on me that the Miles Davis album was no longer spinning.

"So why are you here?" I said, from back at the stove where I turned off the water and drained the pasta, letting it sit inside a big pasta bowl. Turning off the sauce, I came back into the dining room, pushed aside some of my papers, notepads, and newspaper clippings, and sat down with her.

"I feel as though you should know something," she said, nervously dragging on the cigarette.

"You okay?" I said, taking a sip of wine. "You look upset. Or more upset than you were when you tossed me out of Manny's."

She stared at the blue smoke rising up past her face.

"Sure, I'm fine," she lied. But then she exhaled and said, "No, I'm not fine."

"He hit you?"

She shook her head. But I knew in my gut that that was a lie too.

"After what happened this afternoon at the bar," she went on, "I had a talk with Robert. I suggested something to him. Something that made him angry."

"Such as."

"I told him he should tell you the truth."

"The truth about what happened to Sarah?"

She smoked, nodding.

"That's right," she said. "He should tell you everything that happened instead of trying to lie or to deceive everyone. Including the police."

"Why are you doing this?"

"Because eventually Sarah is going to recall what happened and when she does, it will all blow up for Robert."

She was crying again. Smoking and crying.

I said, "What happened on the night of February 18th?"

She wiped more tears and lit another cigarette off the one she had going. She was so tense, the snake on her neck pulsated.

"If I tell you," she said, "can you promise to Holy God above that Robert will never know that I told you anything? He can never know that I came here. Is that understood?"

"I understand completely," I said, drinking down my wine and pouring another.

Daphne sat in silence while she smoked half of her new cigarette. And then she began telling me her version of the truth about what happened on an early, dark and cold morning in February.

38

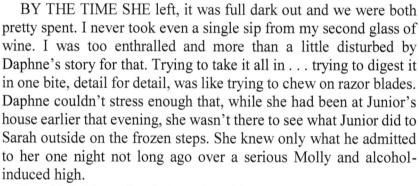

BY THE TIME SHE left, it was full dark out and we were both pretty spent. I never took even a single sip from my second glass of wine. I was too enthralled and more than a little disturbed by Daphne's story for that. Trying to take it all in . . . trying to digest it in one bite, detail for detail, was like trying to chew on razor blades. Daphne couldn't stress enough that, while she had been at Junior's house earlier that evening, she wasn't there to see what Junior did to Sarah outside on the frozen steps. She knew only what he admitted to her one night not long ago over a serious Molly and alcohol-induced high.

I couldn't blame Sarah Levy for trying to run away from Robert David Jr. on the night of February 18th. Not with what I now knew to be true about him. About what he always wanted her to do for him, about how he got his rocks off along with a handful of other deviants who'd obviously read some overly popular novel about getting it on inside a basement dungeon playroom. Daphne included. About his love of blood, pain, and all that is unholy.

The food on the stove was getting cold. But I no longer had much of an appetite for anything.

It had been a few days since I took in some exercise, and I could feel the old bones and muscles begging me for some love, blood, and oxygen. After hearing Daphne's version of the Junior/Sarah story, I felt as though I needed a new skin. Instead of eating, I went into the bedroom, changed into my running shorts, sneakers, and a navy T-shirt that had the words, New York State Department of

Corrections stenciled on the back in white block letters and a simple NYSDOC on the front over a small breast pocket. Grabbing hold of the extra warehouse key I kept on a nylon strap that wrapped around my neck, I exited the apartment by way of the front door and made my way down the short flight of steps to the sidewalk. Glancing over my right shoulder, I looked for Blood.

Blood wasn't there.

The night was still, dark, and humid so that almost as soon as I began the slow jog, I could feel the moist sweat beginning to build up on my skin. I found my pace after a couple of minutes, my breathing controlled, my heart beating steady and good. I made a right onto Lark Street and ran along the sidewalk past the many bars, eateries, and brownstones—their staircases occupied with people sitting outside on the hot night, some of them drinking booze out of bottles wrapped in brown paper bags.

I made a point of running past Manny's, gazing in at the bar as I went past, spotting Daphne and her snake-tattooed neck as she set a cold beer in front of a suited patron. Her face looked pale and her eyes bore the look of a woman who was physically present and accounted for, but whose mind was a million miles away. I looked for Junior, but either he wasn't there or I was moving too fast to notice him. Soon, I arrived at the corner of Lark and Madison where I hooked a right and ran on past The Lark Tavern. Three or four college age kids were smoking outside its big black wood door.

"Better you than me, dude!" one of them barked. "Exercise sucks."

I heard their laughter as I passed by them, knowing that one day in the not too distant future, that same kid would be a middle-aged adult, and he would have no choice but to give up the cigarettes. No choice but to exercise. Or he would be looking at an early grave. Funny how youth springs so eternal. But at the same time, life can be so fleeting.

I entered Washington Square Park less than a minute later. The park was dark with only the inverted arks of sodium lamplight to illuminate the narrow roads that wound through the mostly flat landscape of expansive tree-lined greens. I took a road that ran diagonally through the very center of the park, since it was the only road that offered a trace of an incline. It also ended at a one-hundred-year-old wood and metal pedestrian bridge that spanned the width of the park's long, man-made lake. I could run over the bridge and catch the park's perimeter road on the opposite bank, then catch the State Street exit, and from there, head back to Lark Street and finally, Sherman Street.

I was maybe half way across the diagonal road and close to the top of the incline when I began to feel the short, fine hairs on the back of my neck rise up. There was nothing specific to cause me alarm. Nothing within my line of sight or my periphery. I was alone and it was dark and quiet, and it was just a feeling I had. Something that was causing the alarm to go off inside my gut. The funny thing is, I almost had to laugh. If only it were possible to jog with my .45 still strapped to my chest. But carrying that two and a half pound load while it slapped against my left ribcage was impossible.

Maybe I was still more than a little disturbed by what Daphne told me about Junior. About what he needed from Sarah. About what he demanded of her, but what she refused to give him in the end. About what caused her head injuries, and how even Daphne can't sleep nights knowing what she knows about the man she sleeps with.

Does pure evil exist in the world?

Just take a walk through the cage in any maximum security prison and the answer will reveal itself in the form of "human beings" who are more at peace with rape, torture, and murder than they are living a life of goodness. These people have rights, and we pay for them and their wellness with our tax dollars.

Making a complete three-sixty while maintaining my pace, I scanned my entire horizon and saw nothing there. No one following me. No one visible in the white lamplight. No one lurking in the shadows. Only me, myself, and I.

As I moved on toward the lake and the bridge that would take me across it, I knew that I had been living in the city for far too long. That the constant sounds of cars, people, equipment being loaded and unloaded, garbage trucks, horns, planes overhead, and more had somehow become peaceful music for me. And when it was replaced with silence, I felt nothing but an uncomfortable vulnerability.

It happened just as I was taking the turn off the diagonal road onto a gravel walkway that I felt the impact against my upper back. The pain wasn't sharp, but the impact was immediate—as if I had been slammed with the fat end of a baseball bat. I went down on my chest and face and slid a few inches along the gravel floor because of the momentum.

I knew full well that I had been shot even if I hadn't heard an explosion.

My mortality oozed from my flesh and bones, along with my blood.

For the moment, I maintained full clarity. But I knew it wouldn't last.

The darkness and silence that surrounded me was absolute. Still, I searched with my eyes for someone to reveal him or herself. But I could see nothing. My body was paralyzed and the eyesight I retained was beginning to fade away, much like the filament inside a light bulb that is about to burn out.

I knew more about death and dying than I cared to know. That it could be a pleasant experience as opposed to a frightening one. There was no pain and there was no fear. There was only the feeling of leaving my body and rising above it as if I'd shed not my clothing, but my entire skin. In some ways, I was happy to be leaving myself behind while I rose up and stared down at my sad sack of bleeding flesh and bones.

I caught sight of a white light that was more intense than anything I'd ever encountered. But it was also somehow pleasant. I started moving toward that light and I was giddy happy to be going wherever it was that I was going, even if all I found at the end of it was nothing but a restful and eternal sleep. But then, maybe it wouldn't be eternal sleep. Maybe at the end of that tunnel, Fran would be waiting for me. My true love, Fran.

Sure, I was leaving Val behind. And I was leaving behind some unfinished business. For instance, maybe I would never know the real truth behind the mystery of Sarah Levy's battered head other than what Daphne revealed. That Robert David Jr. would strap her to that wheel and watch while she was play-raped repeatedly and while she screamed for them to stop. While she begged to be released. But her cries of distress were all a part of the game. It made them only attack her and each other all the more. She fed them with her screams and her struggles, and it was as close as anyone could come to summoning the devil in the Albany suburbs. They loved every minute of it. Everyone, that is, except for the main attraction strapped to the wood wheel: Sarah Levy.

Death was no longer a mystery for me. We all owe God a death, and I was paying my final debt in spades. I followed the light and I flew through an eternal black space, and I looked forward to seeing Fran once more.

I never once looked back at this horrid, black earth.

BOOK II

39

I WOKE UP ANGRY inside a big room filled with equipment, bright lights, and people.

An intense pain circulated throughout my upper body. It felt electrically charged. My mouth tasted of dried, caked blood. My head ached as though it had been split down the center with an ax. The pain extended to my right shoulder. I tried to talk, but my jaw felt clamped shut, as though someone had bolted it closed while I laid passed out. But my jaw wasn't clamped shut at all. A thick white plastic tube had been shoved inside it. The tube ran down my throat. It made me feel as though I were choking. Which is why I yanked it out while trying to sit up.

Bells, whistles, and alarms exploded.

A nurse who happened to be walking by stopped and took a good look at me. She was young, strawberry blonde, and blue eyed. She shouted something out that I could not understand. Her voice sounded distant and muffled. More nurses and a doctor approached. The white, ceiling-mounted lights surrounded them like an angelic hue. Someone tried to shove the tube back down my throat. I resisted. Another needle was inserted into my forearm.

Me, the angry but alive patient, fell back into a deep, painless sleep.

40

THE SECOND TIME I woke up, I was alone.

I'd been moved from ICU to my own private room. Or so it didn't take me long to notice. Someone must have pulled some strings.

Miller.

I tried to shift my head on the pillow from my right to my left, but my neck was too stiff and sore. Didn't matter. I knew without having to look that I was alone. The tube in my mouth and throat had been removed, and other than an intravenous line needled to my forearm, I wasn't attached to any equipment. The once intense pain in my upper body had downgraded to a dull, throbbing pain in my right shoulder. I shifted my body and managed to sit up, but only slightly. It dawned on me that maybe I'd died and this is what heaven looked like. No offense to God and His support staff, but if this was paradise then I was about to lodge a complaint. I wondered where the angels were. Where Jesus was hiding. Not a single pearly gate was to be found.

The door opened then, and a man came in.

I looked up at the tall, thin, suit-jacketed man.

"You don't look like Jesus to me," I said, my voice cracking and throat scratchy, as though the skin were peeling back away from it with every word. Detective Nick Miller pulled a chair up and sat down beside me.

"This isn't the first time you've caught a bullet," he said. "Docs tell me you died a clinical death for about a minute. What was it like?"

"God puts on a pretty good light show," I whispered. Then I

asked him for some water. He handed me a little plastic cup that was sitting on the stand beside the bed. It had a straw sticking up out of it. With his help, I was able to suck some water through the straw. It burned the back of my throat. But the water was welcome all the same.

He crossed his long legs.

"You're a lucky man," he said. "Docs tell me the round more or less skidded off the top of the trapezius on your right shoulder. You won't ever see a nickel's worth of skin and flesh again but you didn't lose a whole lot of blood. Shock of the bullet striking you was enough to cause an erratic heartbeat and to stop your heart altogether for a half minute or so when they finally got you on the table in emergency surgery."

"You mean I had a heart attack . . . Exactly how long have I been out?"

"Thirty-six hours," he said. "And cardiac arrest was how it was explained to me. Your heart is otherwise healthy."

"You're not a doctor, but you play one on TV." I looked around. "Where's Val?"

"Sent her home. Before she had an honest to goodness heart attack. She's been tending to you for days with no sleep."

It felt nice being loved.

I shoved myself up a little more against the pillows.

"Who did this to me?"

"We're working on it."

"Ballistics," I said. "I'm guessing a .38."

"Very good. If the shooter were any good, I'd be making plans to attend your funeral."

"Warms the heart. Whose .38 in your opinion exactly?"

"If you had to make a very good guess, who would you choose?"

"The man who tailed me after I interviewed Penny David. The man I let go after he nearly drove off the bridge. The man who carried a .38 which I tossed over the bridge."

"The man who works for the Davids."

"You got him in custody?"

"Not yet."

"Goodie."

"Goodie?"

"'Cause when I get out of this bed, I'm going to kill him."

153

"Perhaps when said man finds out you're not dead yet, he will try for a third time."

"And when he does, you and the entire APD will be waiting for him, right?" If it were possible for me to smile sardonically, I would have. But the fact of the matter is that I couldn't manage to work up a smile at all. Miller, on the other hand, had no trouble smiling. Sardonically.

"I guess you and Sarah Levy have similar problems," Miller said. "The Davids want you silenced."

My throat was moistening so that I could speak almost normally. "Is Sarah safe?" I asked.

"She's safe. And still recovering rapidly. She's been talking, Keeper. She's been coming out with things. Memories from that night."

I shifted myself up a little more. There was some pain, but not a lot. More like discomfort, probably from the few staples that kept the wound on my shoulder closed. So I assumed.

"What has she revealed?"

"She keeps referring to Junior as the devil. Someone she believed was a saint at first. Until he revealed himself in his true form."

I told Miller about my meeting with Daphne, not an hour before I was shot. Told him about what she told me. About the things Junior wanted Sarah to do for him. For the others. How their perverted actions and the sex room they performed them in looked to be entirely inspired by some *shady* book of erotica. When I was through, his face looked as pale as mine must have looked.

"There's something else too," Miller said. "Sarah's been talking about her ex-husband, Michael. It's the first time she's mentioned him in all these months."

"What's she been saying?"

"Something that is sure to piss Junior off even more."

"My ears still work."

Miller exhaled.

"She told her doctors that she still loves him," he said. "That she wants to go back to him."

41

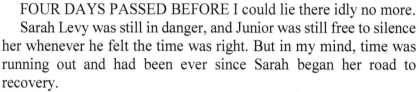

FOUR DAYS PASSED BEFORE I could lie there idly no more. Sarah Levy was still in danger, and Junior was still free to silence her whenever he felt the time was right. But in my mind, time was running out and had been ever since Sarah began her road to recovery.

I slid out of bed and started making preparations to leave the hospital. The doctor, however, insisted that I remain in bed for yet another full week. But time to heal was not a luxury I enjoyed. Not only was Sarah Levy in danger, but I was also a sitting duck. It wasn't a matter of if the goon who shot me would return soon. It was just a matter of precisely where and when he'd strike for a third time.

Val had been with me every night of my hospital stay, on occasion nodding off in the chair and having to crawl home after midnight. When I called her and told her my plans for leaving, she hemmed and hawed about me leaving too early. But knowing me as well as she did, she didn't push the point for too long. She knew how stubborn I could be. At the very least, she wanted to pick me up and take me home, where she would no doubt dote over me like a mother with a sick child. But not only did I not want her underfoot, I couldn't risk placing her life in danger. Someone tried to kill me, after all. Twice. It's possible they would try again for a third time, and this time they might get it right. Better that Val didn't stand between me and the Almighty if or when it happened.

Instead of Val, I called Blood and asked him to use his spare key to enter into my apartment, grab the 4Runner keys and to use it to pick me up ASAP. He told me he'd drop everything to come and get me. I signed off on my discharge, praying that my New York State Law Enforcement Union 82 medical plan would pick up the bill.

Dressed in my now dry but bloodied running clothes, I refused a wheelchair, and took the elevator down to the front entrance of the hospital and waited for the Sentinel of Sherman Street. Turns out, he was already waiting for me. I got in on the passenger side, wincing as I closed the door with my good, left hand.

"You've gone from white-bread to chalk," Blood said, not without a smile.

"Thanks," I said. "Drive. Please."

"Yes, Warden Marconi," he said, and he pulled out of the lot and onto the road that would lead back into the heart of my city.

The way I saw it, I had two overriding problems to contend with.

First and most importantly: Sarah Levy was in danger. If the Davids were after me and willing to execute me out in the open in cold blood, then she no doubt occupied a prominent spot on the to-be-exterminated list. Why hadn't they already gotten her assassination over with by now? Especially with me laid up in a hospital bed for a full week? Two reasons. First, she was more or less protected behind the brick walls and iron bars of that recuperative hospital in Schenectady. And second, her sudden murder would open up an entirely new can of worms for Robert David Jr. and his father. On the other hand, my sudden death would be considered a hazard of the job. Maybe the work of a former inmate or someone I helped put in prison over the years I'd been a private detective.

Another problem: I was coming very close to having all the fuel I'd need not only for Harold Sanders to win his coveted forty million dollar civil suit against the David empire, but more importantly, I'd have the evidence, both circumstantial and real, that would at least give the APD reason to speed up their investigation into Robert David Jr. and what would now be considered the attempted second-degree murder of his fiancée. It might even be enough to place him under arrest. But that might be wishful thinking.

In the end, time was getting short for both me and Junior. That meant Junior was becoming more desperate to keep his name clean and to keep on living the life of privilege that David Sr. had afforded him for so many years. A desperate Junior meant that I had to keep on watching my back. Maybe now more than ever, considering I'd been shot and survived it with only an exaggerated flesh wound and a temporarily broken heart.

What to do next: first things first.
"You get the password for the laptop, Blood?" I asked.
He nodded in the affirmative, his eyes on the road.
"Your man see anything of interest on Junior's hard-drive?"
"You didn't ask us to look at the hard drive. You ask us for the code. We do only what we're told to do. No more. No less."
"I appreciate that."
"We're serious about our work, Keep. You don't stay in business long you start getting nosy in places you don't belong."
"Soon as we get to my place, we can copy the entire hard-drive and then we'll hand the computer over to Detective Miller."
He looked at me quizzically, then returned his eyes to the city street as we came to a stoplight just before Lark Street.
"That laptop is hot," he said. "You sure Miller wants it?"
"We got it all worked out. What I've been doing is trying to work up enough evidence against Junior so that Miller can convince a judge to grant him the search warrant."
"Sometimes you got to resort to some illegal means in order to get at the truth," Blood said.
"Precisely what I learned as a maximum security prison supervisor," I said.

By the time we pulled up outside of Sherman Street, my shoulder was throbbing in waves of pain. It was also bleeding. Maybe Blood couldn't see the wound, but he could see my face. And I could tell he didn't like what he saw.
"Let's get you inside and fixed up," he said.
I grunted a half-hearted, "Okay."
Then I opened my door, and nearly spilled out into the street. A sad, bleeding sack of rags and brittle bones.

42

BUT THERE WAS LITTLE time to worry about my shoulder. As soon as we got through the door, we headed for the bathroom where Blood did his best to clean the wound and change the bandages. A process he was all too familiar with after having grown up and survived in Albany's south end—where Hope Street ended and Desperation Avenue began. We then convened in the kitchen where Junior's computer was sitting on the counter, a plain, white, business-sized envelope resting on top of it.

I picked up the envelope and opened it. Unfolding the standard white copy stock, I found a typed password consisted of five upper case letters: DAVID. I had to laugh. If only I'd thought about using the most obvious of passwords when I was still inside Junior's house I might have examined the computer without having to steal it. Oh well.

I set the paper down, opened the computer and pressed the power button. While it was booting up, I headed into my dining room office, found a spare zip-drive in my desk drawer and brought it with me back to the kitchen where I plugged it into the port. The machine now fully booted, I typed "DAVID" into the designated space for the user password, then went into the laptop's mainframe and typed in the commands that would allow for a total system back-up on to the zip drive.

I pressed Enter and the back-up process began.

Exiting the kitchen for the bedroom, I put on a fresh pair of Levis, my dark brown Tony Lama cowboy boots, and a clean navy blue button-down. I carried my blue blazer and my .45 back into the kitchen with me.

"Need your help again," I said to Blood, handing him the shoulder-holstered piece.

He gently strapped the holster over my wounded shoulder.

"You should have that arm in a sling," he said. "Or you can take care of yourself properly and quit this job while you're still alive. Admit yourself back into the hospital."

I looked at him. His hard face. His deep brown eyes. Today he was wearing a wide-brimmed New York Yankees baseball cap. The cap barely rested on his head and was angled just slightly against his right temple as if defying gravity.

"It's too late for that," I said. "I know too much."

"And Junior knows you know too much."

I looked at the computer. A little white box that appeared on the screen told me the file backup was complete. I pulled out the zip drive and stuffed it into my blazer pocket, then closed the lid on the computer and stuffed it under my good arm.

"You busy?" I asked Blood.

"Workin' for you, buildin' up your tab," he said. "I can see it be tough to drive with that boo-boo in your shoulder."

"One painful boo-boo," I said.

"White peoples are whiners," he smiled, raising his pant leg high, pointing to two nickel-size pieces of scar tissue on his lower thigh. "Uzi done that many years ago in a drive-by. My bro took the bullets out at home with a jackknife. I passed out from the pain. But when I woke up, I strapped on a hand cannon and gave the shooter some real hell."

What Blood meant by "hell," was that he had retaliated by shooting the shooter back. Probably mortally wounding him. That's the way the street worked in Albany. How all personal scores involving guns and knives were settled. Blood was probably only a teenager when it all went down.

"I quit now," I said. "I won't ever put Junior away."

"And that poor girl in Valley View might die."

I tossed him the keys to the 4Runner, and together we left, knowing we had our work cut out for us.

43

BLOOD PULLED UP TO the South Pearl Street precinct of the APD. He double parked in a no loading zone in front of a police station. I told him to wait for me right where he was. He smiled and nodded. I got out and went inside. The desk sergeant told me that Detective Miller was in but that I had to wait inside the waiting room for him. He came through the door to greet me less than a minute later.

"You just got hit," he said. "You should be in the hospital. That wound infects, you'll lose your entire arm at the shoulder."

"Most flesh wounds are worse. How is Sarah?"

"The same. No attempts on her life yet. ."

Struck by his use of the word 'yet,' I handed him Junior's computer.

"Grab a search warrant of Robert David Jr.'s home," I said. "And put this back where I found it in his upstairs office."

"You get a copy of the hard drive?"

"In my pocket."

"You gonna share it with me?"

"Soon as I look at it."

"How should I be so sure obtaining a warrant is the right move right now?"

"Trust me," I said. "Those pictures I sent your way should have been enough to convince a judge. How much longer you gotta wait, Nick? Until someone really gets killed?"

He ran his thick right hand through his closely cropped white hair. I knew he felt almost powerless going up against mega-wealthy citizens like the Davids. He had no choice but to toe the line laid out for him by the very men and women who pulled the strings in Albany. Maybe I was mixing my metaphors here, but the point remained the same. Miller could do only so much.

"Hope you know what you're doing," he said.

"Lots of people tell me that," I said.

"Where you going now?"

"Got a date with a certain employee of David Enterprises."

"Take care of that shoulder."

"Just get that warrant," I said.

But what I really wanted to say was this: "Stop stalling and go get that warrant."

I decided instead to bite my tongue. Better not to piss off the APD more than I had to.

44

BACK OUT IN THE 4Runner, I asked Blood if he was packing. He leaned forward from behind the steering wheel, brought his right hand around his back, and pulled out a Glock.

"Nice piece," I said.

"Glock 9," he said. "Preferred choice of weaponry amongst the rapper elite."

"Get ready to use it," I said.

"Where we heading?"

"First we hit the drive-thru at the Rite Aid pharmacy for some Advil. Then we park outside David Enterprises. Wait to see if a certain goon with a fat face and a silly mustache appears."

"Then what?"

"Albany street justice time."

"You plan on whacking him?"

"No," I said. "Worse than that."

"Me likey again," he said. Then he pulled the 4Runner away from the station.

45

MAYBE'S MOVING AND STORAGE facility was located directly across the street from David Enterprises. It was a big operation with dozens of big trucks moving in and out of the parking lot. There were also all varieties of vehicles parked in the big flat lot which provided very good cover for the 4Runner, even with its fire-engine red paint job making it stick out like a Christmas tree bulb.

Blood and I waited in silence for maybe thirty minutes until the goon appeared just as I knew he would. He walked right out the front door with all the arrogance or stupidity of an untouchable. Dressed in a dark suit, his barrel chest and gut filled the shirt and jacket out to the point of exploding. He looked one way and then the other and started making his way on foot in the direction of the downtown.

"Big fat target's been spotted," I said.

"Affirmative on that, Keep," Blood said.

Blood pulled out of the lot and slowly followed the goon. When we caught up with him, he turned to us, wide-eyed. I stuck my head out the window.

"Remember me?" I said.

Startled, he stopped in his tracks and stole a look at me over his left shoulder through dark aviator sunglasses. He started to run. But Blood pulled ahead, ran the 4Runner up on the sidewalk and blocked his path. He about-faced and tried to make a beeline back the way he came. That's when Blood got out, and with his Glock in hand, chased him down. It wasn't much of a chase for an athlete like Blood. More like a cheetah chasing down an overweight cow. Blood pressed the barrel of the pistol against the goon's spine while gripping his jacket collar with the other. In that manner, Blood dragged the man who shot me back to the 4Runner.

"Get in," I said.

Blood patted him down, found his revolver, and handed it to me. Then he shoved the goon into the backseat.

"Sit still," he said. "And put your seatbelt on."

"Fuck you, coon," said the goon, his upper lip twitching under his half-moon mustache, his face red and puffy.

Blood punched him square on the jaw, causing his bulbous head to snap back. When he raised it up again, his eyes grew glassy and his jaw hung open.

"Speak nicely or don't speak at all," Blood said. "And no one uses 'coon' anymore, honky."

The goon fumbled for the seat belt and snapped it on.

"Safety first," I said.

"Couldn't agree more," said Blood getting back behind the wheel.

"Take us to the train bridge," I said. "The goon and I have a few things to discuss. Don't we, goon?"

But I'm not sure he heard me with the bells still ringing in his honky head.

46

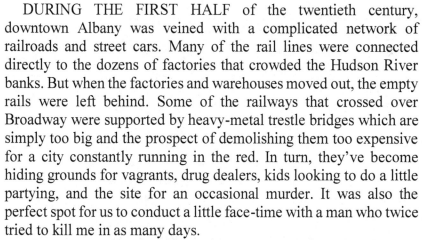

DURING THE FIRST HALF of the twentieth century, downtown Albany was veined with a complicated network of railroads and street cars. Many of the rail lines were connected directly to the dozens of factories that crowded the Hudson River banks. But when the factories and warehouses moved out, the empty rails were left behind. Some of the railways that crossed over Broadway were supported by heavy-metal trestle bridges which are simply too big and the prospect of demolishing them too expensive for a city constantly running in the red. In turn, they've become hiding grounds for vagrants, drug dealers, kids looking to do a little partying, and the site for an occasional murder. It was also the perfect spot for us to conduct a little face-time with a man who twice tried to kill me in as many days.

We drove around the bridge's stone piers and up onto road that led up to the abandoned railroad bridge itself. Behind us was a massive, empty, concrete warehouse that once upon a time was used for cold storage. Beyond that was the highway and the Hudson River that paralleled it. Directly before us stood the steel trestle bridge which no longer supported trains, but instead a couple of burnt out cars, two or three plywood shanties, three or four fifty gallon drums that were used as fireplaces, bags of trash, and scattered liquor and wine bottles. Looking down at my feet, I could also make out some used needles and even a spent shell casing. This was no place to be caught alone and unawares after dark.

Blood killed the engine and got out. He opened the back door and once again pulled the still groggy goon out by his collar, letting him drop hard into the brown gravel road. The goon squirmed and clawed at the gravel while down on his stomach. He looked like a fat fish that had fallen out of the fishbowl. I almost felt insulted that this was the man responsible for carrying out my assassination. You would think a couple of high rollers like the Davids would invest in a much more expensive and sophisticated goon whom they could reliably entrust with the delicate task of prematurely ending my life.

Grabbing the tape recorder from the glove compartment, I popped in a fresh mini-cassette. Then I got out, painfully, and approached him. He turned over onto his back like a wounded cockroach and looked up at me, squinting his black eyes in the late afternoon sun.

"What do you want from me?" he begged.

I thumbed Record on the recorder, not bothering to conceal it.

"You the one who shot me in the park?"

"I don't know what you're talking about," he said, his words heavy and a slightly slurred.

"Yes, you do. You took a shot at me a few days ago and I let you go. You remember that one don't you?"

He nodded, slowly, as though he still couldn't believe I actually let him go when I should have just killed him. Maybe I was all about second chances. Or maybe I was just plain stupid.

"Yeah, sure," he said. "We both know that was me. But I missed." He started giggling. "And you fucking let me go."

He sat up.

Keeping the Record button depressed, I slipped the recorder into the chest pocket on my blazer, knowing it would still easily pick up our conversation. Then I pulled out my .45 with my good, left hand and aimed it at his head.

"So, did the Davids order you to take a second shot at me?"

"What didn't you understand about the first time I told you to fuck off?" he said, trying to get up. "And you already know who I work for."

I thumbed the hammer back. If I shot him in the head at this distance, I'd have to wipe his brains from my boots.

"I just want you to say it," I demanded. "For the record."

"You're not gonna shoot me," he said. "You're one of the good guys and you don't have the balls, Marconi. If you did you would have shot me on that bridge, you dumb fucking whop."

I planted a bead on his left foot and squeezed the trigger. I blew his big toe clean off. He screamed while arterial blood sprayed and spattered. I would have to wipe some of it from my boots, after all.

"Once again, insect," I said. "Did you or did you not shoot me?"

He nodded emphatically while sobbing real tears.

"Okay, yes. Yes. Fucking yes."

"And did the Davids order it?"

"Yes." His tears were getting trapped in his mustache while drool hung down in thick strands off his bottom lip. Then he cried, "You blew my foot in half."

"You blew away half my trap. Now we're even. Answer me again."

"Yes. Mr. David ordered it. I do jobs for him. He paid me personally. In cash."

"Which Mr. David?"

"What the fuck do you mean which Mr. David?" He was screaming now.

"Junior or Senior?"

"There's only one *Mister* David," he said. "And that's the old man."

"Okay," I said. "Does he want you to kill Sarah Levy?"

He looked up at me, and his tears suddenly stopped.

"I don't know nothing about that."

I cocked the hammer back again. He raised up his right hand in surrender.

"Ok," he screamed. "Don't. Please." Then. "There's some talk about taking her out. But she ain't easy to get to. If you know what I mean. Not in that hospital."

"You willing to talk to the cops about it?"

"Are you fucking crazy?"

"Look it . . . What's your real name, insect?"

"Rick," he said. "Rick Rickio."

"Sounds like he in a boy band," Blood chimed in.

"Rick Rickio," I said. "You're bleeding all over this desolate place and all over my boots. My shoulder is bleeding all over the inside of my jacket, thanks to you. And I'm dizzy from pain killers. The way I see it, you got two choices: we can leave you here where you will die before the night is out, not to mention robbed and raped by whatever lives up here during the night. Or, we can take you to the hospital where your foot will be patched up and where you will speak to the police about what you know."

"Not much of a choice," he said.

"Only choice you got," Blood said. "You wanna live."

"Blood," I said, "let's help the wounded Rick Rickio back into the 4Runner."

"Okay," Blood said. "So long as he don't bleed on me."

47

I CALLED MILLER FROM the car while Blood drove us back to the Albany Medical Center.

"They're going to try and hit Sarah," I said. "I have the proof. Got it on tape right from the insect's mouth."

"And ta-da," he sang. "We have our warrant, thanks to you. We're on our way to Marion Avenue now."

I told him all about Rick Rickio. About what happened up on the bridge. While I eyed Rickio laid out in the backseat of the 4Runner, I told Miller that Rickio had been shot in self-defense. That my shooting him had nothing to do with revenge for his having shot my shoulder. My shooting him could not be avoided. While I told him this, I kept my fingers crossed.

Now we were heading to the Albany Medical Center where the goon would receive some much needed emergency medical treatment and that, in exchange for being treated fairly, Rickio would be willing to tell Miller everything he knew about the Davids and what happened on the night of February 18th. He would also confess to having tried to kill me a couple of times and to a possible plot engineered by the Davids to kill Sarah in order to silence her for good.

"Isn't that right, Rick the insect?" I said.

The goon nodded while grinding his teeth in pain.

"What's your next move?" Miller said.

"I'm heading back to Valley View," I said. "Sarah shouldn't be alone for one more second. I think we need to find her some better rehabilitative accommodations away from the Davids' reach, don't

169

you?"

"Some place off the map," he agreed. "Some place top secret. Until this shit storm you're brewing up with your investigation blows over."

"You're reading my mind, Detective."

It was then something struck me. An ice cold sensation that raced up and down my backbone. Like when you were a kid in high school and just handed a math exam for which you knew not a single answer. It was something about Miller's tone. About his present easy-goingness and his willingness to be so damn nice to me. It didn't sit too well with me.

"You go do what you have to do," the cop added in the same uncharacteristic namby pamby tone. "I'll let you know what we dig up at Junior's house."

I hung up, still feeling the cold in my back.

A few minutes later, I made out the brightly illuminated entry sign to the Albany Medical Center. I could also make out the flashing lights of the two cop cruisers Miller had already sent over to greet us.

48

WITH THE GOON IN the hospital under police custody, Blood turned the 4Runner around and drove us through the park toward Route 90, westbound, which would take us to Schenectady and Valley View Rehabilitation Center. In the meantime, I did something I should have done a long time ago. I pulled out my cell and dialed 411 caller information. When the operator came on the line, I asked for Michael Levy, crossing my fingers that the local novelist wasn't so famous that he avoided being listed.

Turns out luck was on our side. He was listed. The computerized operator gave me his number and even dialed it for me. While I waited for him to pick up, Blood turned onto the highway and gunned it. After a series of five or six rings, I knew that Michael Levy wasn't picking up. Maybe he was out and about. Or maybe he was writing. The answering machine came on and I left him a detailed message telling him who I was and why I was calling and that he needed to call me back right away. I gave him my cell number and hung up.

While we drove, I punched his name into the Google search engine on my smartphone. The first item listed was the author's official website. I clicked on it. A face appeared. It was the pleasant if not ruggedly handsome face of a middle-aged man who sported a closely cropped salt and pepper beard. His hair was graying and cut very close to the scalp like lots of men keep it when the hairline begins to recede at a pace faster than the growth can keep up with it. Below the face was a picture of a bestselling novel called *The Condemned*. There were a couple of blurbs posted beside the novel. One from a bestselling author who called Levy's prose "Hypnotic," and another from the *New York Post* which called the opus, "Brilliant . . . Sensational . . . Masterful."

I wondered what it must have felt like for an author to have something as big and important as the *New York Post* call his work "Brilliant . . . Sensational . . . Masterful." On the other hand, I wondered where an author went from there. Maybe everything he wrote from that point forward would have to be considered brilliant or it would be a disappointment in the eyes of the reading public.

I was still wondering that very conundrum when my phone began to ring.

Judging by the digital readout, it was Michael Levy. I thumbed the green Answer button and put the phone to my ear.

"Marconi," I said.

"Mr. Marconi," he barked, the tension in his voice already apparent. "What the hell is going on?"

I told him.

"You truly believe Sarah's life is in danger?" he posed, after taking almost a full minute to digest everything I said.

"I wouldn't be bothering your writing schedule if I didn't."

"What would you like for me to do?"

"I'm not asking you to do anything. I'm only informing you of what's happening and the dangers posed by Sarah's fiancé, Robert David Jr."

"Former fiancé," Levy said, acid in his tone. But there was something else in his voice also. Something I might have recognized in myself in the months following Fran's sudden death. Something that can arise only from heartbreak. That's when it kind of clicked inside my head. I was reminded of what Miller told me about Sarah admitting to her love for her husband.

"Michael," I said, "do you still have feelings for Sarah?"

I couldn't exactly hear it, but I felt him swallowing something bitter inside a very dry mouth.

"Yes," he said. "I still love her. Love her very much."

"I understand."

"No, you don't. There's something else you should know."

"What is it?" I said, as Blood pulled off the exit, paid the fifty cent toll, and drove on toward Schenectady's State Street.

"Sarah and I had been speaking a lot before her accident. If you want to call it that."

"How much is a lot, Michael? I need the truth here."

More dry swallowing.

"I'll level with you, if you promise to keep things confidential."

"You can trust me," I said. But he needn't tell me the rest since I already knew exactly what he was going to say. Miller has already confirmed what Sarah had been telling her doctors as of late. That she and Michael Levy still loved one another. But maybe I needed to hear it from him anyway in order to believe it.

"We were sleeping together again," he said.

The brick, five-story hospital loomed large in the distance. I expected an admission of love, but not sex.

"And allow me to guess," I said. "Junior somehow got wind of your rekindled love." It was a question.

"Yes," he confirmed. "He was very angry. That night . . . the bad night. February 18th. That was supposed to be the night she was going to tell him and break off the engagement."

"Looks like she told him all right," I said. "Maybe she told him a bunch of things he didn't like."

"Yes, I suppose she did."

"Why didn't you tell all this to the police?"

"I thought it would make Sarah look terrible—like some cheap harlot who couldn't be trusted. A fiancée of one of the area's most powerful and richest men, and she's cheating on him with her ex-husband of all people."

"You should have told the police anyway. They would have understood."

"I realize that, Mr. Marconi. Or, I should say, by the time I realized that, it was already too late. Sarah didn't even remember who I was anymore or that we were in love or even that we had once been married or have a son together. Instead, all she was capable of in her brain-damaged state was professing her love for Junior. It was all quite heartbreaking and strange and more than a little disturbing."

We pulled into the lot and took our parking ticket from the man in the booth.

"I'm at the hospital now, Michael," I said. "I'm going to make a check on her and call you back."

"Don't bother," he said. "I'm on my way. I live only a few minutes away."

"See you here," I said.

49

BLOOD AND I DIDN'T bother with the information booth inside the main vestibule since it was curiously empty. Nor did we wait for an available elevator. Instead, we took the stairs inside the concrete stairwell, bounding them two at a time until we reached the fifth floor. We burst through the solid metal door, with me out in front and Blood close behind. Our surprise entry onto the circular nurse's station caused the three or four people who were occupying it to look up at us in complete surprise.

One of the nurses present was the short, overweight brunette who had taken a disliking to me on my previous visit. I approached her anyway.

"Where's Sarah?" I demanded.

"You are not authorized to be up here," she said, picking up the phone. "I'm calling security."

Blood reached down, pulled the phone out of her hand, and gently hung it back up.

"My partner has asked you a simple question about Sarah Levy and we both feel it deserves an answer."

While her work-mates looked on strangely silent and still, I watched her lips grow tight.

"Mr. Marconi," she said. "Sarah is not available."

I looked into her glassy, squinted eyes.

"You mean like she's presently in therapy," I said.

She shook her head.

"No. She's not in therapy."

"Then where is she?"

"She's gone," she said. "That's all I know."

50

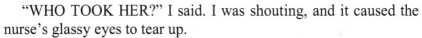

"WHO TOOK HER?" I said. I was shouting, and it caused the nurse's glassy eyes to tear up.

"A man came and checked her out. He followed all the proper procedures."

"What man?" I said. "What was his name?"

She turned to the others with an almost panicked look on her face.

"I don't have to tell you anything," she said, turning back to me. "You should know that we've been warned. And if you do anything to harm us, it will only make things worse."

I found myself shaking my head without thinking about it. I felt that same icy coldness run up and down my spine again. It made my injured shoulder throb all the more. I also felt the concrete floor beneath my boots slowly turning to mud.

"What are you talking about?" I said.

"They're coming," she said.

I heard the elevator doors open then. I heard the sounds of heavy footsteps. Turning, I made out two uniformed security guards coming at Blood and me.

"Don't move!" they shouted.

The security guards weren't alone. They were accompanied by three other men. I recognized Detective Nick Miller easily enough and the two men behind him by the blue uniforms they were wearing. APD uniforms.

"This ain't good," Blood said.

"Nick," I said, "you were going to Junior's house with a search warrant."

"Stay where you are, Keeper," he said, voice terse, strained. His smooth face was pale.

The blue uniforms had their side-arms drawn.

"You three, move out of the way!" Miller shouted at the medical staff standing in the nurse's station. They moved back away from Blood and me. Then he said, "Jack 'Keeper' Marconi, get down on your knees, your hands above your head."

I just stood there.

"Do it!" he shouted, pulling his weapon from his holster.

Crouching, I dropped down to my knees. But because of my bad shoulder, there was no way I was going to raise my hands above my head or at all for that matter.

"You too, Blood!" he said.

Blood did as he was told.

I was immediately disarmed by one of the cops while another cuffed my good arm to my bad arm.

"Nick," I said, feeling the pain of the cuffs cutting into my skin and the strain in my injured shoulder. "Tell. Me. What's. Happening."

"You are under arrest," he said.

"For what impossible reason?"

"For the murder of Daphne Williams."

51

BLOOD AND I WERE carted out to three awaiting blue and whites. A crowd gathered to watch the festivities, including a couple of local reporters who must have been tipped off to the event over their smartphone police scanner apps. Out the corner of my eye, I caught sight of a stocky, eyeglasses wearing middle-aged man who was dressed in jeans, boots, and a T-shirt that was tight around his chest and biceps. He stared at me hard but said not a word as I was escorted past him. So close to him, that I could almost smell his breath.

I harbored little doubt in my mind that the man was none other than Michael Levy, Sarah's ex-husband, and I also had little doubt that he was now as confused as me. Which would explain why I cocked my head over my wounded shoulder and barked, "She's gone, Michael! Somebody took her!"

I would have said more, but the cop behind me told me to "Shut up!" as he opened the backseat door to the cruiser, pushed the back of my head down, and shoved me inside.

Keeper, the defeated.

52

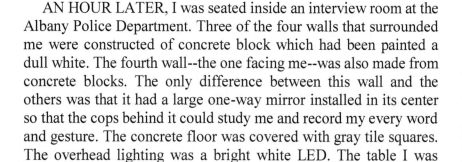

AN HOUR LATER, I was seated inside an interview room at the Albany Police Department. Three of the four walls that surrounded me were constructed of concrete block which had been painted a dull white. The fourth wall--the one facing me--was also made from concrete blocks. The only difference between this wall and the others was that it had a large one-way mirror installed in its center so that the cops behind it could study me and record my every word and gesture. The concrete floor was covered with gray tile squares. The overhead lighting was a bright white LED. The table I was seated at was made entirely of metal. It had a thick metal ring bolted to its underside to which the chains from my shackles were secured and to which the exposed nerves that throbbed in my right shoulder seemed attached.

My watch had been stripped from me, along with most of my clothing, so I had no real idea of what time it was. I could only guess that it must have been around seven in the evening. I was dressed only in my boxer shorts, an orange jumper, and slippers for shoes. I'd been through this song and dance before and I knew full well that Miller was leaving me alone with my thoughts for a while.

My thoughts *and* my pain.

It was a confusion and anxiety-inducing tactic that I knew all too well. I was a former prison warden, after all.

Truth is, I wasn't concerned for myself or for Blood. We hadn't done anything wrong. I was more concerned first for Sarah. Someone had taken her away and it was very possible that someone had been Junior and/or his father or one of the goons working for them. I was also concerned for Daphne, but since she was already dead, my concern amounted to what exactly had happened to her and why Miller was so convinced I'd played a part in it.

When the solid wood door opened, I knew I was about to find out.

Miller entered the room, a manila folder gripped in his right hand. He sat down across from me.

"Allow me to break the fucking ice," I said. "Fastest collar on record for you. Maybe get you promoted to Captain."

He exhaled, ran his left hand over his closely cropped gray and white hair, then loosened the knot on his tie and unbuttoned the top button.

"We knew you'd run," he said, sitting back. "*I* knew you'd run."

"I've been through this shit before. And you're right. I would have run. Fast."

"Exactly," he said. "I wasn't taking any chances."

"And now Junior's snagged Sarah right out from under our noses."

"You don't know that for sure."

"You're kidding, right?"

I glanced at the black glass. I knew that behind it someone was studying me. Studying my words.

Turning back to the dick, I said, "Instead of searching Junior's house, you arrest me. No lawyer, no representation. No due fucking progress. Not even an Advil for my shoulder. Maybe when you get your jarhead out of your ass, you can tell me what's going on and why you're making me out to be a patsy."

"I read you your Miranda's," he said, opening up the folder, pulling out an eight-by-ten color glossy, spinning it around so that I could see it right side up. For a brief second, the picture sucked the air from my lungs. It was Daphne. From what I could gather in the close-up shot, she lay in a bed, her head nearly decapitated from her naked torso.

I looked up at Miller, my empty stomach feeling more than a little queasy.

"Look me in the eye," I said, my mouth going dry, heart racing, "and tell me you think I'm capable of something like this?"

He glanced down at the photograph, picked it up with the tips of

179

his fingers, and returned it to the folder.

"No," he exhaled. "I don't believe you are. But that doesn't mean you didn't do it."

"I was set up."

"She was discovered inside your Sherman Street crib in your bed. Her fucking prints were all over the place. Yours and hers. No one else's."

"It was a setup. I enjoy the use of only one arm right now. I'm not physically capable of that knife work, and you know it. How'd you find her?"

"Anonymous tip."

"From who? Junior?"

"I just told you, it was anonymous."

"The same anonymous who stole Sarah from Valley View?"

He shot me a hard look. I was getting to him.

"Daphne came to see me the same evening I was shot. She had things to tell me about Junior. Bad things, Nick. Things he made Sarah do with other people. Things he got off on. His fifty shades of play-rape."

More staring. Staring without blinking.

"Come on, Nick, I have an alibi," I went on. "Blood will back me up."

"A noted drug dealer," he whispered.

"Former drug dealer."

"That's your opinion."

"Did you or did you not raid Junior's house?"

He nodded.

"Did you put the computer back that *we both* stole?" I said it loud while looking directly at the one-way glass so there would be no mistaking what I said.

Miller issued me a one thousand mile stare. Then, raising both his hands up, he crossed them rapidly signaling something to stop.

"That's it," he said. "That's enough. Show's over."

He stood up. A voice sounded over the intercom.

"You want us to stop recording?" said the tinny voice.

"Yes, that's what I just fucking said."

An even brighter overhead light came on as it does in the movie theaters as they start rolling the credits.

"I had no choice but to bust you, Keeper," he said. "The evidence against you is overwhelming . . . Physical. Evidence." He smiled, cynically. "Okay, maybe too overwhelming. But I have a job to do and I did it. And yeah, I suspect the anonymous tip could have very well come from Junior or someone working for the Davids."

When I pulled on the shackles, it sent a shock wave of pain up into my wounded shoulder.

"Where's Sarah?"

He didn't answer.

"Where's Sarah?" I repeated, raising my voice.

He exhaled again.

"We don't know," he said.

"You. Don't. Know."

"She went to bed last night, and this morning she was gone."

"Cameras must have picked up an image of her leaving the facility."

"You would think that wouldn't you," he said. "But there's an issue of some missing surveillance video."

"What happened?"

"My personal opinion?" he said. "Somebody paid somebody to sabotage the facility's security system for the entire time it took Sarah to be stolen."

"Witnesses?"

He shook his head.

If my hands weren't bound in shackles, I would have pounded the table.

"You alert her father?"

"And her ex-husband," he said. "He arrived on the scene same time you did. When we busted you."

"I saw him," I said.

"Frankly, we think Michael Levy has been very quiet."

"You focusing on him now? You think he could have stolen her?"

He smiled, but I knew then that they didn't consider the writer a suspect. Or they didn't consider him a suspect any longer anyway.

"Hey, we thought you might have cut a woman's head off," he said further stressing his confusion and helplessness in this case.

"I get it," I said. "Anything is possible. You're leaving no stone unturned." I pulled on the shackles again. "Can you please get me out of these?"

He looked into the one-way glass again, cocked his head in my direction. A few seconds later, a man came in. He was overweight and dressed in civies. Without a word, he unlocked me.

"My clothes?" I said to the man.

"Somebody will retrieve them for you," he said and left the room, taking the shackles with him.

"Coffee," I said turning to Miller. "I need coffee. And Advil."

"How about something stronger?" he said, standing.

"Least you can do."

"My office," he said.

I followed.

53

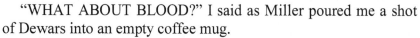

"WHAT ABOUT BLOOD?" I said as Miller poured me a shot of Dewars into an empty coffee mug.

We occupied his small office located on the opposite side of the precinct's first floor booking room. The blinds on his windows and door were closed so that no one could look in. Cop or criminal. My shoulder ached and throbbed. I knew the bandage should be changed, but for now I was shit out of luck. Visions of an infection filled my brain. Amputation. No choice but to ignore it.

"I sent him back home along with your 4Runner," he said, pouring his own shot into a blue coffee mug that had the letters NYPD printed on it in white lettering. "You might find a more savory sidekick."

"He's not a sidekick and he's one of the most upright people I know. The world dished him a shit sandwich when he was born to a fourteen-year-old mother and a father he never once met. He did what he had to do to survive and it landed him in my prison. He's still doing what he has to do to survive, only differently. He helps other people who've been handed a shit sandwich in life."

"He sells drugs."

"Not really."

"He still works the other side of the tracks, even if indirectly."

I downed my shot.

"Can we talk about the real reason we're here?" I said. "We don't have much time. If Junior took Sarah, and we can only assume he's the one who did it, then she could already be dead or fast on her way to getting there."

He downed his shot and poured another. And another for me.

"One very big problem," he said. "We have no fucking clue in the world where he could have taken her. Again, assuming he did the taking in the first place."

"Why don't you put every man you've got on finding Sarah? But first maybe it's a good idea to pull Junior and Senior in. Make them open up for once. Damn their benevolence and generosity."

He nodded. It was the kind of nod that said he's working on it, but not getting very far.

I said, "You find anything at the house that might give you cause to bring one or both of them in?"

He looked at me hard.

"Right backatcha," he said. "You find anything inside Junior's computer that might cause me to cut to the chase and bring him in right now? You might have shared the laptop password with us. Being as we're the cops and all."

I thought about the zip drive that contained all the information from Junior's hard-drive. Photos, videos, and who the hell knew what else. I knew that if Harold Sanders had been right about his future son-in-law, his home surveillance video would be on there too and that it might actually reveal what happened on the night of February 18th, frame by frame. A day ago, I might have sat down with Miller and looked at the C-drive information together. But now that they were pinning me with Daphne's murder, or at least making me the number one suspect, or should I say patsy, I needed all the leverage I could muster. That zip drive would prove to be some very heavy leverage if it assured without a doubt that Junior attacked Sarah Levy and nearly killed her. The only problem was, I wasn't presently in possession of my clothing. And I'd stored the zip drive inside my interior blazer pocket. I could only hope that it hadn't been snatched up by some overly curious cop.

"I have no idea," I said, in answer to Miller's zip-drive question. He looked at me as though I were lying, but then I was telling the truth. Just not the whole truth and nothing but the truth. So help me Christ.

"To answer your question," he said after a silent beat, "we tore Junior's joint apart. We found that room in the basement where he made Sarah, and probably a couple dozen others, do things for him." He drank his shot and set the cup back down. "But nothing that would lead me to believe he tried to kill her. The place is the home of a pervert. Maybe even a Satan loving, vampire-like pervert who's recreating some stupid bestselling book. So what, Keeper? We live in a free country and Junior knows we can't bust him for having that weird room and for what he decides to do inside it along with some consenting adults."

"So now Daphne's dead," I said. "That's so fucking what. In my house of all places." I did my shot and slapped the mug down onto his wood desk. "Christ Nick, the Davids are playing you like a broken fiddle. They've already tried to kill me on two occasions. They've killed Daphne while trying to set me up as the perp, and now they've taken Sarah and probably already killed her too. And you still can't find cause to bring them in."

He rubbed the back of his muscular neck with his hand.

"Listen, Keeper," he said. "I'm gonna tell you something that goes only as far as my lips. You understand?"

"Clock's ticking, so let's hear it."

"Robert David Sr. is a wealthy man. A very. Wealthy. Man. This city's mayor considers him a man of outstanding character and moral aptitude. As you are already aware, he is the largest donor not only to the Neighborhood Watch Committee Association of Albany, but also to the Albany Police Department Benevolence Society. He also is personally responsible for putting eight new blue and whites on the streets just last year alone. You catching my thread here?"

I felt my blood heating at what I was hearing. This wasn't the first time I'd been informed of special treatment extended to someone who was a benevolent supporter of crime fighting in Albany. It certainly wouldn't be the last. If the general public knew precisely how things worked in law enforcement and how the wheels of efficiency truly got oiled, they wouldn't sleep nights. The greasing didn't just start and stop on a local level either. Even in maximum security prison, there were cold-blooded killers who could demand special treatment simply because they had the money to pay off corrections officers. Usually, these killers had direct ties to the mob and enough influence and power on the outside to make a prison official's teeth rattle with fear if they didn't play along. Now I was facing the same thing again, only not with the mob, but with an organization that was perhaps even more dangerous precisely because it appeared to be an honest and legitimate organization:

David Enterprises.

"Who's holding you back on this thing, Nick?" I said. "Who's been pulling your strings from the start?"

He unscrewed the cap on the Dewars and poured yet another, larger shot.

"It's not strings that are being pulled, Keep," he said. "It's more like a chain leash that's wrapped around my neck and yanked every time I even come within spitting distance of either Junior or his father."

"There's something you're not telling me. Something that goes beyond some nice contributions and a few blue and whites."

He drank some more booze and exhaled. Coming around his desk, he went to the door and pulled down on the Venetian blind just enough to get a peek outside onto the precinct booking room floor. Then he snapped the aluminum blinds closed and quickly reassumed his position back behind his desk.

"This goes no further," he said. "But the very union myself and my support staff patronize, Local 2841 of Council 82—"

"—my old union," I jumped in.

"Yes," he nodded. "The very same. Fifty percent of the pool was invested in Madoff's Ponzi scheme. The loss we took was monumental. Over fifteen million in cash just disappeared overnight."

"I'm a member of that same union," I said. "I never heard word one about the loss."

"That's because the fifteen million was replaced almost immediately and news of the transaction held in absolute check."

"It was replaced?" I said. "You don't just locate another fifteen million bucks that easily."

"It was replaced," he said. "But it wasn't replaced for free."

That's when the imaginary light bulb flicked on above my head.

"The Davids," I said.

"You got it," he said. "You just might say the Davids own half the APD and then some."

I felt the adrenalin filling my brain. It caused a slight internal buzzing noise.

"Dear God in heaven," I said. "But you still somehow managed the warrant for searching his house."

"Yeah, I got the warrant," he said, "but the place was so clean

186

you could have eaten soup off the floor."

"They knew you were coming," I exhaled.

"And then some. I'm surprised they're not barking about our little computer robbery."

"You replaced it," I said with a shake of my head. "I'm wondering if Junior even noticed it missing in the first place. Maybe he hasn't even been home in the past week while he goes to great lengths trying to kill me, kill his present girlfriend and kill his old girlfriend. Home will probably be the last place you find him."

He nodded and drank once more.

"Of course, I put the computer back," he confirmed. "But I put it back with the promise that you'd share its information with me. Gotta tell you, Keep, I'm feeling more than a little double-crossed here."

"That's before you arrested me," I said. "Come on, who's yanking the leash and allowing the Davids to run the city?"

"The mayor," he said. "And the county prosecutor." Waving his hands in the air. "Other cops, for all I know."

"Jesus," I said. "Double and triple whammy."

"Mayor Jennings and Prosecutor Waters are like a brother and sister in arms. You know that. They *are* the capital city of Albany. So even without some of my brothers and sisters in arms giving me evil glares when I pass by them in the hall, I am effectively powerless. That is, I want to keep my fucking job. My pension. Maybe even my life."

It was all beginning to make some sense. I pictured the vestibule walls of David Enterprises. Pictures of Robert Sr. with the tall, tanned, and thick black-haired mayor. Photos of David Sr. with the blonde, blue-eyed, and forever smiling and stunning county prosecutor.

"Meanwhile, my shoulder has been shot through, I'm suspected of practically cutting a young woman's head off, Sarah Levy is nowhere to be found, and I have a bad case of heartburn."

"The leash is buckled tight around my neck, Keeper," Miller said. "It's cutting into my skin. But I'm gonna continue to be honest with you. While you remain the number one suspect in the murder of Daphne Williams, I've just realized that I might have been hasty in my decision to arrest you. Now that I think about it, I just don't have enough evidence on hand to detain you any longer."

He looked me in the eye without blinking. He was letting me go. Freeing me regardless of the evidence against me. It told me I was his one and only hope of not only getting Sarah back, but seeing the Davids come to justice.

"I guess that means I'm going to get my clothes back now," I said. Once more I thought about the zip drive. I prayed no one had found it yet.

"Yes, you're getting your clothes back," he said. Then, setting both hands flat on his desk, he leaned into me. "The head of security at Valley View is a former APD cop, goes by the new moniker of James Slater."

"Why the name change?"

"He had a rough time here at the department after he was caught in blow-job-for-leniency scheme."

I raised up my eyebrows.

"He'd wait outside a bar for a drunk patron to get behind the wheel of his or her vehicle," Miller went on. "He'd follow them for a while and when the opportunity presented itself, he'd pull them over. Offer them a deal they couldn't refuse."

"His cock, their mouth. Women *and* men too, huh?"

"Hey, this is Albany, don't forget."

"As much as I try . . ."

"Think you and your sidekick can put enough pressure on this S.O.B. for him to give up what he knows? Short of cutting his over-used cock off?"

"What about this mess with Daphne's head in my bed?"

"I'm happy to see it all go away. After all, we both know you aren't capable of such a heinous crime." His tone verged on sarcastic. But I knew that he knew that there was no way in hell I killed her.

"And if I can't make the happy former cop-speak?"

He smiled.

"We'll cross that bridge when we come to it. I'm acting under direct orders from Mayer Jennings. They want you in lockup. No bail. I can keep the heat off you, but for no more than a few hours. I need you to find Sarah now. Dead or alive. I can't guarantee it, but it's possible I can arrange for some backup. Maybe a couple of cruisers."

I stood up.

188

"No cops. Not yet. Not with what I know about the Davids' financing half the cop pensions. Junior sniffs something like that out, he'll kill Sarah and make a run for the border. I'm begging you to leave it up to Blood and me to find her and bring her back alive."

He bit down on his lip. I knew he didn't like the fact that I was going after her when I was a major suspect in a brutal murder case. But I also knew that what he didn't like more was my going after her and not his own APD. I also sensed he knew that I was right. If he were to organize a posse to go after Sarah, there was a good chance there'd be a leak, and Junior would get wind of it and run. Miller just couldn't risk that at this point. We both knew that in the end, I was the only jerk who could possibly go after her.

"Keeper," he added. "If Sarah's alive, I want her brought back safely, and I want her to talk."

"What if she is alive, and what if she points the fingers at the Davids, your benefactors?"

"So be it."

"It will mean the end of your career in Albany. Maybe without a pension."

He cocked his head over his left shoulder.

"Been thinking about starting up my own landscaping business. Be my own boss."

"No more leashes. Give that neck of yours a break."

"Exactly."

"Where are my clothes?"

"Let's go find them," he said, and together we made our way out of his office.

54

SOON AS I EXITED the precinct building, I checked the Ziploc plastic baggy that contained my personal effects for the zip drive. It was still there, lodged behind my wallet. Then, exhaling a sigh of profound relief, I pulled out my cell, called Blood, asked him to pick me up. He arrived a few minutes later in my 4Runner. As I got in, he tossed a couple of sheets of paper in my lap. The paper consisted of computer printouts of the local *Albany Times Union*. By the looks of it, Ted Bolous's updated blog about the Davids.

"Check that shit out," Blood said, pulling away from the curb. "You getting famous."

The food critic's blog started out by reporting about David Enterprise's most generous donation of one million dollars to the Albany Food Pantry just yesterday afternoon. An unprecedented amount that would keep Albany's bums, junkies and drunks in soup and bread for ten years or more. There was a picture of both the old man and Junior standing beside Mayor Jennings outside the brick walls of the Albany Shelter, a red, white and blue neon sign shaped like a Christian cross illuminated above them, the words "Jesus Loves You" embossed into its crossbeam. In my mind, it contrasted well with the portrait of the red Satan on his basement ceiling.

The Davids and the mayor were each wearing lightweight summertime suits and they were smiling confidently as if Jesus really was on their side of the law. I knew that during the time the photo shoot was taking place, Junior's house was being raided by the cops and Daphne Williams was begging for what remained of her short happy life. Or who knows, maybe she was dead already, the knife having severed most of her neck and that Satan-like serpent along with it.

As if reading my mind, Bolous's blog then went on to say that in related news, the murdered corpse of Manny's Restaurant employee, Daphne Williams, was discovered inside the bedroom of an apartment belonging to local private detective, Jack "Keeper" Marconi, on early Sunday morning. It said that I'd been hired by Sarah Levy's father to investigate the truth behind the incident that occurred on February 18th at Robert David Jr.'s Albany home. It also said that Sarah Levy had recently checked out of the facility and that at the same time, I'd been arrested as the number-one suspect in Daphne Williams's murder and hauled into the APD for questioning.

I took a glance at some of the comments left behind, the first one of which said, "Could be that Marconi has stepped into a hornet's nest." Another said, "Leave the Davids alone. They are very generous to Albany and Albany loves them." Another, "Marconi ought to watch his back. The Davids can make his life a living hell if they want. They have the money and the power." And yet another, "Why would Sarah Levy be checked out from Sunny View Rehabilitation if she was still under their care for serious brain injuries? Sounds like she was forcibly removed. Perhaps by someone who doesn't wish for her to recover. Because, after all, her recovery will mean that she can remember everything that happened to her on that cold night back in February. And when that happens, all stiff little fingers will point to Robert David Jr." The last comment was signed, "Anonymous." I could only wonder the true identity behind "Anonymous." Maybe Harold Sanders himself. Maybe Michael Levy.

I set the papers down and winced from the pain in my shoulder. I filled Blood in on our timeline and what would be our little unannounced come-to-Jesus with fallen APD blue angel, James Slater. But first I wanted him to take us to his place to change my bandages and to grab up some weaponry now that the APD was holding onto my .45. There was a lot of work to do in a very small amount of time. I couldn't afford to waste even another second. Neither could Sarah Levy.

55

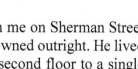

BLOOD LIVED DOWN THE road from me on Sherman Street in a nondescript brick townhouse which he owned outright. He lived alone on the first floor while he rented the second floor to a single mother of two pre-adolescent boys. While he never said a word about it, I suspected he gave her the place for free or close to it, while I often found him playing stickball in the street with the two boys, or carting them off to their charter school or Pop Warner football practice. I even sometimes caught him carrying in plastic sacks of groceries. Blood might have been born of the streets and a survivor with the scars to show for it, but he was also a soft touch.

Once inside his apartment, he escorted me to the bathroom where he changed my bandage and gave me four Advil for the pain, which I swallowed along with a cold glass of tap water. With my shirt off, we then went into his kitchen where he made coffee while I logged onto his computer and made a *Google* search of "David Enterprises" along with "Albany Mayor Jennings" and "Prosecutor Waters." Instead of searching for articles, I cut to the chase, searching instead for images. When I clicked on Search, I was faced not with a few photos, but literally dozens.

The images were all different versions of the same theme. Robert David Sr. standing outside some new building alongside Mayer Jennings, a pair of scissors in the Mayor's hand positioned to cut a yellow ribbon that would signal the facility's grand opening. Both Davids standing beside Prosecutor Waters at a fundraiser for the Albany Boy's Club, the prosecutor looking ravishing in her black mini-dress and perfect shoulder-length blonde hair and, of course, that whiter-than-white Pepsodent smile. The photo-ops seemed never ending.

But that wasn't the most interesting thing about the photo collection. Because what really caught my eye were the half dozen or so more recent shots which were taken at a pre-ground-breaking ceremony on the western edge of the city limits near the state university. It was the site for the new Nanotech research facility, which was arguably one of the most expensive facilities ever to be constructed in Albany. It would also provide jobs to brilliant minds from all over the world. Judging from the picture, the line-up of happy-faced dignitaries at the ceremony didn't just include Mayor Jennings and the David boys, but it also included Prosecutor Waters and one more smiley faced big shot: My present employer, Harold Sanders.

My heart started to pound, my shoulder throbbing more than ever.

Seeing Sanders standing beside his present enemy nearly robbed me of my breath. Funny how he didn't think to inform me of his professional working relationship with the Davids. Or perhaps he conveniently held the information back. But for what reason, I had no idea.

For now, there were more pressing issues to attend to. Reaching into the interior pocket of my blazer, I pulled out the zip drive that contained information stored on Junior's laptop. If Sanders was right, I knew it would contain the surveillance video of the exterior of his house. If it contained the video, I could only hope that Junior was too stupid to have deleted it. Or perhaps the sadist in him made him want to view the video again and again.

I popped the zip-drive in and waited for it to boot up. I clicked onto videos and opened up a few dozen which for certain had been shot inside his basement sex play-room. I didn't have time to run through them, but the still shots of the videos that appeared on the screen contained enough of a visual to give me a precise idea of what went on down there. Several men and women dressed all in leather, all of them wearing black masks, all of them holding whips and chains, and doing things to a naked woman who was bound to that big wood wheel. The woman being tortured and raped in each case was Sarah.

I had to ignore these videos and instead look for the surveillance video. There was a series of dates listed vertically. Maybe one hundred or about three months' worth of them. I scanned the dates. When I found one dated February 18, I knew I had a winner.

I clicked on it.

The video contained two simultaneous black-and-white, side-by-side shots. One of the home's front and the other of the backyard. The sides of the house were evidently ignored since they didn't contain any egress openings or present any possibility of security breaches. Naturally I focused most of my attention of the video being shot of the home's front exterior.

There was a time counter set in the upper right-hand corner of the video. By using the tool at the bottom of the video, I fast-forwarded until the time on the counter read 7:08 p.m. That's when a car pulled up in the driveway. A new model red Volvo wagon. The woman who got out of the Volvo was Sarah. She was carrying a leather overnight bag over her shoulder as she made her way up the steps, careful not to slip on the ice. She used her key to let herself into the front door, and then she disappeared.

I kept watching for a while until I fast forwarded to 8:00 PM. That's when several cars showed up all at once. Expensive cars. Foreign makes, all of them. One of the people who got out was Daphne. She too was carrying an overnight bag. Several men got out whom I could not recognize in the grainy black and white digital film. But I was able to recognize one of them. I shared a donut with him not too long ago inside the front seat of my 4Runner. It was the *Albany Times Union* food blogger, Ted Bolous. I recognized two more people too. The last two who parked their car at the very end of the driveway. It was a man and a woman. The man was Robert David Sr. and the woman was his new wife, Penny. Apparently it wasn't enough for Penny to play around with her stepson. She also enjoyed a little extra S&M quality time with her stepson's fiancée. Good to keep things in the family.

I quickly scanned three more hours of film until the guests politely took their leave, including Daphne and David Sr. But not Penny. By midnight, the only car left in the driveway was Sarah's. Obviously, she had made plans to spend the night, but with David *and* Penny? Was Robert Sr. allowing this to happen? Maybe he didn't have a choice. Maybe Penny did what Penny wanted and that's that.

More hours passed with nothing happening. Nothing that is, except for the weather, which had gone from clear and dry to snow mixed with ice. Using the fast forward tool one last time, I set the time for two in the morning. At precisely three minutes after two, the front door opened again and out stepped Sarah onto an ice and snow-covered landing illuminated in bright light from several exterior wall-mounted fixtures. She was wearing her coat and her leather bag was once more slung over her shoulder. She stepped outside onto the slippery top step but turned and shouted something back inside. That's when I saw Junior take hold of her arm while apparently attempting to pull her back inside.

She yanked her arm back and freed it from his grasp. She then tried to claw him in the face. But did so unsuccessfully.

The T-shirt clad Junior stepped out onto the landing. At one point, he turned and shouted something back into the house through the open door as if there were another person standing inside and out of camera range.

Penny.

Without sound, it was difficult to tell precisely what he was doing or make out what he was saying. But there was no mistaking his actions when, turning back to Sarah, he took hold of her arms and from the look of things, began pleading with her. But once more, she yanked her arms back and started clawing at him again. But as much as she lashed out at him, he was able to deflect her attacks. That's when she slid and almost lost her balance entirely.

Even in the grainy black and white you could see the fear in her face.

But the fear did nothing to stop the rage and violence that was spewing out of her like a suddenly opened vein.

Reaching out with both her arms, she attempted to claw at his face yet again. But he managed to avoid her by grabbing her right wrist, tearing apart her bracelet, the beads of which scattered all over the now ice-covered sidewalk. He then grabbed her by the hair, as if he had no other choice. She dropped her bag and began to scream again, in obvious pain. I could only wonder how the neighbors didn't hear her. But then the neighbors on Marion Avenue not only lived in castles surrounded by lots of land, but the homes would be locked up tighter than a snare drum in the middle of a cold winter's night.

I kept watching until Junior did precisely what I suspected he'd do.

He let go of Sarah's hair, grabbed her arm, and tried to pull her back in the house. But she let loose with her right leg, kicking him in the crotch. At the same time, she lost all her footing and the momentum of the kick propelled her backward. She went down hard on the ice-covered steps and dropped down and down, bouncing off each tread like a rag doll, until she landed hard at the bottom.

The video showed what appeared to be a panicked Junior racing down the steps, slipping once onto his backside just before he came to the bottom. He tried to revive her there, but she was unconscious. He tried picking her up, but he kept dropping her onto the pavement as if her dead weight were impossible for him to manage. And it was. That's when he stood up straight. He looked one way, then the other. Reaching into his pocket, he pulled out his cell phone and began to dial. He talked on the phone for a minute or two. Then he shoved the phone back into his pocket.

Junior ran up to the house then, slipping once onto his chest as he climbed. When he came back out, he was holding a blanket, which he draped over Sarah's unconscious body. A few minutes later, David Sr. reappeared in his black Lexus. He got out and the two of them examined the still unconscious Sarah. Together, they shoved her into the backseat of the Lexus and drove her away.

End of a story which neither proved nor disproved that Junior tried to intentionally harm Sarah. But what it did prove is that he would be liable for her injuries. Not only did the video reveal his picking her up and dropping her, but no doubt a judge would see to it that he was responsible for physically fighting with Sarah on a set of steps that hadn't yet been properly de-iced.

I stood up, glanced at my watch.

"We need to go," I said to Blood who handed me a coffee with milk in it.

"We're already on our way," he said. "Allow me to gather the hardware."

He disappeared into his bedroom with his own cup of coffee in hand. Meanwhile, I thought about the pictures of Sanders and Robert David Sr. Especially the ones taken at the groundbreaking for the Nanotech facility. Is it possible the Davids and Sanders had been working together prior to Sarah's brain damaging incident outside Junior's house? And if they were, did it really make any difference at all what projects they did or did not work on together? I could only suppose that it didn't. But then, why was I finding it hard to ignore this nagging, tight feeling in my gut that told me something more was at play here. The Davids and Sanders both were richer than God and the devil put together. Maybe they were working together to get richer.

One thing is for certain, David Sr. and his new young wife had been doing bad things to his son's fiancée in the basement of that Albany Marion Avenue home. For all I knew, she welcomed their participation in their bizarre sex games. For a while anyway. But what about her father and my employer? What about Michael Levy, her ex-husband? Had they been aware of the dangerous games being played inside that basement playroom? And if they were, wouldn't they have tried to put a stop to them?

Questions. But no answers. Not right now. The only thing I did know for sure was how the local food blogger got his rocks off at night and now he was enjoying his little moment in the sun by blogging about the Davids. If anybody should know all about playing with fire and how badly you can get burned, it should be a food blogger.

Blood came back into the kitchen. He handed me a 9 mm Smith & Wesson. An identical model and make of the APD standard issue. He also handed me two extra clips. I stood up, thumbed back the clip it already housed, checked the existing load. Cocking a round into the chamber, I then thumbed the safety on, and stuffed the barrel into my waistband and hid the exposed butt with my blazer.

I couldn't see any weapons on Blood, but I knew he was packing. Probably his Glock 9 stuffed in his waist and a smaller caliber revolver around his ankle. Somewhere in the mix would be a knife. Blood was good with a knife.

"You driving?" I said, popping the zip drive out and stuffing into my blazer pocket.

"You gotta ask?" he said.

We exited his Sherman Street house, headed for the 4Runner.

Marconi Released on Lack of Evidence
By Ted Bolous, *Albany Times Union* Senior Food Blogger

So, dear food lover, yesterday I reported a mouthful to you about the Davids and their generous donation to the Albany Food Pantry. You also read the tragic news about Manny's employee, Daphne Williams, losing her head, literally, in the bed of Harold Sander's personal private detective-for-hire, Jack 'Keeper' Marconi. While Marconi was arrested yesterday afternoon for the murder, it seems that now the APD have changed their mind and decided they didn't have enough evidence to keep the gumshoe behind bars.

Huh? Williams was found inside his home, in his bed.

Meanwhile, the search continues for a missing Sarah Levy.

Before you all go off half-cocked once more pointing the blame-game fingers at the Davids, perhaps you should take another look at this Marconi character. Funny how he keeps popping up like a Butterball thermometer and all around him people either go missing or go very dead.

As usual, your comments will be scrutinized carefully for their ingredients.

Comment by HiImBi
Really, Teddy boy, seems to me this Marconi guy is just doing his job. You ever heard of the term "setup?" If the Davids have enough money to block the police from doing their job in the Sarah Levy head injury case, they sure as heck can take care of a big mouth like Daphne Williams and make it look as though the private detective is the perp.

Comment by Robert
As I said from the start, this whole thing stinks. And now poor Sarah is gone and someone else is dead. Things are imploding. If this were a mystery novel, I'd say the ever crucial climax is about to reveal itself."

56

THIS TIME WHEN WE arrived at the Valley View Rehabilitation Facility, we didn't park in the designated parking lot where my 4Runner would surely be spotted by the parking lot attendant. Instead, we drove around back to the maintenance entrance. Before we made the drive in, Blood stopped the 4Runner. I got out and immediately got back in via the vehicle's backseat, where I lay down on the floor, making myself invisible. Blood drove slowly until he came to a stop at the guard shack.

The guard asked him his business.

"I've got a job interview with Mr. James Slater."

A few seconds of silence ensued as if the guard were checking his manifest for information confirming the interview. Naturally, he wouldn't find anything no matter how much he looked.

"You sure he's expecting you?" the guard said.

"He just called me. Told me I could come right away if I wasn't busy, and since I'm not busy, here I am. Probably hasn't had the time to tell you. You want me to wait here while you call him? I got no problem with that."

Blood was bluffing. I could only hope that the guard did not call it.

"No problem. You can go ahead."

"Thanks, man," Blood said. "Hoping to be wearing the same uniform as you pretty soon."

"Good luck," said the guard.

Blood drove on.

We stopped outside a pair of glass sliding doors. Blood made a three-point turn and then backed the 4Runner into place. You never knew if we might need to make a hasty exit. I got out and so did Blood, pocketing the keys.

"Let's do this," I said, as we approached the doors which automatically opened for us.

There was a big plastic board mounted to the painted block wall to our right. It offered a listing of all the basement level offices in two neat vertical columns, along with the office numbers and the names of the occupants. I found "James Slater, Director for Security" easily enough and made a mental note of his office number.

"Lucky thirteen," I said to Blood.

"Lucky for us," he said. "Bad luck for Mr. Slater."

We proceeded through the dimly lit, dungeon-like basement corridor, passing by the many steel and glass doors until we came to number 13. Blood stood on one side of the door and I stood on the other, each of us glancing in through the wire-reinforced glass at a man seated behind a metal desk. The man was middle-aged, balding, and he was talking to someone on the phone. He was wearing a pink polo shirt with the collar standing up at attention. Over the polo shirt, he wore a big gray hooded sweatshirt that had the word "Nantucket" printed across the chest in big bold white letters. A pair of reading glasses hung down against his chest by a leather strap attached to the earpieces. He was sitting far back in his swivel chair and smoking a cigarette while laughing his ass off with whoever occupied the other end of his connection.

"Doesn't look like much of a director of security to me," Blood said.

"More like a preppy boy just come off the golf course," I said.

"Sure we gonna need guns?" he said. "Maybe we attack him with some tennis rackets."

"Or toss some golf balls at him."

I reached out for the doorknob, slowly twisted it. The door was unlocked. Then, pushing the door open with my good shoulder, I pulled the 9 mm from my pant waist with my left hand.

"You going to take lookout?" I said.

"'Less you want me to torture the preppy by pulling his collar down."

"That's inhumane."

I opened the door. Slowly. Walked on through.

I saw Slater look up wide-eyed, the phone still pressed against his ear.

"I'll call you back," he said into the receiver and hung up. Then, eyes locked on my own. "Who the fuck are you?"

I didn't point the gun at him. I merely allowed the barrel to dangle down by my lower thigh, the piece aimed at the painted concrete floor. But he got the message clear enough.

"I'm the guy who's going to make you tell me who took Sarah Levy and where they took her to."

I gazed quickly over my bad shoulder, saw that Blood was standing hidden to the left side of the closed door, his eyes peering out the glass in anticipation of anyone who might want to barge in while I was having my little one-on-one with preppy Mr. Slater.

Slater sat up straight, then stood. He was on the shorter side, and he was wearing tan Bermuda shorts.

"Thought you were the head of security?" I said.

"I am," he said.

"Strange uniform you got there."

"I happen to be leaving for the Cape in a half hour. Not that it's any of your goddamn business."

I thumbed back the hammer on the .9mm. Inside the little office, the mechanical noise sounded louder and more powerful than the metal bars slamming closed on an inmate's cell.

"Back to my original question," I said. "Who stole Sarah Levy? Who paid you off to make it happen?"

His tan pallor went pale.

"Listen, Slater," I pressed, "I'm aware that Slater isn't your real name and that you got kicked out of the cops for taking a few too many hum jobs from the boys and girls of your choice."

Now his pale pallor turned a distinct shade of green. Matched perfectly with his pink collar.

"You don't know what you're talking about," he said.

"I do, actually. Lots of security support staff roaming these grounds. Be a shame to have to tell them the nasty secret about their boss."

The Adam's apple bobbing up and down in his throat told me he was swallowing something dry and bitter. What he was swallowing was the truth about his past and from what I'm told, those skeletons don't go down too easy.

He glanced down at his desk, flung open his drawer, pulled out a snub-nosed Saturday night special. His speed took me by surprise. Raising up the 9mm, I swung and slapped the revolver from his hand, and then swiped his forehead on the back swing. He dropped back down into the chair like a hole in one.

"You still with me, Slater?" I said.

He nodded, a large black and purple lump now rising on his forehead.

"Who paid you off to kill the security system while Sarah was being kidnaped?"

His eyes were glassy. It was possible that if I hit him again, he'd pass out. I didn't have the time to wait around for him to come to. Someone from his support staff could come in at any moment. I raised the pistol up anyway and made like I was going to hit him again.

"Okay, okay," he mumbled. "Enough."

"How we doing, Blood?" I asked.

"All right so far. But tell preppy man to hurry up with what we already know."

Turning back to Lewis: "It was Robert David Sr. wasn't it?" I said.

He shook his head.

"No," he said. "It was the kid. He paid me a couple of grand to shut things down for ten minutes. That's all it took to get her out."

"Where'd he take her?"

He shook his head again.

"I don't know that," he said, his eyes peering down at his hands in his lap.

I reared back and hit him again. This time across the jaw. I figured if I hit him there with the tip of the barrel, it wouldn't knock him out so much as knock some sense into him.

"Where'd he fucking take the girl?"

Fresh blood was dripping from his mouth onto his Nantucket sweatshirt. He'd have to buy a new one.

"He didn't tell me."

"Did he give you a clue?"

He paused for a moment, wiping the blood from his mouth with the back of his hand.

"The girl with him. A big blonde girl. Kind of hot. She said something about a bar. Their bar. The basement. A wine cellar. I don't know, maybe you'll fucking find her there."

It made sense to me. Hiding Sarah in the wine cellar of Manny's was as good a place as any to store her. A wine cellar in a century old building like Manny's would be deep, wide, and dark. I also knew now that Daphne had still been alive at the time of the kidnapping. Junior must have killed her very soon after. It must have all been a part of some master plan.

"Thanks for your time, Mr. Slater," I said, turning back to Blood.

"Coast still clear, Keeper," he said.

"Door," I said.

He opened it and stepped on out. I stepped out right behind him. We double-timed it back down the corridor and out the sliding glass doors. We hadn't yet made it to the 4Runner before the Valley View campus alarm sounded.

57

WE JUMPED BACK IN the 4Runner.

Blood behind the wheel. Me in the shotgun seat.

The sirens were blaring not only from the alarm speaker system attached to the building behind us, but also from the campus security vehicles that were closing in on us. Blood hit the gas and made for the exit which meant we'd have to speed directly past the guard shack. It was the only way in and out of the otherwise fenced-in facility. The guard assigned to the shack was standing in our way, at the end of the drive, just beyond the now lowered, horizontally-positioned yellow and black gate. Standing four-square, sidearm gripped in hand, combat position, the burly guard planted a bead directly at our heads.

"You don't think he'd actually pull the trigger, do you, Blood?" I asked as we began running out of the parking lot.

"Never mess with a flunky cop," Blood said.

The pistol barrel stared us down like a tiny black eternity. For a brief instant, I thought Blood was going to run the guard over. But that's when a yellow and white four-door Jeep pulled out in front of us and stopped on a dime. Blood slammed on the brakes while the two uniformed men who occupied the driver and shotgun seats jumped out. The one closest to us hid behind his open door for protection, his piece planted on us. The tall driver pointed his gun at us over the roof of the vehicle.

I gripped the 9mm in my left hand while my right shoulder throbbed and my heart beat against my ribs.

"Options," I barked.

"Only one option," Blood said.

"Not sure I want to know what it is."

He shifted the 4Runner in reverse and gunned it. The tires spun out on the pavement beneath us until they caught and lurched us backward. He hit the brakes and then shifted the 4Runner transmission into neutral.

"Stop right there!" screamed the armed guard closest to us. "Stop or we will fire on you!"

Blood revved the 8-cylinder. As the engine roared, you could see the jagged purple veins popping out on the both of the guard's foreheads. Or maybe I was just seeing things. But I knew they hadn't seen this kind of action in a long time. Probably more true that they'd never seen this kind of action. Ever.

"I'll be a dumb son of a bitch, Blood," I said. "You're gonna do this, aren't you?"

"They're not the cops," he said. "Cops would be a different story. But they people like you and me."

"Or not," I said.

"Or not," he repeated, revving the engine once more. Then he added, "Duck your head and hang on, Warden."

Shifting the tranny into drive, my former inmate punched the gas.

58

THE 4RUNNER SHOT FORWARD like a big, red projectile.

The face of the guard closest to us went wide-eyed, mouth ajar. He dropped his pistol and leaped out from behind the open Jeep door. Just as we slammed into the Jeep's front grill, careening the 4-wheel drive vehicle sideways.

Propelled by the Jeep, the guard on the driver's side was thrust onto his back on the pavement. Somehow he managed to secure his service weapon in his shooting hand. Turning, I watched him plant a bead for the 4Runner. I saw the flashes of the spent rounds as they blew out the tailgate glass and made three nickel-sized holes in my brand new windshield.

"Go!" I screamed at Blood, as he tapped the brakes before entering the exit road that would take us past the guard shack.

"Man up ahead ain't moving," he said, bringing the vehicle to a full stop.

"He'll move," I barked. "Trust me."

"Your call, boss," he said.

"Just go!" I repeated.

I heard his right foot stomp down on the gas as the 4Runner headed straight for the third guard.

59

THE GUARD FIRED AT us.

Pointblank.

The new windshield exploded just as we heard the shots.

The guard turned out to be a brave soul. He stood his ground directly behind the lowered gate as if it were somehow going to protect him from two tons of speeding SUV.

I felt Blood's free hand grip my blazer collar while he pulled me down onto the center console as he braved the gunfire. Then I felt a slight jolt as we rammed the gate. I waited for the dreaded thud that would occur when we made road-kill of the stubborn guard. But he must have jumped out of the way at the last possible second. Maybe cops and soldiers sometimes feel it their duty to die in the line of fire, but no rent-a-cop was ever called a martyr. Bravery or no bravery.

Blood pulled out onto the street, hooked a right onto the road that would lead us back to the highway. He let go of me, and I gradually straightened myself up. Now that the gunplay was over, I was back to feeling the throbbing pain in my right shoulder. I was getting too old for this shit.

"You hit?" Blood said. "Excuse me . . . You hit *again*?"

"Just about to ask you the same thing."

"That's what I like about you. You one caring white bread man."

"I voted for Obama."

"You think anything tailing us?"

"Not a question of if," I said, "but when."

"We got to ditch this bright red elephant, Keep. They know it's yours, and they know you arrested for a murder."

"Think we can make it back to Sherman Street without being spotted?"

He laughed.

"Yeah," I added. "Thought you were going to say something like that."

Up ahead was a church parking lot. The lot was filled with cars. Parked in the very front of the church, a black funeral hearse and two black stretch limousines lined up behind it.

"Pull in there," I said. "Park in back."

Blood did it.

"You still good at hacking cars?" I asked him, as he parked the 4Runner in one of the empty spaces.

"Depends on the year and make."

I took a quick look around and spotted a Volkswagen Rabbit from the mid-1980s. It was still in very good shape. No rust.

"How about that?" I said, pointing to it.

"Give it a whirl. You be the lookout. Those rent-a-cops ain't about to chase us out here, but the Schenectady cops are already on their way."

He pulled a switch blade from the interior pocket on his leather jacket and got out. He popped the blade as he approached the Rabbit. He immediately began working the blade in the narrow crack-like opening between the hood and the engine block compartment. Within a minute, he was able to pop the hood. Less than a second minute later, he had the engine purring.

"Let's go," he barked, closing the hood. It took him a few seconds to jimmy the driver's side door with the blade, but he did it without breaking a sweat or breaking the blade.

I got out, jogged over to the passenger-side of the compact car. He flipped the manual lock for me and I got in, closing the door behind me. It felt strange being so low to the ground as opposed to the 4Runner where we were high up.

He shifted the manual transmission in reverse and backed out. That's when I began to make out sirens.

"Here they come," I said.

Blood gave it the gas, sped around the cars in the lot, and made it past the church just as two large young men wearing dark suits came barreling out of the front wood doors, shouting at us to stop.

Blood didn't slow for even a second. He pulled out into the road as if we owned it *and* the old Volkswagen Rabbit.

In a big way, we did.

60

WE DIDN'T HAVE AN E-ZPass on us.

Neither did the kid who owned the relic we just ripped off.

We couldn't just zip through the toll booth without stopping.

Knowing we'd have to face another human toll collector who might very well I.D. us, we avoided the highway and took the back roads all the way into the town of Colonie, past the airport, and into West Albany. From there we made our way down the busy four-lane Wolf Road to Central Avenue where we hooked a left. Central Avenue was the main east/west artery for the city, and it would lead us directly to Lark Street and Manny's Restaurant.

I asked Blood for his cell.

He handed it to me without asking me what I wanted it for.

"Your caller ID appears on the receiver's extension?"

He looked at me while he drove.

"Got that shit blocked," he said with a smile.

I dialed the memorized number for David Enterprises. When his assistant, Victoria, answered, I asked to speak with David Sr. Listening to my gut, I took a shot, told her my name was Bill and that I was calling from Harold Sanders office, and that I needed some direction on one of the projects we were working on together.

She said, "Hi there, Bill," in a sing-song, glad-to-hear-from-you voice. Then she told me Mr. David Sr. was unavailable since he was in a meeting with David Jr. Big mistake on the sexy lady's part, but exactly what I suspected I'd hear. It was also exactly what I wanted to hear.

"Can I take a message, Bill?" she said.

"Tell them both to have a nice day," I said, hanging up. Then, turning to Blood. "I got the Davids in the same place, same time. I also got some pretty clear confirmation that Sanders's suit is a fraud. A way for them both to split a big pot at the expense of Sarah's injuries."

"David Enterprises and Harold Sanders Architects acting in cahoots?"

"Yup."

"Shall we blow the place up like they do in the movies?"

"Nope. That would be too good for them. Prison would be better."

Blood smiled.

"Nefarious man, you are. You must have worked in a prison."

We drove toward Albany. I knew it was only a matter of time before the Albany cops caught up to us since the owner of the Rabbit had no doubt already called the stolen vehicle in. But I wasn't the least bit concerned about it as I dialed Detective Nick Miller's cell phone.

When he answered, I told him where I was now and where I was going to be in a matter of a few very long minutes. Then I told him about James Slater and what he revealed about Sarah's possible location. I also told him about the Davids both being present and accounted for at David Enterprises. I let him in on my suspicion being all but confirmed. That the Davids and Harold Sanders were going to split a $40 million pot once I did my job by uncovering evidence that made Junior liable, but not legally responsible.

"Insurance would make the forty mil payout," Miller said. "Junior gets nailed for liability but he doesn't get put away for anything. Brilliant when you think about it."

"Risky," I said, "but yeah, I got to hand it to them."

"You sure Slater can be trusted?" Miller said. "Sure it's not a trap? Slater is one shady motherfucker no doubt on the David payroll. I'm sending over a squad car. One of the ones the Davids paid for."

"No," I spat. "No cops. Not now. I don't want to scare away the pigeons while they still got their feathers on. Leave it up to Blood and me."

"Have it your way."

"You get any word from Harold Sanders or Levy?"

"Levy occupies my office as I speak. He's going nowhere until we find Sarah. As for Sanders, he seems to be nowhere, further confirming your suspicion of plaintiff/defendant collusion. We've been trying to find him since his daughter disappeared."

An imaginary red flag went up before my eyes.

"Something's been telling me from the beginning Sanders isn't exactly the loving, all-concerned, arsty-fartsy dad he's making himself out to be. Kindler's gonna have a shit when he hears he's been takin' for a ride."

"Couldn't agree more," he said. "Before I go searching for Sanders' skinny ass, I need to get some more face time with Junior and his father."

"You know what to do," I said.

"You're thinking I make a real raid on David Enterprises? This time, a raid they don't see coming?"

"I'm not telling you how to do your job, Nick, but I think that would provide enough of a diversion for Blood and me to safely grab up Sarah from the wine cellar. That is if she's there in the first place. You need to get the Davids in custody now while you have the chance. Don't wait. They're both trying to figure a way out of this inside their Broadway offices. Don't give them a chance to flee the state. Or flee the damn country. Lord knows they have the money and the resources."

He then told me about a report that came in about a stolen car. That my shot up 4Runner had been abandoned at the scene of the carjacking.

"Tell your people to back off."

"Technically speaking, you're still the number one suspect in the murder of Daphne Williams," he said. "I'll continue to do what I can to keep you on the hunt for Sarah without getting busted by my people. In the meantime, stay out of sight until I can organize a raid on David Enterprises without giving our number one benefactor an excuse to scream police brutality and harassment while he cancels his checks."

"That's the idea," I said. "But hustle it. Who knows what condition Sarah is in."

"Give me a half hour."

"Done," I said.

"I'll be in touch," he said.

61

BLOOD DROVE THE RABBIT down State Street and parked it on the south-eastern edge of Washington Park. He left the keys inside it with the window open. The cops would come upon it soon, seize it and hold it as evidence against me. Until a time when I was proven innocent of having anything to do with Daphne's murder.

We moved together on foot toward Manny's.

The corner of State and Lark was always congested with cars, trucks, taxis, and people crowding its concrete sidewalks and today was no exception. I caught a glimpse of the big exterior windows embedded into Manny's big brick wall and could see right away that the lights in the place weren't on. It was close to happy hour. Manny's traditionally opened up for the lunch crowd and stayed open through the day and night. But not today. Something definitely wasn't right. But then, I already knew that.

Blood and I sifted through the crowd until we found ourselves outside the building's front door. I tried pulling on it.

"Locked," I said, tugging on the closer.

"They know we coming," observed Blood.

I took a look around, searching for another way in.

"There's got to be a service entrance," I said. "Where they take their deliveries and bring out the trash."

"That there is," said Blood. "Around back."

We walked State Street for a short distance until we came to an alley that led directly to a small back lot behind Manny's. Problem was, there was a chain link fence blocking off access to it. I shot Blood a look and he shot me one back.

"You ain't gonna let a fence stop you," he said like a question.

"Been a while," I said. "Bum shoulder."

"You still got the guns, Keep," he said. "They just a little older and more shot up then they used to be. I'll give you a boost."

"Warranty ran out a while ago," I said as I set the tip of my booted right foot into one of the square-shaped chain links, grabbed hold of the fence with both hands and, with Blood's help, heaved myself up.

Once at the top of the fence, I felt the searing burn in my right shoulder. I was pretty sure that whatever bleeding had stopped had started right back up again. With Sarah's pale face foremost in my brain, I threw my right leg around, then my left, and dropped down onto the lot. I fell hard, dropping down onto my good, left side, but still feeling the concussion in my right side.

Blood jumped and landed on both feet. He probably could have hurdled it had he been given a running start. But to him, that would have been like showing off. He already had his gun out, and his eyes were examining the back of the building.

Picking myself up, I pulled the 9 mm out of my pant waist, thumbed the safety off, and slowly moved in the direction of Manny's back door.

Find Sarah!
By Ted Bolous, *Albany Times Union* Senior Food Blogger

If anyone has any information regarding the whereabouts of Sarah Levy, please post it here.

62

THE EXTERIOR WALL OF the building was made of old, common brick. It looked as if it hadn't been cleaned since the day the bricks were laid maybe one hundred or more years ago. In the center of the four-story brick wall was a solid metal door and beside it, a steel roll-up door. To the right of the building sat a beat up blue dumpster that bore the letters BFI.

The area behind the building was dark since the brick buildings that surrounded it blocked out the sun. Directly behind us was the service road. It too was blocked off with padlocked chain-link gates topped with razor wire. The place seemed more like Fort Knox than a place for innocent food deliveries.

Blood and I approached the door. I tried the opener, but it was closed tighter than a bank vault.

"Think you can jimmy that?" I asked Blood.

"You got the time, I can jimmy anything."

"Ain't got the time," I said.

"Back up," he said, pressing the barrel of his hand cannon to the closer.

I backed up.

He squeezed the trigger and the closer exploded into a dozen fragments. Blood reached into the round machined hole where the closer had been installed, pulled out the bolt, and dropped it to the ground. Then, using the same hole, he pulled the door open. There was no alarm. I sensed that, like Junior's home, it would sound silently. Not that I cared. Miller knew precisely where and what we were doing. I could only wonder if Junior and his father knew what we were doing.

We entered the kitchen. It was dark, and I felt along the wall for a switch. I found one and flipped it on. The place was white, like a morgue. There were stainless steel prep tables set up in the middle of the floor, several stainless steel freezers, and a walk-in cooler. There were also several professional grade gas stoves, a wood-fired pizza oven, and a couple of regular ovens.

"Wine cellar," said Blood.

Our guns aimed for what lie ahead, we exited the kitchen directly into the bar back. It might have been early evening, but it most definitely was not happy hour.

"Here," Blood said, pointing down at the worn wood floor behind the long wood bar. "An opening," he said.

I shuffled over to him. There was a rectangular panel embedded into the floor with a retractable opener.

"Step away," I said, as I crouched down, fingered the opener, and pulled it up. The panel opened easily, revealing a basement that was accessible by a set of narrow wood plank stairs.

"Got a light?" Blood said.

I reached in, ran the fingers on my left hand along the wood wall, and found a round, old–fashioned, surface-mounted fixture. I flicked the switch on and a dull bulb cast an eerie yellowish glow inside the basement.

"Perfection before brains," I said.

"I'm smarter than you," he said. "Played you like a violin at Green Haven for many years."

He smiled because he was right and he knew it.

"Must be nice to be perfect."

He grimaced as he placed his right foot on the first tread and then began his descent into the cramped basement. I immediately followed, praying we were entering into a wine cellar and not into hell itself.

63

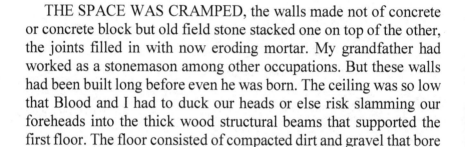

THE SPACE WAS CRAMPED, the walls made not of concrete or concrete block but old field stone stacked one on top of the other, the joints filled in with now eroding mortar. My grandfather had worked as a stonemason among other occupations. But these walls had been built long before even he was born. The ceiling was so low that Blood and I had to duck our heads or else risk slamming our foreheads into the thick wood structural beams that supported the first floor. The floor consisted of compacted dirt and gravel that bore a damp mustiness to it. Someone had thought enough to install a series of wood planks over the dirt so that you weren't forced to walk on it and, therefore, drag the dirt upstairs to the restaurant.

We followed the path of the planks to a series of wood wine racks that contained dozens if not a couple hundred bottles stacked horizontally to the ceiling. Some of the bottles bore a coating of white dust while others looked as though they'd just been placed there.

"Why don't we pop a cork and get drunk?" Blood said.

"Thought you don't drink anymore," I said.

"Don't do drugs or liquors," he said, examining some of the bottles. "But when it comes to a very good bottle of wine . . ." He allowed thought to trail off. "Got a red here bottled in 1969. Must be expensive."

"Not for a man of your means."

"True that," he said, gently setting the dusty bottle back on the rack.

"You see anything that tells you Sarah Levy is down here?" I said, walking the length of the racks until I came to another stone wall.

"That preppy James Slater was lying to us," Blood said.

"Maybe not. He said he overheard Junior taking about a wine cellar."

"You giving that creepy Slater the benefit of the doubt?"

"I was raised a Christian."

"Turn the other cheek."

"She's not down here," I exhaled.

"My sentiments exactly," he said. "Lots of wine though. I almost hate to leave this place."

"Stay as long as you want," I said, heading back across the wood planks for the staircase. "Plenty of spiders and snakes to keep you company."

"Not on your life," Blood said, following close behind. "Man's got to know the limitations of his bravery."

64

WHEN WE CAME UP for air, closing the floor panel behind us, a group of three or four business-suited men were pulling on the door, trying to get in.

"Stay down," I said to Blood.

"Those businessmen need to wet their whistles," he said. "They not used to the joint being closed up."

"Makes me wonder if Junior and the old man have already fled the city and the state."

"You wanna call Miller? See how he doing with the raid?"

I shook my head while someone yelled out to "Open the damn door!"

"Follow me," I said.

Crouching, I made my way from the bar, through the swinging door, and back into the kitchen. Blood stayed close behind. When we were both safely inside the kitchen, I took one last look around.

"Goose chase," I said. "Any ideas?"

Blood wasn't answering me. His hawk-like eyes were focused on something else instead. He moved on past me and made his way to the walk-in cooler. He took a knee and pressed his index finger to the floor. He smelled the pad of his index finger as if something now coated it.

"What is it?" I said.

"You really wanna know?" he said.

"The cooler," I said, feeling my stomach drop. "Sarah's in the cooler."

65

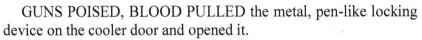

GUNS POISED, BLOOD PULLED the metal, pen-like locking device on the cooler door and opened it.

We stepped inside.

First, we were hit by a blast of cold air. Then we were hit with something else.

A body, hanging from a meat hook, directly beside two separate sides of raw beef.

The body of Sarah Levy.

66

HER EYES WERE CLOSED and her body, which was dressed only in her underwear, was hanging perfectly still while beneath her, a puddle of urine had collected. It was the urine that Blood had smelled on his fingertips.

"Junior," Blood said.

"Looks like his work," I said.

Upon closer inspection, I could see that her back hadn't been pierced by the meat hook. She was hanging by a thin, brown leather belt which had been strapped to the hook and strung under her armpits. Maybe Junior's belt. I set my hand on her body. It was cold, but not as cold as a dead person's body would be.

"Christ she's alive!" I shouted to Blood.

Without a second of pause, he grabbed her by the legs and heaved her up so that the belt detached from the meat hook. Her lifeless, unconscious body draped itself over his shoulder.

"Hospital!" he said.

I back-stepped, turned toward the opening.

That's when the cooler door slammed shut in my face.

67

"OH, SHIT," BLOOD SAID, setting Sarah's body gently onto the floor on her back. Standing up straight, he approached the door, yanked on the interior closer which was just a thin metal pulley. But the door wouldn't budge. He tried ramming it with his shoulder. Even when Blood put all two-hundred and twenty- pounds of solid muscle into it, he couldn't make it move.

He backed up and rubbed the shoulder he used on the door.

"Somebody know we're in here," he said. "Saw us coming."

"That somebody wants us dead," I said, my teeth beginning to chatter.

Blood drew his .9mm from his pant waist. Aimed it at the pulley.

"Save it," I said. "Won't work. This is like a vault door. That bullet will just rattle around inside here like a coin in a piggy bank. One of us might get shot, and I'm sick of being a bullet magnet."

He replaced the pistol into his pant waist and sighed. I knew that even though he would never admit to it, Blood was freezing also.

I pressed my ear up against the door and listened.

I could hear talking. Not shouting, but talking. A man's voice. Junior's voice.

He seemed to be talking to someone else. One of his goons, maybe.

"You going to freeze them to death?" the second man said.

"Don't be an asshole," Junior said. "Takes too long. I'm thinking about something else maybe."

"Like what?"

"This place has got to go away," Junior said. "So how can we make it go away?"

"Burn it."

"Exactly," Junior said. "Send it back to hell."

I turned to Blood.

"They're gonna burn the joint," I said.

"I know," he said. "I've got perfect hearing."

I made a fist, pounded on the door.

"Junior!" I barked. "Let us go! No one else has to die. The police know everything. Do yourself a favor and give it up now while you can still cop a plea."

But it was like spitting into the wind.

I heard Junior laughing.

"You have got to be kidding me, Marconi. Today life ends. For all three of you. I'm just glad you had the stupidity to actually show up."

I turned to Blood. Even in the freezing cooler, he was sharp enough to know precisely what I was thinking. Slater set us up. Junior must have figured that eventually we would get to him and when we did, he would lead us here for which a trap would be set. Blood and I walked right into it.

Blood pulled out his cell phone.

"Almost forgot," he said. "Modern technology."

"Call 911," I said.

He punched in the numbers. I saw his eyes go wide.

"Can't get a signal," he said.

"Shit," I said, pulling my phone out, speed-dialing Miller. Same thing. No signal.

"And if you try your cell phones," Junior said, "they won't work. That cooler is lead-lined. It's topped and surrounded by insulation and steel. You might as well be calling from hell."

"Can you text?" I said to Blood.

On the floor, I could see that Sarah was squirming, coming to. I almost wished she would stay unconscious.

Blood tried to text something. He looked at me with those same big, disappointed eyes. Shook his head.

I heard some commotion going on outside the door. Some doors opening and closing. Some orders being given. Then I smelled something toxic. I looked down at my feet and saw liquid seeping into the cooler. I bent down, touched the liquid with my fingertips, brought it to my nose.

"Gasoline," I said, looking up at Blood. "Get back."

I stood up and followed Blood to the back of the cooler at the precise moment the gas flashed and burst into flame.

68

THE THREE OF US were trapped inside Junior's version of hell. The entire front wall of the cooler was going up in a hot, red flame.

The more gas that was poured into the cooler, the more intense it got. The flame was tickling the toes of Sarah Levy. It was beginning to cook the sides of beef. You could smell the beef beginning to roast. I bent down, took hold of Sarah's hands, dragged her to the back of the cooler. She was mumbling something.

"Michael," she said. "Michael."

"We're dead meat," said Blood. He pulled out his gun. "You want to shoot one another? Cut to the chase?"

I looked at him, heart in throat, veins mainlining blood and adrenalin.

"No one dies," I said.

Blood laughed.

"You believe that?"

I looked around. Trying to find an opening. A vent or a breach. Something that would allow me the chance to claw my way through the ceiling or a wall. But there was nothing.

I looked at the door. It was entirely engulfed in red-orange flames along with the wall. I saw more gasoline being poured in. The air was being sucked away by the flame and the heat. I couldn't breathe. The flame spread across the entire ceiling as though it were a live animal. I knew it was about to flash, and that once it did, our bodies would be consumed in white-hot flame.

The interior of our lungs were searing.

Blood dropped to his knees.

I saw him press the barrel of the pistol to his head. He was intent on cutting to the chase rather than bear the torture of being burned alive. It's something all inmates feared the most. Being locked in a prison cell while the place burned all around them.

I felt my eyes tear up. But the moisture burned away as fast as my tear ducts could produce it.

I too dropped to my knees, lungs burning, air gone, my world blinded by flame and heat and death. I lay atop the body of Sarah Levy as if I could somehow protect her from the flames that were about to roast us.

Then came the gunshot.

69

WHEN I CAME TO, I was lying on the kitchen floor. I was coughing, my mouth tasting of ash, soot, and burnt gasoline. There was the smell of burnt meat. It combined with the acrid odor of burnt hair. I felt my face, ran my hands over my cropped head, and could immediately tell that my eyebrows had been singed and that some of the hair on my head had been burned off. But otherwise, I was no worse off than when I'd first entered the cooler.

I sat up and looked to my right.

Blood was standing beside me. He was downing a bottle of spring water as if all humanity depended upon it.

"I thought you were dead," I said.

He pulled the bottle away from his mouth.

"Thought the same about you," he said, handing me the bottle.

I took a deep drink, and my lungs felt as if they had been doused with ice water.

"I heard a gunshot," I said, coming up for air, handing Blood the bottle back.

"Wasn't one of our guns," he said.

I stood up, a bit wobbly and out of balance. As my eyes and ears adjusted, I could see that we weren't alone. Not by a long shot. The kitchen was crawling with APD. Lying in the center of the floor were two bodies. Black rubber sheets concealed their identities.

Freshly spilled blood stained the floor along with the charred wood, plastic, and metal. Behind me, the cooler door was wide open, water having doused the charred meat still hanging from the meat hooks. I looked around the room, but Sarah Levy was nowhere to be seen. I felt relieved to see that she was no longer present. I could only hope that like Blood and me, she had survived the cooler inferno.

I turned back to the sheet-covered bodies. I made my way over to them, kneeling down before the first one. Taking hold of the rubber sheet's edge, I pulled it back. I should have known all along who the face belonged to. After all, the man wanted me dead for what I was revealing about his life. About the life he'd led with Sarah Levy. The life that may have resulted in her death. But it was the second face that took me by surprise. When I pulled the sheet off it, my heart sped up and my breath was once more sucked from my lungs.

70

I REPLACED THE SHEETS over the faces of Robert David Jr. and the man who would have been his father-in-law, Harold Sanders, and then I stood up straight.

"Ain't he the man who hired you?" Blood said.

"Yes," I said.

"Looks like he try and shoot Junior, but Junior shoot him first. Or vice versa."

I shook my head.

"They shot each other," I said. "At exactly the same time. Imagine that."

"That's why it sound like one big gunshot."

"Must be their forty million dollar wet dream was going south fast."

"Thanks to your fine detective work."

"And your fine assistance."

A uniformed EMT came in. A young, well-built man. He placed a blanket around my shoulders. He tried to place one around Blood's shoulders, but Blood refused.

"I ain't never been no baby," he said. "Ain't about to start now."

"My hero," I said pulling the blanket off, handing it back to the medical tech.

"Follow me outside please," the EMT said. "Both of you."

We did. Even in the summer heat, the fresh air felt like a gift from God.

There were two EMT vans backed up to the overhead door which were parked directly beside a fire truck. Plus there was an assortment of blue and white cop cruisers, their lights flashing but their sirens turned off. All around us was a zoo of firemen, cops, and medical technicians all busy doing something.

Lying on a gurney just outside the open doors to the first EMT van was Sarah Levy. There was a translucent breathing apparatus strapped to her face. Without thinking about it, I found myself going to her. When I got there, I stared down at her and was amazed to see how little and fragile she appeared. She was conscious now and she looked up at me with her big brown eyes. It was difficult to see her mouth through the plastic mask, but I saw enough to know she was smiling. I took her hand in mine, squeezing it gently. She squeezed back with all the strength of a wilting rose petal. That smile was all that needed to be said between us.

The team of EMTs pushed her body into the back of the van, then swiftly closed the doors. They jumped into the front of the vehicle, turned on the lights and sirens, and pulled away. Standing there watching Sarah take her leave, I wondered if she would one day remember everything again. Remember everything about her life.

Maybe it would be better if she didn't.

I felt a hand on my good shoulder. I turned. It was Detective Miller.

"You okay?" he asked.

"Believe it or not," I said, "I'm going to live."

He pursed his lips, nodding.

"I should have been here sooner," he said. "When I got a match on both Sarah's and Junior's prints on that little bracelet bead, I knew I had at least some tangible proof that a violent and criminal act more than likely went down on Marion Avenue on February 18th. It's all the fuel I needed to start rounding up the unusual suspects. Just wish I could have helped you with saving Sarah."

"You needed to go after the Davids while you had the chance," I said. "While they were confirmed in the same place at the same time. And wherever the Davids were, Harold Sanders was sure to be close by."

"We missed Junior and Sanders by just a minute or two. I knew we'd run them down in a matter of minutes. Not like this though. Not dead."

He nodded sadly, stuffed his hands in his trouser pockets. I tried to get a real sense what he was thinking, and I think I succeeded. If

I had to make a guess, I'd say he was thinking that if the Davids didn't have so much money and power . . . that if they didn't have their hands in the mayor's pockets . . . that if they didn't bankroll half the cop's union pension . . . he might have made an arrest on Robert David Jr. long ago. That the life of Daphne Williams might have been saved and Sarah's head wouldn't be injured.

But in the end, money sings a sad, hard song. And having viewed the home surveillance video of February 18th, I'm not sure Junior was directly liable for Sarah's injuries in the first place. He certainly didn't appear as though he was trying to hurt her. More like he was trying to calm her down. But then, they'd just spent hours inside the basement playroom playing a satanic game of rape the fiancée. Maybe Sarah had finally had enough. Maybe she'd finally lost her love for a creep like Junior. One thing was for sure: she most definitely wanted to go back to her ex-husband. Start all over again with him and their child.

"Junior and Harold Sanders," I said. "Theories?"

Miller cocked his head.

"Harold was greasing Junior for the design on the Nanotech center. One hundred fifty million bucks. Biggest construction project to hit Albany since Rockefeller tore down the entire east side to build the Empire State Plaza. And it just so happens the land on which the Nanotech Center is to be constructed belongs to Albany's biggest developer and philanthropist, David Enterprises. Robert David Sr. was not only providing the land, but he was the dominant investor in the project. He alone owns fifty-one percent of that facility. He alone gets to make the design consultation decisions."

"Junior was seeing Harold's daughter. They were engaged. In love. Why would Junior expect to be greased by Sanders when they were practically family?"

"Because Robert Sr. wanted to use a design outfit out of London. Harold Sanders is good, but not that good. He can put up an office building, but a state-of-the-art high-tech laboratory, forget it. Plus, a London firm would be big news and it would make David Enterprises a global player."

"So Junior started begging the future father-in-law for bribes," I deduced, "in exchange for the promise that Sanders architectural services would oversee the development of the Nanotech facility."

Miller pursed his lips and nodded in the affirmative.

"Turns out the old man kept Junior on a pretty tight financial reign. He made sure the kid had everything he wanted in terms of housing and employment, but at the same time, he made sure to curb his spending habits."

"That's one way to control Junior's cocaine and Molly habit."

"There were other complications," Miller said. "Harold was flat broke and couldn't begin to make the payouts that Junior kept demanding. But Sanders knew all about the *Fifty Shades*-inspired sex games Junior was playing with Sarah. About what they were doing to her on that wheel in the basement. He also knew that Robert Sr. was involved with it. That Penny David was involved. He threatened to expose it and in there lay his leverage.

"But then Sarah gets hurt and the cops, yours truly included, haven't got a thing on Junior. So Sanders proposes something to Junior in secret. He devises this lawsuit in order to collect forty million which he can then split with the kid."

Now I was seeing clearly. Seeing where Miller was going with this.

"That's why Sanders hired me," I said. "To validate his fake lawsuit. He knew that no matter what kind of evidence I came up with, the cops would never touch the case since the Davids own half the APD's union pensions and half the cops are on their side. But a civil suit would be something else entirely. Being responsible for an icy staircase that resulted in his girlfriend's injuries doesn't necessarily make Junior look like a bad guy—just a careless groundskeeper."

"Sad when you think about," Miller added. "Sanders wasn't really interested in exposing how his daughter got hurt or even seeing her survive Junior's wrath. He already knew how she got hurt. Maybe he even felt she deserved what she got by playing Junior's games. What he wanted was money in order to further his stalled career and refill his bank accounts. Instead, all he got is dead. And how's the old saying go? The dead look really dead when they're dead."

"But Sarah lives," Blood chimed in. "We win."

"But I nearly got us killed in the process."

"You didn't mean for us to get killed, Keep," Blood said. "Just the way it worked out."

I exhaled and felt a soreness in my bad shoulder. Soon, I would have to visit the hospital to have the wound redressed before infection set in. I heard some commotion behind me, and when I turned to look, I saw the black-bagged bodies of both Junior and Harold Sanders being wheeled out of the building on two separate gurneys. In silence, all three of us looked on while the EMTs stuffed the bodies into the back bays of the two vans.

"Guess this means I won't be collecting my full fee," I said.

"Maybe you can go after Senior for it," Miller said. "He can pay you from Green Haven where he'll be doing quite the stretch along with his young wife, Penny."

"Penny," I said, picturing the blonde, blue-eyed femme fatal and her impressive physique. "Why Penny?"

"Daphne Williams," Miller said. "Someone who's good with a knife had her way with her immediately after Junior asphyxiated her. She honed her skills by spending many years in some of the best restaurant kitchens of the world. She's a killer cook."

I recalled Penny cutting up the lemons and limes with all the professional skill of a five-star chef.

"Jesus," I said. "What kind of human being does something like that?"

"A cold, heartless, psycho witch who was also present when Sarah Levy was pushed down the steps."

I recalled the surveillance video shot outside Junior's house. Recalled how, just before he pulled Sarah's hair, he turned and yelled something in the direction of the still open front door. The information Daphne revealed to me inside my apartment on the night I got shot turned out to be true. Junior must have been arguing with Penny while she was insisting he toss Sarah down the steps.

Miller went on, "Penny's been arrested and has already admitted to being on site when Sarah went down those steps and connected with each brick along the way."

"Let me guess," I said. "Penny's looking for leniency. Who ratted her out?"

"Her husband, of course," he said. "She wants a reduction of her two pending charges. The first for conspiring to commit homicide in the second degree, in which she prompted Junior to push Sarah down those steps, and the second for the successful murder in the first of Daphne Williams."

"Did Junior really act on her orders?" I said. "If he did, why would she admit to it? The woman's hanging herself."

"Remorse, my warden friend," he said. "Simple fucking remorse and guilt. Remember what I just said about the dead? Well, the guilty look very guilty when they're guilty. In any case, she's been singing like a bird and begging Jesus for forgiveness, and that's the kind of music that makes me a smile. It also allows me to hang on to my precious job."

The second EMT van drove out of the lot, their flashers going but the sirens muted. With the cargo they were carrying, they wouldn't be in any rush to get to the morgue. Was I supposed to believe that Junior didn't act on his own when it came to the near killing of one innocent girlfriend and the successful killing of another? I guess maybe it did make sense. He was forty-one years old but hadn't yet assumed responsibility for anything. He was a child trapped in an adult's body who could be led around by his nose if need be. Maybe the little devil didn't even comprehend the enormity of his actions when he went on harming Sarah in the basement of his house, or when he fought with her on those icy steps, or when he wrapped his hands around Daphne's throat and choked her to death. Maybe even when he pushed his mother off that stepladder ten years ago.

I looked Miller in the eye.

"Joan David," I said. "Tell me the truth, Nick. What's the official *unofficial* word on her death underneath the backyard grape arbor?"

He nodded and bit down on his lower lip.

"Blood," he said. "You mind?"

"Got to make a couple of calls anyway," Blood said, pulling his cell phone from his pants pocket and stepping away from us, out of earshot.

71

"DOESN'T MATTER MUCH TO ME anymore why or how intentionally Junior hurt Sarah," Miller went on. "Doesn't matter if Penny David ordered him to do it or the devil made him do it. Doesn't matter at this point. Because he's so dead and he's the devil's problem now. All I know now is that he did, in fact, hurt Sarah Levy bad, and he hurt Daphne Williams worse, but they were not the first victims of that motherfucker's wrath. That first victim was his mother."

I pictured a much young Junior coming up on his mother from behind where she stood precariously balanced atop a rickety stepladder. I saw him thrusting out both his hands against the ladder, saw Joan dropping onto her side, her head bouncing off the stone pavers like a pumpkin.

"But I thought he had an alibi? He was in the South of France. In cooking school."

"We know now that he flew back to New York the same weekend his mother was killed. Within six hours of her death, daddy put him on another flight back to France. 'Mums' the word, of course. Or so were my orders from my APD command via our illustrious and handsome mayor."

I shook my head, pictured the tan, chubby face of Mayor Jennings. I knew that sooner or later I would have a run in with him.

"But why kill your own mother?"

He pursed his lips, cocked his head.

"Who knows? There were any number of reasons why he could have done it. Money, or the lack of it. Frustration. Boredom. Maybe

Joan was harping on him to become his own man. To grow up, so to speak. Maybe she wouldn't let him watch back-to-back episodes of *SpongeBob SquarePants*. In the end, it doesn't take much to make an inherently evil man angry enough to commit homicide. Men like Junior are born angry and angry they will die."

As if on cue, we both stole a glance at the back of the second EMT van, knowing full well that an angry dead body was stored inside it. I also couldn't get Daphne Williams out of my mind. I recalled the panic-stricken woman who visited me the night I was shot. I wondered if I could have saved her life by carting her and her story to the police. But then, I wondered if she would have agreed to accompany me in the first place. Probably not. She would have been too afraid of Junior and what he would do to her should he find out. And from the looks of things, the police might not have been able to do a goddamned thing for her.

"You need me for anything else?" I said to Miller. "My shoulder hurts and I need a shower." But really, I just wanted to get the hell away from that place.

"I'll need you and Blood to come in for a statement later or early tomorrow."

"I can do that," Blood said, making his way back over to us.

"Swell," Miller said. "My night's only just begun with interviewing Robert Sr. and Penny David and playing their stories against one another."

"Good luck with that," I said. "Glad to know you still have a job."

He smiled sadly, brushed his cropped gray hair with his right hand, about-faced, and headed back in the direction of the nearest APD cruiser. His face and the silence that draped it spoke volumes.

I patted the pockets on my blazer.

"Crap, Blood," I said. "I forgot all about the 4Runner."

He laughed.

"She been impounded by now."

For a brief second, I thought about having Miller help me get it out of hock. But then, knowing that he would be going without sleep for a while, I guessed it could wait until morning. Besides, Blood and I were in walking distance of Sherman Street.

"Beer?" I said to Blood.

"You know I don't drink much," he said. "But there is a quaint wine bar just a couple hundred feet from here. Play some nice jazz too."

"How sophisticated, Blood," I said. "Tonight is a special occasion, however."

"You buying?" he said.

I shoved both hands in my pockets.

"No cash," I said. "Just add it to my tab."

"Tab gettin' awfully big," he said. "But I guess you good for it."

I reached out with my good arm, slapped him on the back.

"Blood," I said, "I believe this is just the start of a beautiful friendship."

"*Casablanca*," he said. "I don't put much stock in sentimentality."

"Don't worry," I said, "I don't fall in love so easy."

He laughed.

I laughed.

It seemed strange. Laughing in the face of all that death. But then, it was far too late for tears. And who exactly would we cry for anyway? The good news was that Sarah was alive and that she would continue to recover. Maybe even remarry her ex-husband and raise that little boy of hers.

Together, Blood and I walked through the open chain link gates in search of a quaint wine bar down on Lark Street. Directly behind us, the EMT van carted off the bodies of Robert David Jr. and my former employer, Harold Sanders. I knew that if a hell did indeed exist, it now housed two new residents.

As Blood and I walked, the hot summer sun set on the city. There didn't seem to be any relief from the unrelenting heat. Summer wasn't even half over yet. I wondered how much longer the extreme heat would last. But then, that was up to God or the devil to decide..

THE END

If you enjoyed this Jack Marconi thriller, than you need to check out *The Innocent* (A Jack Marconi Mystery No. 1) and *Godchild* (A Jack Marconi Mystery No. 2).

ABOUT THE AUTHOR

Vincent Zandri is the *New York Times* and *USA Today* best-selling author of more than sixteen novels, including *Everything Burns*, *The Innocent*, *The Remains*, *Moonlight Falls*, and the Suspense Magazine "Best of" award-winning, *The Shroud Key*. A freelance photojournalist and traveler, he is also the author of the blog *The Vincent Zandri Vox*. He lives in New York and Florence, Italy. For more information and to join Vincent's "For Your Eyes Only" Mailing List, go to http://www.vincentzandri.com/.

Made in the USA
San Bernardino, CA
17 September 2017